Left standing on the side while their contemporaries marry into society, four young ladies forge a bond to guard each other from a similar fate . . .

Finishing school failed to make a proper lady of Penelope Arrington. But as a Wallflower of West Lane, Poppy has a far more vital role—she and her three best friends have made a pact to protect each other from the clutches of dangerous, disreputable men. So when one of them is about to be married off to a duke sight unseen, Poppy makes it her mission to divine the prospective husband's true character. If only she didn't require the aid of London's most unsuitable rake.

Rhys Draper, Earl of Marsden, has known the headstrong Poppy since she was a young girl, naïve to the ways of men. To her eternal chagrin—and to his vague amusement—they have been at odds over the memory of their embarrassing first encounter all these years. Now, with his services in need, Rhys sees a chance to finally clear the air between them. Instead, he is surprised by the heat of their feelings. If the two do not tread carefully, they may end up in a most agreeably compromising position . . .

Visit us at www.kensingtonbooks.com

Books by A.S. Fenichel

The Demon Hunter Series
Ascension
Deception
Betrayal

Forever Brides Series
Tainted Bride
Foolish Bride
Desperate Bride

The Everton Domestic Society
A Lady's Honor
A Lady's Escape
A Lady's Virtue

The Wallflowers of West Lane
The Earl Not Taken

Published by Kensington Publishing Corporation

The Earl Not Taken

The Wallflowers of West Lane

A.S. Fenichel

LYRICAL PRESS
Kensington Publishing Corp.
www.kensingtonbooks.com

LYRICAL PRESS BOOKS are published by
Kensington Publishing Corp.
119 West 40th Street
New York, NY 10018

All Kensington titles, imprints, and distributed lines are available at special quantity discounts for bulk purchases for sales promotion, premiums, fund-raising, educational, or institutional use.

Special book excerpts or customized printings can also be created to fit specific needs. For details, write or phone the office of the Kensington Sales Manager: Kensington Publishing Corp., 119 West 40th Street, New York, NY 10018. Attn. Sales Department. Phone: 1-800-221-2647.

Lyrical Press and Lyrical Press logo Reg. U.S. Pat. & TM Off.

First Electronic Edition: March 2020
eISBN-13: 978-1-5161-1051-3
eISBN-10:1-5161-1051-X

First Print Edition: March 2020
ISBN-13: 978-1-5161-1054-4
ISBN-10: 1-5161-1054-4

Printed in the United States of America

This book is dedicated to those of you who have felt out of place or been pushed aside. If you've ever been the girl or boy standing alone at a party or felt like an intruder in someone else's group of friends, this book is for you. The Wallflowers of West Lane sympathize and want you to know, you are not alone.

For my husband, Dave, because you are where romance begins.

Prologue

Helmsbury Manor was grand and comfortable, but Poppy's new friend Aurora had been right about her mother's lectures. By her third day as a guest, Poppy was so tired of the droning on about behaving like a proper lady, she sneaked out before tea and went for a long walk around the property. After all, Aurora might have to listen, but Poppy had her own mother and had heard her fair share of the same kind of drivel over the years.

She'd been sent from home dreading her fate at Miss Agatha Wormbattle's School for Young Ladies, and now she wished they would leave sooner. They would leave in five days and meet two other girls in London before they all would travel to Lucerne together and spend three years learning to behave like proper young ladies. Father thought it a punishment for bad behavior, but anything that took her out of his purview was a blessing.

It was a beautiful day with a light breeze and blue skies. She trudged across a lawn toward a line of trees at the top of the hill, stumbled, and smudged a grass stain on her pale blue dress. Brushing at the newest stain, she resigned herself to always having a stain or two on her clothes. Tea would have been nice, but enjoying a long walk was far better. All she had to do was figure out how to avoid the countess for the remaining two days of her stay. Then she and her lovely new friend would be free of critical parents while they attended the Swiss boarding school. Poppy only hoped that Aurora was right about their ability to handle Headmistress Agatha Wormbattle. Admittedly, they were both clever girls who'd managed a fair amount of mischief. Letting the lively thought fill her, she reached the crest of the hill and froze.

Shirtless, Aurora's elder brother, Rhys, had a woman with long brown hair and her dress bunched around her waist pressed against a tree. It was scandalous behavior for a man who would one day be the Earl of Marsden. He'd been nuzzling the woman's neck, his golden hair falling to his collar when Poppy stepped into the stand of trees.

She must have gasped at the unexpected sight, as Rhys's head snapped up. Their gazes met.

Not knowing what to do, she fumbled for words. "Satan's beard. I'm…I…I beg your pardon." Turning, she ran back toward the house with her cheeks on fire.

Laughter, both masculine and feminine, followed her as she dashed away from the tawdry scene.

Despite her bravado in most situations, she had never seen a man with so little clothes on before. Rhys Draper's neck was corded, his shoulders wide and muscular, while his waist narrowed where his golden flesh disappeared beneath tan breeches. She had trouble catching her breath, and she was not at all sure it was from the dash back to the house.

"Poppy, are you all right?" Aurora called from the gazebo where she sat with a book.

So close to escaping to the house and running to her bedroom where she might claim a headache and avoid seeing anyone for the rest of the day, Poppy sighed and meandered closer. "I'm fine. Just a bit tired and was going to go upstairs for a rest."

Putting her book aside, Aurora narrowed her gaze. "You looked flushed, and you were running as if you'd seen a snake. What happened to your dress?"

"It's nothing. I'm quite all right." Poppy sat across from Aurora in the gazebo. "What are you reading?"

"I'm not. I'm pretending to read *A Lady Must Always Be a Solemn Creature* in order to avoid Mother." She changed to a soft conspiratorial whisper. "I would like to read the Gretchen Tormblat novel *Danger Deep at Sea* I bought the last time I walked to town. But that will have to wait for the journey. I've been collecting reading material and plan to continue as we travel."

Glad for the subject to turn away from her, Poppy said, "I haven't read that one. I managed to borrow a copy of Mrs. Tormblat's *The Pirate Cave* from my neighbor's daughter back home, and I found it very distracting."

"That's what I love about the books, so thrilling and filled with adventure. You may read any you like from my collection. My maid will sneak them in my bag once Mother has made her inspection."

Poppy pulled her feet up on the bench and wrapped her arms around her knees. "My mother inspected my trunk as well. Unfortunately, Willa has not been my maid but a week. I could not trust her to hide reading material. Mother found three romantic novels by Priscilla Prettifield at the bottom and promptly tossed them in the trash. I was quite vexed."

Aurora shook her head. "Do not fret; we shall replace those books. Did your parents give you pin money?"

"Yes, and I have some saved they didn't know about. I'm quite solvent." Proud of herself, Poppy hoped her new friend was trustworthy.

"Excellent. I have also been saving. Ever since they told me I would be sent away, I've been saving half of my pin money in case I need it while we're in Switzerland. I have made Mother believe I'm sad about being sent away, but truly, I can't wait." Aurora leaned her head back against one of six posts that held the roof and smiled.

It was impossible not to like Aurora, and Poppy was thrilled to have a friend to rely on for the next three years. "You may be right, Aurora. We shall have a marvelous adventure."

Her joy fled an instant later when Rhys appeared from around the shrubs at the other side of the garden and strode toward them.

"Hello, Rhys," Aurora said. "Why are your clothes so wrinkled?"

Poppy wanted to crawl away and hide. Cheeks heating, she was sure her blush was obvious. The last thing she wanted was for Rhys to know how embarrassed she was by what she'd seen. It was impossible to seem worldly when a man's bare back sent her running across the countryside.

Rhys raised his eyebrows and stared at Poppy for a long moment. "I was frolicking with someone from town. A bit of fun."

Aurora smiled. "Well, don't let Father see you looking so messy. He'll throw a fit."

Those sharp eyes of his settled on her for a long moment, perhaps waiting for a comment. "I'm going to clean up now," he assured his sister. "Lady Penelope, what did you do with your afternoon?" A wicked smile twisted his full lips.

Were they so red because of kissing that woman? Poppy didn't know and couldn't imagine why she cared. Her stomach was in knots. She knew one thing for certain: as much as she liked Aurora, if she never saw Rhys Draper again it would be too soon. "Nothing of note. I took a walk around the property."

"And how did you like the views?"

Perhaps he was teasing, but Poppy wanted to die. She wouldn't have it. This being made to feel small by a boy would not do. "While the vistas are lovely here, I saw nothing notable."

Frowning, he examined his shoes. "I see. Well, perhaps your next visit to our home will be more interesting."

"As you know, I'll be far away for three years learning how to behave like a proper lady. You'll likely be married off to some very fine lady by that time and we shall never meet again." Preferring the strong tone of her voice, she didn't care that her words were cutting.

Aurora watched, looking from one to the other. "I feel as if I've missed something. But I am sure Rhys will not be married before I return from school. I'll be very annoyed if you were to marry without me."

He kissed his sister's cheek. "And I would never do so. I wish I could talk Father out of this, Rora. I have tried to keep you home, but you do yourself disservice with your constant disobedience."

Smiling, she shrugged and stood up. "I am what I am, Rhys. I cannot change to please Father and not even for you."

He hugged her tight. "I would not have you change, just obey enough to keep you at home where I know you're safe."

She swatted his chest. "They are sending us to a fortress in the mountains. We'll be perfectly safe and far enough away so I will no longer embarrass our esteemed parents. Speaking of our parents, I promised Mother I would meet with her before dressing for dinner. I must go. Will you escort Poppy in?"

"Of course."

Aurora rushed to the house and was gone.

The awkward silence hung between them. Rhys remained guarding the entrance to the gazebo, and Poppy had no way out but to push him aside. Not wanting him to suspect how uncomfortable he made her, she held her place. "Are you just going to stand there and glare at me?"

"I'm trying to figure out why you didn't tell my sister what you witnessed." He stepped a few feet away and scratched his head.

Poppy took advantage and made a quick exit from her trapped position. "I like your sister and she obviously thinks the world of you. I have no desire to hurt her with the truth."

Narrowing his gaze, he closed the gap between them. "What truth is that?"

"Perhaps I am mistaken, but to debauch young women in the woods is not exactly gentlemanly. If you thought it was acceptable behavior, you wouldn't be so relieved I kept your secret." She backed away until the path to the house was beside her.

"I haven't done anything wrong. Mimi is more than willing. You make me sound lecherous." He gripped the edge of his coat and kicked the pebbled path.

Pulling back her shoulders, she looked into those winter-sky eyes. "I think you are well on your way to becoming a perfect English gentleman."

"And what of you with your bad behavior and stained dress? You're not exactly on your way to becoming a well-bred lady."

"I never claimed to be. Besides, I don't think my stumbling and ruining a dress is comparable to what you've been doing with who knows who. You're a scoundrel, I'm just a lummox."

His frown deepened, and something dark glared in his eyes. "You have no right to judge me."

"Hades's blood, I only tell what I see." Her heart pounded in her throat. He stepped toward her.

Poppy ran to the house and up to her room without looking back.

Chapter 1

"I'm sorry if I offend anyone, but I am glad he's dead." Poppy hated funerals, but as she walked into Aurora's home on West Lane, she was happy her friend was free of that monster. The Earl of Radcliff had deserved what he'd gotten, and her friend's three-year marriage had been too long. Poppy had behaved herself all morning. Now with only her three closest friends and Aurora's brother, Rhys, to hear her, she had to let it out.

Rhys Draper, recently elevated to the Earl of Marsden after his father's passing, frowned at her. "Really, Penelope. Must you say such things?" He stood with his arms crossed over his wide chest leaning against the wall near the window, and his blond hair touched his collar. All remnants of the skinny boy had been replaced by muscle over the last few years, but Poppy was determined not to notice. His roguish behavior far outweighed any pleasure she might take from his good looks.

The lady's parlor of Aurora's townhouse on West Lane was their gathering place. The Earl of Radcliff's death was the only reason Rhys had tagged along after the funeral. It was the only room in the house with a feminine flair, cream-colored walls and a buttery rug. The overstuffed furniture was covered in a similar fabric, and lace curtains shielded them from the street.

Aurora pulled the black veil off her face and over the brim of her hat before removing the pins and tossing the hat on the table near the door. It bumped a vase of flowers sent by someone with condolences and slid to the floor. Her golden hair was coiled at the back of her head in tiny braids, and her pale blue eyes were clear. All the fear, which had marred them for three years, had died with Bertram Sherbourn, Earl of Radcliff. "You'll get no argument from me, Poppy."

Faith picked up the hat and placed it more firmly on the table. Taking a deep breath accentuated her full curves as she tucked her wild brown hair behind her ear. She took Aurora's hand, and the two sat on the divan. "He was a miserable sod and none of us are sorry he's gone. Still, Poppy, it's not nice to speak ill of the dead." Her sweet voice was in direct contrast with her words.

Holding back a chuckle at the double standard Faith set, Poppy shared a knowing look with Mercy, who shrugged and smiled. "I suppose I must say nothing at all then. I certainly won't say anything nice about him." Poppy sat on the chair to Aurora's left.

Curling up on the chaise, her long legs bending until she took up little space despite her tall stature, Mercy pushed her spectacles up on her nose. Her strawberry-blond waves pulled up to expose an elegant neck and shoulders. "Then we shall find another subject or sit in silence. What do you want to talk about, Aurora?"

"I think I'd just like to call for tea and sit here. Can we do that? Can we forget I was ever married and act as if we were just getting home from Lucerne, four wallflowers hell-bent on embarrassing our families?"

Patting her hand, Faith narrowed her eyes on Poppy as if daring her to continue the unwanted conversation. "Of course we can."

Poppy stifled a chuckle and held up her hands in defeat. Faith rarely put her foot down, and it was clear this was one of those times.

"Should I leave you ladies?" Rhys asked, still manning his post against the wall.

Aurora smiled. "No. Come and sit with us, Rhys."

"Ring for tea before you sit," Poppy added with a smile. She had never gotten along with Aurora's older brother. Her experience with him as a child had colored her opinion, and from the stories she'd heard over the years, he'd changed little.

There was that frown again. A typical man, he couldn't bear one small order from a woman. Still, he pulled the cord and a maid ran in a moment later.

Aurora sent the girl for their tea.

The frown lines around Rhys's mouth deepened, and his brows drew together. "I know Radcliff was a difficult man, but does he deserve so little respect in death? He did leave you a living, a title, and this house."

All focus was on Aurora. She had kept her situation a secret from her brother because there was nothing he could have done about it. Their father had made the contract with the Earl of Radcliff while the girls were still away at Miss Agatha Wormbattle's School for Young Ladies in Switzerland. They had all been excited about the first of their misguided group to get married and about coming home after a three-year exile for bad behavior. The reality was far different and had kept the rest of them from accepting any proposals since.

"I don't know if I can tell him." Aurora looked at Mercy and Poppy with eyes filled with tears, not for her dead husband but for the pain she was about to inflict on her brother.

"Shall I do it?" Poppy would open a vein for any of the Wallflowers. Telling a horror story to an arrogant earl was nothing.

Aurora nodded and wiped her eyes.

Arms once again crossed over his broad chest and his mass of blond hair hiding one eye, Rhys peered across the coffee table at Poppy. Awkward in the ornate French country-style chair, he waited. "Well?"

Where he had been gentle with Aurora, his tone was harsh when he addressed Poppy.

For her friend's sake, she would be as kind as possible. "Demon's breath. Bertram Sherbourn was a monster. He abused your sister on a daily basis when he bothered to come home."

"Poppy?" Mercy pushed her glasses up on her nose, her eyes holding a warning.

Poppy glanced in Mercy's direction before returning her attention to Rhys and continuing. "It's best to tell him the truth at this point. Besides calling her all manner of names and forcing his attentions on her, he beat her so badly that on several occasions, we had to call a doctor. Once she lay unconscious for two days...."

"Penelope..." Faith's tawny eyes widened with alarm, and she shook her head.

Rhys flinched as if he'd been struck in the stomach with a bludgeon. "This cannot be true."

"Of course it's true," Poppy said. "Your father married her to an earl because that was all he cared about. He did not bother to check to make sure she would be safe with a villain."

White faced, his eyes begged for someone to contradict her. "Rora?"

Poppy felt a pang of remorse for her lack of grace with words.

"I'm sorry, Rhys. I'm afraid it's true." Aurora looked at her brother and then at her own hands twisting in her lap.

Faith patted Aurora's hands and finally fought through her grip so she could hold one. "We would not lie to you, Rhys."

He jumped up, and the chair fell backward, crashing to the floor. Staring into the corner of the room, his face burned bright red and his chest rose and fell in sharp breaths. His strong jaw ticked with strain before he picked up the chair and stood, gripping the wooden frame. "Why did you never tell me this while he was alive?"

Mercy said in a level voice, "There was nothing you could do. Aurora did not want you to harm yourself in some vain effort to save her."

"You had no right to keep this from me. After Father died, I became the head of this family. I would have helped you. You could have come home this last year, Rora." He clung to the chair as if he wanted to hurl it across the room, but he held his temper.

Poppy had to admit, she was impressed with his restraint. Though she would never tell him that.

Standing, Aurora's smile was weak. She went to her brother and kissed his cheek. "He would have come after me. I was his property. There is no law to keep me away from him. He would have been even angrier and more violent and one of us would have died. Either me, because Bertram would have gone too far, or you because you came after him and he killed you. I couldn't live with the possibility."

"I can take care of myself. I would have bested Radcliff and you might have been free of him sooner." Pain etched lines around Rhys's mouth. His full and maddeningly interesting lips pulled taught. He ran his hand through his hair.

Cocking her head and pressing her palm to his cheek, she sighed. "And then what of you? You think you could have killed an earl and not endured some consequence? As it turns out, he took care of it himself."

"Well, with the help of the owner of the gaming hell he tried to cheat." Poppy couldn't stop herself.

Faith gave her a stern look.

Mercy hid a chuckle behind her hand.

"I should have known." He hugged her tight. "I'm sorry, Rora. Father should have judged his character before allowing you to be betrothed."

With a last pat on his back, Aurora eased away from him. Always the most elegant of their quartet, she glided back to the divan. Aurora's figure was slim but stronger now that the fear of her husband was gone. "Yes. Well, Father was only interested in my becoming a countess, and he got that before he died. I was no longer an embarrassment to the Draper name and well married. I'm sure he thought he'd done right by me. Not to mention, the piece of land somewhere in the north he received in trade for my hand and dowry."

"I wondered where that Cheshire property came from." He paced the rug. "I would give that property to you, if you want, Rora. It seems the least the family can do."

Tipping her head, she put her pinky on her lip. It was what she always did when considering something. "That is very generous, Rhys. Let me think about it."

The maid brought tea and some sweets. Once they were all served, Faith cleared her throat. It meant she had news but she was uncomfortable sharing. Another polite ahem and she sipped her tea.

"What is it, Faith?" Mercy asked, her amusement clear behind her spectacles. Mercy's keen sense of all that was ridiculous in their lives had gotten Poppy through many hard days at school. She only wished she had shared some of her grace. While Poppy was clumsy, Mercy was lithe and agile like the goddess Diana.

"What? Oh, it's nothing." She took a large bite of biscuit and had to work to chew such a mouthful. It would take her a moment to decide she was going to tell whatever was on her mind.

There was little doubt she would eventually open a discussion. They just had to be patient.

Rhys sat in the chair, sipping tea and watching with interest. He had a knack for keeping quiet and observing. Poppy had seen him sit in the background on several occasions over the last six years of their acquaintance. He was quite young when Poppy stopped at Helmsbury Manor, his family estate, on the way to school, but even then, he took everything in and if possible would use the information later. Even though they always bickered when they met, she admired his patience and wished more young men were as mindful.

Putting her cup and saucer on the table, Faith plastered a fake smile on her face. It was a most annoying expression. "I'm to be married to the Duke of Breckenridge."

"What?" Aurora's eyes widened.

"When?" Mercy's hand flew to her chest.

"How?" Poppy's heart dropped.

The simultaneous questions didn't seem to faze Faith. She folded her hands in her lap and tipped up her pert chin. The effect was meant to make her look as if she had a leaner elegant figure, but it did nothing to hide the voluptuous curves that more than one man noticed each time they attended a ball. "Mother arranged it. I haven't met him yet. He's been in France for some months and only arrived back in England last week. I thought he might come to call but he hasn't. Not yet."

"Has your mother met him?" Poppy jumped up, hands flying in the air. She already guessed the answer but hoped for better.

Faith sniffed. "No. It was all arranged through letters. I read the letters when Mother informed me last week, and he seems quite…intelligent."

Coming out of her skin, Poppy paced the room. She stumbled on the edge of the rug but righted herself. While her friends had become nimble young ladies, Poppy remained the clumsy oaf she'd always been. "We are not going through this again. You cannot marry a man we don't know. I don't care if he's a duke or the prince himself."

"I don't see that I have a choice. It would be nice to meet him and perhaps for you three to get a look at him. Maybe then we'd know what I was getting into." Another sniff and she pulled her handkerchief out of her sleeve and dabbed her eyes.

Mercy turned to Rhys. "Do you know him, my lord?"

"I think you can call me Rhys in this setting, Mercedes. I've known all of you since you were girls just shipped off to Switzerland to be turned into fine young ladies." His gaze settled on Poppy before he continued. "Unfortunately, I have never met the Duke of Breckenridge. All I know is he's well respected in the House of Lords and has a massive estate in Hertfordshire. Supposed to be one of the nicest homes in all of England."

"What's he been doing in France?" Aurora also abandoned her tea with the troubling news.

Rhys shrugged. "I'm sorry. I have no idea. It could be he has property or business in France, and he is checking how it all fared after Napoleon. Perhaps he just likes to travel, and it is safe to visit the Continent once again."

Poppy didn't like the way Rhys seemed fine with not knowing. "Well that's not good enough. I'm not watching another of my dearest friends walk into the arms of a monster. I need to know who he is and what kind of character he has. I say we do some investigating and ferret him out."

"You're mad." Rhys stood to face her. "You intend to spy on a duke. And just how will you go about it, Penelope? Will you slink by his home at night, listen at doors, break into White's?"

Fury heated her cheeks and neck. "I'll do whatever is necessary, and so will the rest of the Wallflowers of West Lane. We are all we have to protect ourselves."

They had been called wallflowers when still at school. Instead of letting mean girls offend them, the foursome had adopted the name as their own. Once Aurora was married and they were meeting at her West

Lane townhouse for tea on Tuesdays, they had let the address become part of the moniker.

Faith clapped and smiled. "I feel much better."

"Do you have any idea when you will meet him, Faith?" Usually smiling and laughing, Mercy's expression was drawn and serious as she uncurled herself and faced the divan fully.

"Mother said we will attend the Sottonfield ball and that is where I will finally meet him."

Pacing again, Poppy started a list of things to do. "We have a week to get ready. Of course, Aurora will not be able to attend since she's in mourning. What about you, Mercy, can you be there?"

"We leave tomorrow for the country. Aunt Phyllis wanted to leave already but stayed so I could attend the funeral. "I'm sorry. I'll try to shorten the trip." Worry etched in the corners of Mercy's mouth, and her green eyes flashed with regret. She had no choice but to travel at the whim of the relations who had raised her after her parents' deaths.

Dabbing her eyes again, Faith nodded. "It will all be fine."

"Not to worry. I'll be there with you, Faith." Poppy rounded the furniture and kissed Faith's cheek.

"Perhaps I can be of service," Rhys said.

They all stared at him, but Aurora spoke. "You are going to the Sottonfield ball?"

He got up and folded his hands behind his back. "You four cannot do this without someone who might actually get close to Breckenridge. I know Lady Penelope means well, but she can be somewhat graceless in a ballroom. I'm willing to help. It seems the least I can do after failing Rora so completely."

That he had never before agreed with anything Poppy said had her nervous, but it was hard to argue with his logic or his assessment of her. He was a member of the same gentleman's club. He was a man and could, once introduced, befriend Breckenridge. The mention of her clumsiness hurt more than it should from someone whom she had no respect for, but the sting couldn't be denied. "I have no idea how to explain you to my mother, and I can assure you she will be with me at the ball," she said.

He gnawed on his thumbnail. "I suggest you tell her nothing. She'll assume I'm courting you, but we can sort that out later."

"You obviously don't know my mother." She'd said it under her breath, but from the quizzical look on Rhys's face, she gathered he'd heard her. The idea of anyone, her mother included, thinking she would marry someone as arrogant and wild as Rhys Draper made Poppy nauseous. Mother's own marriage might have been an embittering ordeal, but that didn't mean she was immune to the notion of her daughter becoming a countess. It seemed to Gwendolyn Arrington being well married made up for her husband's debauched behavior and mean spirit.

Even after he excused himself to take care of some business, she still worried about a venture that included Rhys and herself. How would they save Faith when they couldn't be in a room together without bickering? There was no help for it. Someone had to make sure the same fate didn't befall Faith as what had happened to Aurora.

"You will all still come for tea weekly, I hope," Aurora said when the four of them were alone and the servants told not to disturb them.

Mercy pulled her strawberry-blond tresses back into her bun. She rarely did more than a simple chignon with her soft waves, and they often pulled loose—the problems of not having a lady's maid because her aunt was too stingy to employ one for her. "I'll only be away a few weeks, then I'll be here each and every Tuesday. More often if you need me."

Patting Aurora's hand, Faith forced her horrid bland expression. "You never need worry about that. Anyone I marry will have to understand Tuesday afternoons are dedicated to the three of you."

"Even Radcliff seemed to understand." After pacing the room since Rhys left, Poppy sat. "He was the worst man, but at least he never tried to separate us."

"Only Headmistress Agatha ever dared try." Mercy's grin lit the room.

Aurora chuckled. "That did not work out very well for her."

"No. Poppy put a frog in her bed and salt in her oats." Faith covered her giggles.

"I seem to remember you putting salt in Miss Agatha's tonic." There was no way Poppy would let Faith pretend she'd had nothing to do with the strategic attack on the headmistress.

Aurora clapped. "Poor woman was only trying to teach us to behave like ladies, but she should never have dared separate us. After all, we arrived at Miss Agatha Wormbattle's School for Young Ladies together and we made a pact. Nothing was ever going to keep us apart."

Mercy laughed. "Even hateful Mary Yates calling us wallflowers after that first ball could not daunt us. We made it our own, embracing the title."

"Then tea here at West Lane each Tuesday sealed our little club's title." Poppy loved each moment spent with her friends, and over the years they had become like sisters. Nothing would change that.

Faith took her hand. "No matter our marital status, we shall always be the Wallflowers of West Lane."

It was true they could not be separated. Any one of them would fight to remain together. Poppy worried about Aurora all alone in her West Lane townhouse. "I realized Radcliff was not company, but will you be lonely here, Aurora?"

Looking around the room then down at her hands, Aurora sighed. "I had a mad thought that you three might like to move in here with me. We could hire more lady's maids and until we do we can all share Gillian. Perhaps the upstairs maid, Jane, would also do. She's been with me a long time."

Mercy's eyes lit up. "I see nothing mad about it. It won't take much convincing. My aunt will be happy to be rid of her aging ward. I will tell her my plans while we're in the country and move in here directly upon our return."

Faith's eyes were as wide as saucers. "My mother will not like the idea. I will tell her I am only staying here as a guest until you are feeling more yourself. Yes. That will work for a while anyway."

It was a grand idea, and Poppy was not immune to the attraction of being away from Mother and Father on a daily basis. She had never been the daughter they dreamed of. In fact they had never failed to express their disappointment. Father wished for a son, and mother wished for a paragon. Poppy was neither. While Aurora was prattling on about the need for servants, Poppy was already planning what she would tell her parents. "I will speak to Father about an allowance and move in tomorrow if you are certain this is what you want, Aurora."

Her smile was wide and filled with more joy than Poppy had seen in years. "If I'm certain? Of course, I'm certain. The four of us under one roof is all I have ever wanted. Now, with my new widowed status, I can serve as chaperone for the three of you."

Giggling, Faith covered her mouth. "You as a chaperone is the funniest thing I've heard. As if you would ever censure any of us."

"That sounds like the perfect chaperone to me." Mercy's sarcasm rang true with Poppy as well.

"It's a pity you can't go to balls and theater as you please yet," Poppy complained. "I think it ridiculous you should have to wear black and stay home in mourning for a man who was not worth a halfpenny."

"I agree," Mercy said. "In fact, I think we must find ways of getting you out of this house. It would be nice to get out of the city together for a few weeks. I know we all can't go now, as I have to accompany my aunt. But perhaps in a month or so, the Landons might invite us all for a fortnight?"

Faith's eyes grew wide. "That's a marvelous idea. I must make Father and Mother believe it was their notion, but I'll get to work on it. They adore Aurora, and I'll find a way to let them know they'd be helping her in her grief."

It was impossible not to laugh. Poppy said, "Oh Faith, I do love you. Always so prim and proper until trickery and mischief is necessary. Maybe your mother would like to invite Nicholas Ellsworth to attend the house party as well?"

Frowning, she sighed. "It means I'll have to pay him some attention, but at least it would give us a chance to find out if he's a nice man."

"That is the point, Faith," Mercy said. "Unless you've already decided against him and you just want us to figure out a way for him to become unsuitable."

"Let me decide after I meet him. Then perhaps we'll need a secondary plan of attack." Faith smoothed her skirt and fussed with a wrinkle, which wouldn't release.

Aurora stood, went to the cabinet in the corner, and pulled out a decanter of wine. "Shall we toast our new covenant?"

"Oh yes," Faith, said clapping and practically bouncing with excitement.

Poppy went over to help with the glasses, and once poured, she brought one for Mercy and one for herself, which she sloshed several drops of on the table. When they each had a glass and stood in a circle, she said, "To the Wallflowers of West Lane. No harm shall ever come to any of us every again."

"Never again," Mercy repeated.

"No harm," Faith said.

Aurora nodded, and they all touched glasses with a musical clink of crystal.

Chapter 2

Rhys hated teahouses and the petty gossip floating around them as if the frilly curtains and white table linen demanded it. He'd needed a place where he could meet with Poppy, which was not at his sister's home and publicly suitable. In spite of the unacceptable thoughts running through his head since offering to help her, he would behave like the gentleman he was. Poppy Arrington was a mess. She always said the wrong thing, had no sense of fashion, and was far too headstrong and opinionated. Besides, she didn't like him one bit. When he married, which wouldn't be for some time, he hoped his wife would tolerate him to some degree.

The rain and early hour had kept most of George's clientele away. He didn't think such a small thing would keep Poppy from showing up, though it had occurred to him she might leave him waiting just to punish him. At least a good fire burned in the hearth to warm him on the dreary day.

For three years he had tried to fathom why she disliked him so. While she and his sister were away in Switzerland he had visited twice, but he'd spent little time with Poppy. He obtained permission to take Aurora away, and they went into the Kingdom of Sardinia to eat and catch up on gossip. The last time he'd brought his best friend Garrett Winslow with him, and that visit had been very merry and vexing, as the ladies often were.

His father had disliked Poppy and deemed her a bad influence on Aurora. He had been horrifically in error about his choice for Aurora's husband. Rhys should have been more attentive rather than running about town with friends and mistresses. Maybe if he'd paid better attention, Aurora's suffering would have been lessened. He forced his anger down and focused on the task before him.

Father's opinions were rarely correct. Rhys preferred to form his own opinion, and while Poppy mocked society's rules, she was intelligent, funny, and kind to everyone. Though he seemed to be the exception to Poppy's benevolent nature.

Only one other table was occupied, and the three ladies sitting there were engaged in their own conversation when the bell above the door jingled and a slightly wet and delightfully flushed Poppy stumbled in.

"By the Kraken, it's awful out there." Poppy shook out her umbrella. Rhys stood, shook his head over her exclamation, and bowed. "May I help you?"

Narrowing her eyes, she studied him. "You may take my overcoat if you like. I don't know why we couldn't meet at the West Lane house."

Taking her overcoat and umbrella, he placed them both on the hooks near the door. "I thought it best to leave Faith and Aurora out of the planning."

Other than a few wet strands of warm brown hair clinging to her face from the damp and the bottom few inches of her dress, she'd managed to stay dry. Sitting, she gave him a hard look. "I don't see why. I will tell them everything anyway."

Lord, he wished he could see something other than disdain in those deep blue eyes when she glared at him. "I'm well aware of that. Still, too many plotters can muddy the plan. Since Aurora can't participate and Faith shouldn't be included should she actually marry Breckenridge, I thought it best to keep it between us."

One thing he'd always admired about Poppy was her keen mind and ability to recognize when something was right or wrong. Her eyes focused on a spot on the whitewashed wall, and slowly her expression softened. "I see your point."

Rhys sat. "Good. I knew you would. Shall I tell you what I think?"

There was her narrowed gaze again. "I don't suppose I can stop you."

It did no good to fawn over and coddle her. He had tried to get her to like him over the years, and she only became suspicious. It was better to be himself and let her think what she would. "You may tell me your plan first if you like."

Eyebrows raised and lips in a pout, she made him want to kiss her senseless. Lord, where had that come from? He shook off the impulse. Nothing about Poppy was right. Her dress was out of fashion, and the cream color washed her out. Her hair was tied in a tight knot, but bits had fought loose and stuck out in every direction. He had given too much thought to her and decided it was her lack of interest that drew him in. Since he'd left school, he'd been chased by every marriage mart mama in England and their silly daughters. Poppy was the first who dismissed him as a pariah. If he could turn her opinion around, he could shed his unwanted feelings. It was brilliant. They would save Faith if need be, and he would divest himself of his notions about Poppy all at the same time.

"Rhys, why are you helping me?" She leaned forward, pressing her breasts against the table in the most delectable way.

His mouth went dry. "I told you. It's the least I can do after allowing Aurora to be hurt all those years. I thought you were going to tell me your plan?"

The way her gaze softened, she was beautiful rather than just pretty. "You were not at fault. It was your father and Radcliff who were culpable and hopefully they are both in hell for their crimes."

Despite his father's many flaws, he couldn't let her say such things. "My father could not have known what Radcliff was. I did not approve of many things my father did and said, but he would not have intentionally harmed Aurora. You must know that."

Eyes cast down, she flushed. "I'm sorry. It is one of my many character flaws to say what I'm thinking. Most of the time thinking it is more than enough. I should not speak of the dead in such a way."

It cost her the loss of some pride to offer him an apology. The agony of it wrinkled her pert nose and shadowed her eyes.

"Tell me what you think we should do to begin this investigation," he said.

Nodding, she waited while the server placed a tray with tea and two cups on the table.

Once the girl curtsied and rushed off, Poppy poured the tea. "The Sottonfield ball is a good opportunity. I hope to dance with Nicholas Ellsworth and do a little prying. I doubt he'll pour out his heart to me in the span of one dance, but it's a start. Beyond that, we must look for other times when we can get him alone."

Despite having never met the Duke of Breckenridge, the idea of him dancing and sharing secrets with Poppy twisted inside Rhys. It would be a bad start to hate the man before they began their research. "Perhaps my sister can give you some help with your attire and tips on dancing without damaging your partner."

"I can dress myself."

He looked from her messy hair to her muddy, worn boots and sighed. "I will make inquiries with some of my friends and see if anyone knows him or knows what he was doing in France for so long."

She cocked her head. "Why do you look vexed? Is it because of what I said about your father? I have already apologized and truly, I never had the impression you admired him much when he was alive."

That mouth of hers would get her into trouble one day. He shook off the ridiculous jealousy. "I am not vexed, but you really should monitor yourself, Penelope. I have known you for six years and you constantly say the most outrageous things."

"Are you saying you had affection for your late father?" Her nose wrinkled in the most adorable way.

He sipped his tea. "My father was a difficult man as you well know. When he sent Aurora away, it was hard for me to forgive him. I worried she would be unprotected in Switzerland."

"Aurora told me you tried to keep her home and even after we went away, you continued to badger his lordship. It always made me wish for a sibling to stand up for me. Of course I had none. If Mother had delivered a son, then Father wouldn't have bothered with me at all. It would have been better. However, after me, Mother could have no others. I ruined all their plans."

"Your parents should also monitor what they say and perhaps even what they think. I would not wish for a sibling if I were you, as all my attempts to keep my sister at home failed as you well know." Old anger for his stubborn father roiled inside him.

With a shrug, Poppy sipped her tea. "I'm rather glad you failed. If you had managed to change your father's mind, I might have lost Aurora. We were happy at the Wormbattle School. It might not have been the most common way to finish a lady's education, but it got us away from London's prying eyes. I, for one, was glad to be gone from here and wish I could go back."

Poppy's attention drifted to a platter of biscuits fresh from the oven. The warm vanilla and spices wafted through the shop.

Rhys signaled the server to bring some of the sweets over. Watching Poppy's eyes light up and her pink tongue peeking out between those full lips would be worth the cost of a thousand pastries. "If you could go back, what would you gain? You hardly seem the type to hide yourself away."

As she closed her lips around the biscuit, her eyes closed in a rapturous expression. "Delicious."

Swallowing down his desire, he took a biscuit and ate it while attempting to ignore her delight.

Sipping her tea, she gazed at him over the rim of her cup. "I've never liked the demands of society, and you have continually noted my lack of social graces."

"I have seen you fumble around the ballrooms and embarrass a few hostesses. Yet your card is always full and you never lack for male attention."

The snick of her cup in the saucer was the first sign he had said something wrong. "I go to balls because it is required, and I dance with stupid men like you for the same reason. My card is full because my father has placed a giant dowry on my head like bait for the fish. You know nothing of my troubles, Rhys Draper. All you know of is your fancy title and the multitude of women who want to be the next Countess of Marsden."

Standing, she forced him to rise. The change in her demeanor was enough to set his head spinning. "I don't see why you have become upset."

Her chest heaved, and the effect was more distracting than he cared to admit. "You don't see anything. You and your kind always think the worst of those ladies trying to find husbands. Has it ever occurred to you they may want something else but have no options?"

She grabbed her wet overcoat and umbrella and was out the door before he had time to respond.

Something had just happened, but Rhys didn't know what it was. Through the window, he spied Poppy standing in the rain trying to hail a hack. The ladies at the other table were watching now as Poppy's last words had been in full voice.

"My sister is vexed with me," he told the ladies watching and hoped he was not recognized as he left money on the table, donned his overcoat, and ran after her.

Poppy stood straight as a tree with her hands fisted at her sides. Her overcoat hung on her, hiding her lovely curves as the rain soaked her cream-colored hat and ran in rivers downward. Curls of hair stuck to her face, and she kept her focus on the street as he approached.

The steady rain dripped off the rim of his hat. "What is wrong with you? I will drive you home. There is no need to stand out here getting soaked through."

"I don't need anything from you, Rhys Draper. I can manage to get myself home, and I can keep Faith safe without you mucking everything up."

He was not in the habit of being confused, but the last few minutes had him bewildered.

Clearly, he had struck a nerve, but how, he couldn't fathom. "I am well aware that you are a capable young woman. You don't need to prove anything to me."

Her face was covered in raindrops, but there might have been tears mixed in. "No. Of course, I don't."

Perhaps he was going about it wrong. He was used to Poppy being a fierce yet fumbling lioness, but here was a kitten he'd never seen before. "Poppy, whatever I said to upset you, it was not my intent. I agree that men, myself included, are ignorant about the lives and needs of young ladies. Let me take you home in my carriage and you can rail at me all the way as penance for my bad behavior."

Fisting her left hand at her side, she gave a nod.

Rhys waved his driver Patrick forward, and rather than allowing her to wait and get further soaked, he opened the door, tossed her umbrella inside, and lifted her into the carriage. She gasped as his hands wrapped around her waist. The warmth emanating through her coat, dress, and corset remained on his fingers even after he'd launched himself into the carriage as sat across from her.

The carriage rolled down the street. She gazed at her gloved hands in her lap and pulled at the wet fabric. "I should not have reacted so…loudly. People will talk."

"The ladies at the other table did not look familiar or like they would run in the same society. I told them you are my sister. Hopefully that will be enough to stave off any gossip. You and Aurora don't look alike, but as I said, the clientele was not from our immediate associations."

"Still, I should be more careful." The kitten was gone, but the lioness was missing too. Across from him sat the personification of a perfect English lady. Rhys might become sick. He wanted the lioness. "There is no harm done. But perhaps you might tell me why you became so upset."

"I'd rather not." She tugged at her glove, pulling the soggy cloth from her tapered fingers.

"If we are to work together to save Faith, it would be helpful to know what is going to send you into a rage." He should let it go, but he couldn't stop himself.

"It was not a rage." There was his lioness.

Lord, it was deadly to enjoy her temper so much. "Are we going to argue every point? Shall we bicker about whether we bickered?"

She cocked her pretty head, studied him, and then giggled. "All right, I admit to a small rage."

It was better than winning a hundred pounds on a pair of twos. "And the reason?"

"I don't like the way you assumed all women are clamoring to marry because it is what we want. The fact is, it is the only thing we can do to better our position in life. You can go out and buy land, build a factory, open a shipping business, if you choose. You can find ways to increase the production of your fields or decide you prefer a quieter life and retire to the country with a small income from your holdings. Men have choices. The only option I have is to marry someone who won't make me miserable or worse, beat me to death." The final words were forced out through a tight throat.

Rhys's heart broke for his sister, and he thanked God Radcliff was in the ground already. "I understand. I didn't mean to sound unfeeling toward the plight of women. Try to look at it from my perspective, just for a moment."

She wrinkled her nose and ran her fingers along the piped trim on the ruby-colored velvet on the cushion. "What do you mean?"

"I shall give you a specific example of why I rarely go to balls. Three weeks ago, my good friend Thurman Nash asked me to attend his sister's coming-out ball. Rebecca is a nice enough girl whom I met when she was still a child as Thurman and I were at school together."

"I know Becca Nash. She is a bit shy, but very nice." Despite her favorable words, Poppy frowned.

He would have called the girl mousy, but her description was kinder. "Indeed. I arrived at the Nash's townhome at a fashionable hour, and immediately I knew it had been a mistake. Mrs. Nash rushed toward me, her face bright red. If you know her at all, you must know she is rather terrifying under good circumstances."

At least Poppy had the good grace to try to hide her giggle, though it stirred something wonderful inside him to bring her joy, even at his own expense.

Mrs. Nash was near to six feet tall and had a bosom that preceded her by several seconds. She always wore her hair piled high and therefore towered over most everyone in any room. "Clearly, you have met her."

Another giggle.

"She was waving her hands, and her hair swayed from side to side. I thought surely it would topple and I would be smothered. She yelled, 'Marsden, you must come quickly and dance with Rebecca. All is lost.' I thought, good Lord, has the girl ruined herself at her first ball? I like Thurman, but what am I to do in such a case? I said I would be happy to dance with her and was dragged across the ballroom and thrust at poor Rebecca, who had spilled a good deal of wine down the front of her white gown and looked as if the incident had caused some hysteria. As soon as the dance was over, I suggested she might want to retire to her room and have her maid help her into a different gown. I was trying to help, and clearly her mother had lost her mind to not let the girl go and change. An hour later when she returned to the ballroom, both she and her mother were telling anyone who would listen I was sure to propose at any moment. I barely know the girl, she is too young at just sixteen, and I never gave any indication of special regard. I was badgered and embarrassed within five seconds of entering the house, and I'm afraid to go anywhere near my friend Thurman lest he be in on the conspiracy."

Poppy recovered from her laughter. "Odin's wolves. I can see why you might shy away from the ballroom and perhaps where you have gotten your opinion of women.. But you must understand Becca is only doing what she has been raised to do. From the moment we are born our mothers tell us we must find a husband, run a house, be an obedient daughter."

"And that is not what you want?" He longed to know what went on inside Poppy's mind.

All laughter fled, and there sat the perfect lady again. "Of course, it's what I want. What else could a person of my kind hope to have?"

Sensing there was more to the story, he longed to probe her, but the carriage rolled to a stop outside his sister's West Lane townhouse.

Patrick hopped down and pulled the door and step for her. The rain had slowed to a drizzle.

Before she could escape, Rhys pulled the door closed. "I hope you will consider telling me the truth someday, Penelope. I'm not the monster you think I am."

Sitting at the edge of the bench brought her so close all he need do was lean an inch forward and he could press his lips to hers. She might slap him or scream, but there was the chance she would return his attention and perhaps rid him of his fantasy.

A gaze filled with fire lifted to his. "My lord, just because your sister is my dear friend does not mean we have reached that level of confidence. However, you shouldn't fret. You are exactly as you should be, a perfect gentleman with all the privilege and purpose that goes with it. You have always known what you would be and how you would live."

As always, she'd put him in his place. Nothing she said was false. He had always known he would become an earl, and she was required by society to marry someone regardless of her feelings. "I understand. Perhaps for the sake of having an amicable association and for the sake of Faith's future, you and I should find a neutral ground. I shall attempt to be less the arrogant fob you think I am, and you can withhold your opinions of me and men of my sort."

She pushed open the carriage door, and passion filled her eyes. "I can only be who I am, but for Faith, I will do my best to keep peace between us."

Watching her stride up the stairs without a backward glance tightened something inside him. Giving himself a shake, he called up to Patrick to take him to the home of a very pretty actress. Melissa had been his mistress, but when his father died, he'd broken off the arrangement.

They reached Melissa's home twenty minutes later, and Patrick opened the door for him. Rhys sat staring up at the windows of Melissa's rooms. The building was in a respectable part of town. Not rich by any means, well frequented by good society. Many men of his class kept mistresses, but he found it impossible to keep the meaningless relationship for any length of time.

He thought his desire to get Poppy out of his head would spark interest in Melissa. "Take me home, Patrick."

Closing the door, Patrick gave him a knowing smile. "Yes, my lord."

Soft brown hair and startling blue eyes haunted him on the ride home. It wouldn't do. He had to rid himself of Poppy Arrington. His gut twisted at the thought. Perhaps it was the fact that she didn't like him that was so attractive. If he wooed her into desiring him, he would lose interest. Of course, the first woman to dismiss him was a challenge. That was all this was. She would vanish from his mind as soon as she wanted him.

A seed of doubt lingered despite his revelation. Rhys pounded a fist on the carriage's window frame.

Chapter 3

Poppy and her mother, the Countess of Merkwood, arrived at the Sottonfield ball just as Faith and her parents, the Earl and Countess of Dornbury, were greeting their hosts. While their parents became reacquainted and spoke of the difficulty of getting a daughter properly married, Faith and Poppy scooted away, hoping the crowded ballroom would obscure them from disappointed parents.

Taking Faith's arm, Poppy tugged her into the ballroom. "Mother picked me up just a moment after you and your parents pulled away from West Lane. I think this living away from home again is going to work out just fine."

"Mother and Father have no complaints about my living with Aurora as long as I continue with my duty to marry well." Faith pulled a long face and crossed her eyes. "It's a wonder they didn't force the issue three years ago like the Earl of Marsden did with Aurora. They are happy to be rid of me."

"Perhaps they became used to our absence while we were in Switzerland, and all these years they were lamenting bringing us home." Despite her chuckle, Poppy knew this was probable.

"You look beautiful, Poppy," Faith said as they walked arm in arm, slowly circling the elaborate room. "Lavender looks very good on you, and Aurora's lady's maid did a wonderful job with your hair."

"I feel like a doll twisted up for a glass case." Poppy held her breath against the painful corset. The large ballroom had eight enormous round pillars equally spaced to hold up the ceiling. She was sure one of the bumble-footed men would ram her into a pillar before the night was over.

Gilded walls and a thousand crystals reflected the hundreds of candles on each of four chandeliers and a dozen sconces. The arched ceiling, frescoed in the colors of an evening sky, made it questionable if they had ever come inside. "Let's see if we can catch a glimpse of your duke, Faith."

"Do you think we should wait for Rhys?" Faith clutched her arm tighter.

Patting Faith's hand, Poppy cringed at the reminder she had somehow become partnered with the arrogant earl. "I suppose he'll find us if he arrives. I'm not waiting around for any man."

"That attitude will not go over well with your mother." Faith frowned.

It was true; her mother had enough of Poppy's unconcerned attitude toward the marriage mart. The one poor marquis who dared like her enough to ask for her hand had been summarily dismissed as too stupid to spend a lifetime with. "I have never cared much for my mother's opinion where men are concerned. It was a mistake to bring Rhys into what should have remained a Wallflower endeavor."

"But if he can help?" Faith's eyes were wide.

Poppy pulled her arm closer. "Don't fret. I will utilize Rhys's advantages as a man, and we will not let you be married to a monster or even a dunderhead. Only the best men will ever be allowed to marry my friends going forward. I only wish we had known more three years ago and spared Aurora."

"You cannot change the past, Poppy, and beating yourself up about it will do no one any good." Faith had a kind of wisdom that was righteous and well-timed.

"Of course." Yet memories of her friend's battered body haunted her day and night. She shook off the dark thoughts. "Now, do you know what Nicholas Ellsworth looks like?"

"I understand he is very tall." Faith surveyed the room.

There were so many people about, it was difficult to see much. "Not much of a description."

"As I told you, Mother arranged everything through letters." Faith's eyes filled with worry, but she kept her expression neutral and pleasant. It was an expression trained into every young lady. Hiding one's emotions was an essential part of success among the ton. Of course, among close friends, the expressions hid very little.

From across the room a tall man with a shock of dark hair drew the attention of everyone in the room as he excused himself through the crowd and headed for them.

"I think this must be him now," Poppy said.

"He wouldn't. We haven't been introduced." Faith's expression was comical, a cross between shock and admiration.

Stopping a few feet in front of the ladies, he bowed. A bit of hair escaped his queue, and he brushed it back. His blue eyes were alight as if he were excited to meet them, and a hint of amusement ticked at the corner of his lips. The sharp angles of his face gave him distinction, the overall effect an extremely handsome man. "I apologize. I know this is rather strange, but it seemed ridiculous to stand across the room and wait for a common acquaintance to introduce us. I am Nicholas Ellsworth, Lady Faith. I trust your very fine mother has told you about me?"

Faith's big eyes grew impossibly bigger and her mouth formed an O before she recovered and pulled her curvaceous figure to full height of just over five feet. "I hardly know what to say, Your Grace. This is not done. "Faith spoke just over a whisper but plastered a smile on her face for the crowd. "I suppose there is no help for it now." She curtsied. "I am Faith Landon, as you appear to know already. Of course, Mother has told me about your correspondence. I had hoped for a more formal introduction." She sighed and shook her head. As if to show him the way, she added, "This is my close friend, Lady Penelope Arrington."

Nicholas bowed to Poppy. "A pleasure to make your acquaintance, my lady. I apologize to both of you for my rudeness. I'll admit I find all these rules tedious. Perhaps you might forgive me?" His smile could charm a queen, and Faith was not immune.

Faith gave a slight nod. "They are tedious, but they are still the rules we live by, Your Grace."

Raising an eyebrow, he leaned in. "I'm surprised such things matter to you, Lady Faith."

"Why would you say that?" Faith cocked her head; her lips pulled into a tight line.

"I was told you had to be sent away to the Wormbattle School. This usually indicates some disregard for societal rules."

Unable to help herself, Poppy hid a giggle behind her gloved hand. "We managed to return to England with some semblance of right and wrong, Your Grace."

Shrugging, he said, "A pity."

Faith gasped.

The music started and Nicholas asked, "Would you honor me with this dance, my lady?"

She accepted his arm, but her frown hid just below the surface of her calm facade. He'd left her no choice with the entire ballroom focused on them. Faith didn't like being manipulated. It was a mark in the negative column for the duke.

They looked good together. In her light blue gown, Faith was lovely with her dark curls tamed for the time being by pins. He was as tall as was reported and dressed all in black with only a dark blue cummerbund. It was as if they had arranged to both wear blue.

Poppy saw it as an opportunity for them to get to know each other, and it was safe because there was no way she would let the pair out of her sight. It was obvious Faith was stubbornly refusing to speak while Nicholas chatted throughout the dance. By halfway into the music, he gave up, and Faith appeared annoyed.

"Well, I see they've met." Rhys stood beside her, but Poppy had no idea where he'd come from. She never saw him approach.

"Yes. He's a bit unconventional. Introduced himself." Her skin warmed even though he was several inches from touching her. It was aggravating to have her body in direct conflict with her logical mind. She didn't like Rhys, and yet he made her uncomfortable in a very female way whenever he was near. Hades' blood, it was most inconvenient.

"Interesting." Rhys leaned closer. "I made some inquiries, but whatever he was up to in France is not public knowledge. I was able to confirm he has been back in England for a week, and he has visited number four Bow Street several times since. He was at White's two nights ago and avoided any gossip."

The warm scents of leather, woodsmoke, and something distinctly Rhys filled the air and made Poppy want to step closer and take a deep breath. Of course, that was not an option. He was arrogant and pushy. His only redeeming quality was his love for his sister. It was a love they had in common. "Not very much to go on. Nothing really. Though, the fact that he visited the Bow Street Magistrate is interesting. Perhaps he was in France in some official capacity for the Crown."

"It is possible. Still, it seems strange it would be such a tightly held secret. Why does Faith look as though she's eaten a frog?" He straightened his crisp white cravat and gave a crooked grin.

"I think she is trying to dislike His Grace despite his attempts to win her over. Even in the few moments I met him, he was charming. Did you see Aurora today?"

He frowned. "I stopped in for tea. I thought you might be there but found only my mother and Rora bickering with Faith trying to make peace."

Poppy sighed. "They never have gotten along very well. I spoke to her earlier and found her quite sad, but I had several errands to run before preparing for the ball. Faith was staying with her."

Gripping her arm, he pulled her away from the edge of the floor. "I thought she hated Radcliff. Why is she sad?"

It was a difficult thing to explain to a man, let alone a man like Rhys Draper, who thought he knew everything. Men like Rhys and her father had no regard for what women really thought. "It is complicated."

The music ended, and Nicholas escorted Faith over to her mother on the opposite side of the ballroom. They chatted, and the Countess of Dornbury laughed at something he said.

Rhys tightened his hold. "I'm not an idiot, no matter what you might think of me, Penelope."

"Why must you call me that when you know I hate it?" She had never liked her given name, and the only time it was used was by her mother or for formal address. But Rhys insisted on calling her Penelope since they were first introduced a week before the Wallflowers left for Miss Agatha's.

"That is exactly why I call you Penelope. Now, tell me why my sister is sad over the death of a man who mistreated her."

"This is not the place for such a conversation, my lord." She tugged her arm out of his hand but missed the heat of the contact. Damn him for being so nice to look at and warm to touch. And why did he have to smell so good? Woodsmoke and something wild in nature always filled her senses when he was near.

A waltz started, and colorful dancers took to the floor in pairs.

"Dance with me, then. We look foolish standing here on the outskirts of the dance floor gawking."

He aggravated her more and more. Crossing her arms over her chest, she stomped her foot. It was petulant, but that was how she felt. "I don't dance with men who use an address they know will offend me. Nor do I dance with rakes who run about town deflowering innocent women."

His warm breath tickled the shell of her ear and sent a tingle through her that settled low in her belly. "As a matter of fact, I have never deflowered an innocent. At least, not yet. Dance with me, Poppy."

The warmth of his breath on her skin spread lower until it pulsed between her thighs. Pushing aside her body's response, she faced him. "Are you flirting with me?"

Eyes the same pale blue as his sister's but filled with mirth and mischief, he winked. "I'm trying to get you to dance so you'll tell me what I can do to help Rora."

At once, Poppy was disappointed and relieved. "Fine. I'll dance with you but only for Aurora's sake."

A better dancer than she'd expected, Rhys whirled her around the floor with ease and grace. "You look very pretty tonight."

"There is no need to sound so shocked." She'd been primped and poked for hours so she would look presentable for spying on a duke. Foolish as it was, she had to admit, she'd hardly recognized herself in the glass when Gillian was done.

His full lips tipped up on one side in a maddening half smile. "I'm not shocked you can look lovely, only that you would make the effort."

"I think the process is a waste of time. I'll probably trip and tear the gown or fall and dirty it anyway, so it hardly seems worth the trouble." She stepped on his foot and made a quick apology.

Rhys chuckled and righted her. "We will have to work on your dancing skills. However, in my opinion, the effort was well worth it."

"Thank you. You are surprisingly handsome." It was true, but she had no idea why she'd told him so.

The way his smile lit his eyes made it worth the compliment. As fast as the delight had flashed there, it was gone, replaced by fury, which might have frightened someone who didn't know him well. "I love my sister, you know. If I had known Radcliff was harming her, I would have killed him."

It didn't matter that she disliked Rhys. His pain still shot a knife to her heart. "I know. Aurora knew too. That's why she made the three of us swear to never tell you. I cannot begin to count how many times I wanted to tell you the truth, but it was Aurora's to tell, and she thought you would land in Bedlam or worse if you knew."

His jaw ticked, and his grip around her waist tightened. He maneuvered them around one of the pillars with dexterity and even kept Poppy on her feet. "She was probably correct. I wish I could raise Radcliff from the dead so I could strangle him now."

The heat of his hand on her back spread with their shared love for Aurora. "Do you think we're foolish to think we can avoid Aurora's fate?"

"No. You cannot be forced to marry against your will. If you refuse, you may have issues with your parents, but better that then to be trapped with a villain. Besides, now you are under Rora's roof and it will be easier to disobey." He eased her closer just as she missed a step, righted her, and the breath went out of her. "Why is Rora sad?"

Far too comfortable in his arms, she made the space between them an inch greater. "Because she wasted three years. Because she didn't have a child. The only good thing she had hoped for was the beast to give her a baby to love, and he couldn't even manage that. Now she's a widow and damaged in ways that cannot be seen." Poppy ached for her friend.

A creased formed between his eyes. "I refuse to believe she cannot recover from this."

"You asked me why she is sad. I didn't say I believed all of what she's feeling is true."

One last turn and the music ended. The warmth of Rhys's smile shot a lightning bolt through Poppy, and she had to remind herself to breathe. Whatever had just passed between them, it was only a momentary lapse.

"Thank you for the dance, Lady Penelope. I will see if I can gain an introduction to His Grace and find you later to compare notes."

Somehow her given name suddenly sounded nicer coming from his full lips. Making a curtsy, she said, "I wish you luck."

As they separated, Poppy wandered toward a large fireplace. Being out of Rhys's arms left her with a chill she struggled to shake but determined it was some slight ailment trying to claim her. It couldn't be anything else. She had always hated Rhys Draper with all of her being. The only thing that had changed in six years was now he was bigger, with a grander title, and more women would throw themselves at him. His only saving graces were his love for Aurora and his willingness to help the Wallflowers, though she still questioned his motives for helping. It was maddening when he was nice and easy to speak to.

Faith sauntered over, frowning. "He has no manners at all. All he spoke of was some property he's trying to convert into a four-crop rotation or some such nonsense. I asked about his travels, and he wouldn't tell me a single thing. He hushed as if I'd asked for admittance to see the prince."

"His lack of details about his travels is interesting. There must be some mystery there. Rhys couldn't uncover anything either. I wonder what the big secret is." Poppy turned her back to Decklan Garrott, a young man who often sought out her attention and with whom she had no interest. "I will have to dance with this nit. Will you be all right?"

Wide eyed, Faith spotted Decklan over Poppy's shoulder. "Yes, of course. But I wanted to ask about you dancing the waltz with Rhys. You two danced very well together."

"Ha! I stepped on his toes no less than three times."

Faith shrugged. "That's quite good for you."

"A ruse to keep people from thinking it odd we were chatting so intently at the edge of the dance floor."

"It didn't look like a ruse." Faith's voice took on a singsong quality.

"Lady Penelope, may I have the next dance?" Decklan stepped into the small space next to them and bowed low.

Turning on a sigh, she had no excuse to offer. "Hello, Mr. Garrott. I would be charmed to dance with you."

So with no other choice and a farewell giggle from Faith, Poppy danced the quadrille with a very stupid man who really did like her but who she could never like. She managed the feat without falling or making too much of a fool of herself. A minor miracle.

The moment the dance ended she found a quiet corner to hide from the crowd and her mother. Faith sat with a group of women, including her mother, and might be about to cry with boredom. Before she had time to catch her breath, Rhys strode over with Faith's duke in tow. "Lady Penelope, may I introduce my new friend Nicholas Ellsworth, the Duke of Breckenridge. Lady Penelope is a close friend of my family's."

With a slight nod and a wry smile, Breckenridge said, "The lady and I have already been introduced. I had no idea your acquaintance was so vast, Lady Penelope."

"Oh yes, Your Grace, I have many dear friends. If you had not been out of England for so long perhaps you might count yourself among their numbers." She was flirting, but perhaps it was one way to discover his character.

Rhys's face turned red, and he mumbled something under his breath.

"I'm certain that would be the case. Perhaps we should dance to begin our acquaintance?"

Lord but Nicholas was charming. Faith might be in trouble. "I would be delighted." Taking his arm, she walked with him to the dance floor.

A moment into the dance, he said, "I take it you are a particular friend of Lady Faith's."

"Yes, we went to Miss Agatha's School together. You know, the school for girls who scoff at society's rules." She refused to be cowed by his title or his inquiry.

His lips twitched, and she thought he might laugh. "I meant it as a compliment, though it seems it was not taken as such."

"On the contrary, Your Grace. We Wormbattle girls are fond of crossing wits with any manner of man who dares challenge us. I admit I was a spirited youth who didn't always do as I was told. I often escaped our home to see a show or a traveling circus. I enjoyed the company of the farmer's daughters more than that of the stuffy gentry in our neighborhood. For my heinous crimes, I was packed off to Switzerland for three years. I'm sure my parents thought it a fitting punishment, and it might have been so if I had not met three other young criminals who made the adventure worth taking." Poppy watched his expression change from pity to admiration, and she pushed down the notion of liking the Duke of Breckenridge. This was the man trying to steal Faith from them. He was the enemy.

"I assume Lady Faith was among those three?"

The dance moved her out of his hearing for several turns but then back to him. "She was."

"And what were her crimes?" His expression remained soft and without malice.

"You will have to ask Faith for that information if you really want to know. I have only my own secrets to divulge, Your Grace." Unsure of how he'd managed to investigate her instead of the other way around, Poppy swallowed down the effects of his charm, and counted out the time of the dance before she made a fool of herself. "What of you, Your Grace? You have been out of England for many years. What manner of trouble did you get yourself into and why have you come back now?"

The crooked smile returned. "I traveled about the Continent until it was time to come home and do my duty. I'm no different than any other young rake ready to settle down."

It was not quite a lie, but Poppy could tell it was not the truth either. There was something about the way his neck colored and his eyes lost their humor that told her he was not telling the truth. "Is that so? Rakish young men all return to England to settle down after writing a dozen letters to the mother of a young woman whom they have never met? Rakish young men propose marriage via those same letters? I must say, I have been acquainted with several rogues and rakes and have never heard of this type of action being taken from abroad. What was it about my dear friend that made you think she was the one woman who might make you happy?"

The music ended too soon, and he bowed over her hand. "Thank you for the dance, Lady Penelope."

"I prefer Poppy, Your Grace. If you are going to court Faith, you may as well get used to me too." It was a risk to have given so much information, but sometimes one had to get closer to the enemy in order to strike the killing blow.

As he stared for a long moment, skepticism then amusement faded in and out of his eyes. "My friends call me Nick or Nicholas. Perhaps you would do me the honor, Poppy?"

She made a pretty curtsy and allowed him to return her to the edge of the ballroom where Faith waited, and he asked her for the next dance.

Frowning, Faith took his arm and they disappeared into the crush of dancers.

"You seemed very cozy dancing with Breckenridge." The tone of Rhys's voice grated and filled with something Poppy hadn't heard before. It might have been jealousy, but that wasn't likely.

"He's not what I imagined. Not like any other duke I've ever met."

Closing the gap between them, he moved so he stood over her, and her face was only inches from his chest. Poppy had to crane her neck to look at him; his anger was palpable. "Are you in love with him?"

It took her several beats to translate what had to be a mistake. Perhaps Rhys had lost his mind. She blinked, hoping to clear her head of the nonsense. "Are you mad? First of all, I've only just met the man. Second, I'm not inclined to love anyone romantically at this time or ever. Third and finally, he is for Faith, not me, so my only interest is in the strength of his character."

Rhys took a step back, and his expression smoothed. "I see. Well, it was an honest mistake with the way you were talking about him."

"I don't see how. I merely said he's not what I expected. He's unconventional. That doesn't mean he's not a monster. We still need to find out his opinions on women, animals, servants—and we need to know what he was up to for the last few years." Poppy had no idea why she had divulged so much to Rhys about herself. She'd only meant to discredit his assumption, but she'd managed to vomit out her lack of desire for men in general.

"Animals and servants?" He crossed his arms over her broad chest and leaned against the wall, looking out over the ballroom.

Taking a similar stance, she breathed deep. She had to explain everything to him. "Yes. If a man is kind to his servants and loves animals, it shows sympathy and empathy for others no matter their station. For instance, my father has seven maids working in his house and I can promise you, he doesn't know the names of five of them. Those women have worked for him for ten years, but he never bothered to learn their names. He ignores them. Mother makes sure there are no attractive women working in the house so Father will keep his hands to himself under their roof. Whatever he does outside, she chooses to ignore."

Again, she had told him too much. Something about the way he listened without judgment made her tongue loose. Her cheeks heated, and she searched for some way to extricate herself from his company.

Turning his head just enough to catch her gaze, he asked, "Is that why you are not inclined to love anyone romantically?"

Poppy pulled back her shoulders and kept her chin up. "It is one reason."

"Not every man behaves like your father, Penelope. Some men take their vows quite seriously."

"Spoken like the rake you are. You would no more be faithful to one woman than you would dance naked in Piccadilly Square."

He unfolded his arms and turned to face her. "For the moment I'm going to put aside your mention of me dancing naked, though I'm interested to find out how you imagine such a thing. Why do you suppose I wouldn't be faithful to someone to whom I pledge my troth?"

Cheeks on fire, she wanted to hide behind the heavy draperies. How had she gotten herself into such a topic with such a man? "I am not discussing this with you. This is not the time or the place. Pledge your troth, by Medusa's snakes."

Head cocked, he narrowed his eyes. "You insult me in the basest way, then refuse to back up those accusations? I thought you had more grit than that, Penelope. And where do these ridiculous phrases come from?"

"Stop calling me that!" Her temper flared.

"Why? Why do you hate your name so vehemently?" He leaned forward until his nose was only inches from hers.

A group of men had turned to gape when she raised her voice. Now several other parties were watching them.

Poppy stepped away and spoke in the barest whisper. "That is none of your business."

It was the coward's way out, but she ran from the ballroom and out into the cool night. What she needed was a long walk in the garden and as much space between herself and Rhys Draper as possible.

Chapter 4

Rhys closed his mouth and watched Poppy run out of the ballroom. Her lavender gown billowed like clouds behind her. Her shoulders pulled tight, almost to her ears, as she clutched her fists to her sides. He had no idea why she had gotten so upset. He was the one who had been insulted. She'd said he was incapable of being faithful. Granted, her father was notoriously loose, but what did that have to do with him?

She had never liked him, he knew, but he hadn't realized her opinion of him was so terrible. It was likely her opinion of all men, and he shouldn't take it personally, but the way she said he would run about after marriage grated on him.

Brooding in the corner, he couldn't shake the sting of Poppy's bad opinion. He'd watched partygoers laughing and talking around him. The musicians signaled they would begin again, and a large group stepped onto the dance floor for La Boulangere. Couples formed groups of eight. The light, upbeat music should have put him in a better mood, but he couldn't shake his malaise.

Faith walked over and smiled. Folding her hands in front of her, she scanned the room before bringing her attention back to him. "Why do you look so mean?"

Masking his emotional state with a practiced calm expression, he asked, "Why does Penelope dislike me so much?"

There was something about the way Faith fidgeted that made Rhys uncomfortable. She was the most practical of his sister's friends. She at least made an effort to comply with society's rules, though she didn't always succeed. Her physical attributes were often spoken about behind closed doors among the men, and Rhys had on two occasions censured young men for their comments. Faith was a sweet girl and deserved respect.

Poppy's more gentle curves and the way they might feel distracted him, and he almost missed Faith's response.

"I think you will have to ask her, Rhys. Wallflowers never gossip about each other."

"Is it gossip to tell me why someone dislikes me so intensely? I always thought we were just oil and water and didn't mix, but tonight I have learned it is more than that. She truly hates me, thinks I'm a man of no character. I shouldn't care. Penelope Arrington is nothing to me save my sister's friend. Yet I'm confounded by her rancor."

Faith sighed and patted his arm. "Then I suggest you find a quiet moment to ask Poppy about her feelings."

He laughed. "She is not very forthcoming."

"You may have to be patient." Her gaze flitted across the room.

Rhys followed her gaze and spotted the Duke of Breckenridge, several inches taller than anyone else in the crowd, sneaking along the far wall and out the garden doors. He had obtained his overcoat, but leaving through the back was unusual. "Stay here, or better yet, find your mother and stay near her. I'll follow your duke."

Without waiting for a reply, Rhys walked out the nearest door to the garden. Keeping to the shadows, he followed the sharp footsteps on the cobbled path. The moon gave plenty of light, and several torches had been lit along the path, giving the garden a sense of the primitive. The boxwoods were thick and green, affording him ample cover.

Breckenridge kept his gaze forward as he hurried to the farthest corner of the gardens where several evergreens stood sentinel, creating a wall of trees. Pushing his hands into his pockets, he scanned the area in every direction.

The tall bushes were the perfect place for Rhys to remain hidden yet retain a view of the duke's activities. He felt a bit guilty for spying, but his new acquaintance gave the impression of a man with something to hide. Too bad, since on first meeting, Rhys had liked Breckenridge and thought him a fine match for Faith. He was smart, rich, and somewhat unorthodox, which might suit Faith despite her constant attempts to appear staid and formal. The truth was, none of his sister's friends were typical debutantes. They had keen minds and adventurous souls. Nothing like what most titled men wanted in a wife.

Perhaps his sister and the other Wallflowers were right to investigate the duke further. A man whose past was a mystery and acted as if he had many secrets might not be the best choice of husband. It might turn out to be nothing, but there was no way he would let another woman fall victim because of an opportunistic parent. If his own father were still alive, he'd be tempted to call him out for forcing Aurora into a dangerous marriage. He didn't know how he was going to live with the knowledge he'd been ignorant of her situation. Somehow, he should have known her marriage was more than a bad match. He'd known she disliked Radcliff but thought it was because the man was a fool not a beast.

Taking a breath, he focused on the task at hand. Finding out if Breckenridge's secrets made him a threat was his mission, and he would not fail.

The greenery rustled, and he slipped into a break in the shrubbery. Whoever drew close stopped inches from Rhys's hiding place. The familiar scent of lilacs and Poppy's warmth reached him. The foolish woman was going to get herself in trouble.

Breckenridge's attention was focused toward the back of the garden.

Easing forward, Rhys clasped his hand over Poppy's mouth and dragged her back into his niche. "It's me. Be still and don't scream." Whispering against her ear engulfed him in the heady scent uniquely Poppy. His lips touched the soft skin behind her ear, and his body reacted with violent desire.

Poppy relaxed, which molded her back against his front.

He removed his hand from her mouth but kept the other around her waist. Knowing he should put space between this maddening woman and himself didn't seem to mean a thing when she was soft and pliant in his arms.

Movement at the back of the garden stopped anything Poppy might have said as they both watched a stocky man with black cropped hair and olive skin slip out from between the evergreens. He was dressed for the evening with a smart suit and crisp white cravat tied to perfection with a dramatic flair. Draped across his shoulders was a long, layered cloak, which fanned out like a cape when he walked.

Poppy gasped.

The man turned in their direction. "Were you followed, Your Grace?" he asked in a thick foreign accent.

Looking around, Breckenridge shrugged. "Doubtful anyone inside cares a fig for what I might do in the garden. I'm simply a duke out to get away from the crush and enjoy the night air. No one would think anything different. Do you have the maps, Geb?"

"I heard a woman." Geb narrowed his eyes.

Shrugging, Breckenridge turned in their direction. "I'm sure it's just a couple finding a bit of privacy for activities of a carnal nature."

With one last look in the direction of their hiding place, Geb shrugged. He reached inside his cloak and produced a scroll of parchment. "This is all I could obtain. It's incomplete but a good start."

"Incomplete?" Breckenridge tucked the scroll inside his coat then smoothed the front of the fine material.

Geb shrugged. "Those you seek are not keen to give themselves up. I will keep searching for the rest."

They shook hands, and Breckenridge said, "Thank you, my friend. Do not put yourself in too much danger over this. If you can't find the rest of the map, we shall find another way. I have lost enough friends already and would hate to see you harmed."

Geb slapped his back. "I am like the wind, Your Grace, and cannot be captured."

Laughing, Breckenridge shook Geb's hand. "I will contact you soon."

Slipping out the same way he came, Geb was gone a moment later.

Breckenridge stepped onto the cobbled path and turned toward the house. His direction would bring him past where Poppy and Rhys were hiding. If he turned toward the niche, they would be exposed.

Rhys being caught in the garden would be of little consequence, but Poppy could be ruined by such a transgression. Turning so his back faced the path, he pressed her deeper into the niche. All Breckenridge would see was a man's back with little idea of who was there but a good idea some untoward delight was in progress. Most gentlemen would walk by without investigating as long as it appeared the woman was willing.

His footsteps drew closer.

"What are you doing?" Poppy's eyes sparkled in the moonlight and filled with fire.

"Shh." Rhys pulled her close. Soft in all the right places, she was also surprisingly solid.

Hand on his chest, she pushed back. "Don't you shush me."

As she refused to heed his warning, Rhys did the only thing he could under the circumstances. He kissed her hard in order to keep her pretty mouth from uttering another word and giving herself away. A woman of good breeding caught in a compromising position with a man, in a garden, at night and unchaperoned, would be fatal to her reputation. She struggled for an instant then gasped before relaxing and softening in his arms.

Knowing she didn't care for him didn't make her less lovely or desirable, and the little moan deep in her chest undid him. He eased his grip and nipped her full bottom lip. Silken and warm, she tasted like the perfect confection, and he wanted more. He wanted to gorge himself on Poppy until there was nothing left.

She sighed, and he slipped his tongue between her lips. Gripping his coat with one hand, the other slipped around his neck, and she toyed with his hair.

Longing shot through him from every place she touched. Even her fingers in his hair was somehow erotic. "You taste so good." He devoured her mouth, grazing her teeth and seeking out her sweet tongue.

Boldly, she met every lick and nibble in a duel filled with passion he could never have expected. He kissed his way across her cheek and down her jaw, gaining him a low moan, which vibrated inside her. He pulled her tight against his hard length, and she gasped and clutched his hair tighter.

No fear lurked inside this magnificent woman as she opened her mouth for more of him.

Cupping her cheek, he indulged in running his thumb along the creaminess of her jaw to her ear. He traced the shell, and she gasped and pressed tighter to him.

She was a force, and he was powerless against the gale that was Poppy Arrington. She slipped her hand into his coat and petted the soft cotton of his blouse, driving him to want more than was appropriate for a kiss to save her reputation. If he didn't back away, he would good and truly ruin her.

Oh, but how he longed for more. Not an hour ago, she'd insulted him, and now he wanted to deflower her in the garden. He allowed himself to consider if she'd let him go further but decided not to tempt fate. He'd already taken advantage but couldn't feel bad for a kiss he would remember forever.

The footsteps were long gone when he pulled back, struggling to catch his breath and regain his good sense.

Her chest rose and fell, and she glared at him with wide blue eyes made even starker by the dark lashes that framed them. Drawing her hand slowly out of his coat, she touched her lips. "Thor's hammer. You kissed me."

He gulped in air. "I was trying to hide you from Breckenridge. You were going to give yourself away if you kept talking."

Blinking up at him, she was a vision, and Rhys was not immune. She might always fight with him and make him mad with her contrariness, but he'd always seen her beauty under all her awkwardness. If she had always looked at him as she did now instead of with disdain, he might have courted her years before.

He couldn't believe the path of his thoughts. Court Poppy? It was insanity. She didn't like him, had never liked him.

"You were trying to protect my reputation?" She tipped her head to one side.

THE EARL NOT TAKEN

Beginning to wonder if that was his only motivation and if his plan to rid himself of desire by winning her over would work, he shook away over examining the moment. "Yes. If he had seen or heard you, we would have a real problem and you would be ruined. I thought to keep my back to the path and block you from sight, but you wouldn't stop talking."

She drew her hand away from his neck, but her gaze stayed with him. "You didn't stop even after the duke was gone."

He missed the contact and almost reached for her hand before thinking better of it. "No. Nor did you push me away."

The rise and fall of her breasts against his chest was more distraction than he could bear, yet he loathed to let her go. She swallowed, and he regretted not tasting her throat to find out if it was half as good as her lips. Damn, what was wrong with him?

Closing her eyes, she pulled her shoulders back. "You may release me now, Rhys. I think it is safe for me to return to the house."

Every instinct inside him said, *Hold on, don't let go.* Yet this was Poppy, a girl he called by her full name for the sole purpose of aggravating her. He let his hand drop from her waist. "I think we should discuss what just happened between us."

"Nothing happened. I thank you for your quick thinking when I almost made another foolish mistake. I appreciate you taking control and keeping my reputation intact. I'm sure you would do the same for any of Aurora's friends." A cool assuredness returned to her expression. Gone were the passions of moments before.

"And that is all? You wish for me to believe you felt nothing and the kiss was meaningless?" The desire to hold her until the sensual woman of a few moments ago returned clawed inside him, and he had to stifle the urge. Perhaps kissing her back to compliance was a better idea. Yet, if it really meant nothing to her, it would be idiotic to push himself on her like some heartsick schoolboy. The Bible proverb "Pride goeth before the fall" rang in his head, but he still refused to make an ass of himself with a woman who hated him.

"Your kisses were quite pleasant. I'll not lie." Even in the moonlight, her cheeks pinked.

Longing to see if the blush warmed her flesh, he fisted his hands and kept them at his sides. "I'm glad you think so. Perhaps you might consider indulging again under less stressful circumstances."

Her breath came faster, and her breasts pushed up and down with a distracting cadence. "Why would I do that? I am not some milkmaid for you to toy with."

Surprised by the vehemence of her tone, he took half a step back. "I would never consider you as such."

A moment passed with her gazing into his eyes. Kissing her was the only thing he wanted in the stretch where time stood still. He'd never wanted anything more, yet it had to be her choice. She already thought him a rutting animal. There was no need to prove her right.

"I must return to the house before I am missed." Skirting him, she stepped onto the path.

It took every ounce of his will to keep from dragging her back into his arms and showing her "pleasant" until she was again breathless and yielding in his embrace. "What about Breckenridge? Don't you want to talk about what we witnessed and heard?"

She glanced toward the trees then back at him. "I will meet you at George's tomorrow and we can discuss it. Will two o'clock suit you?"

Although he was disappointed she had picked the public patisserie and teahouse for a meeting, he could make no complaint that wouldn't sound like he was trying to get her alone. She would think he wanted more kisses, and she would be right. He bowed. "As you wish, Penelope."

Even knowing the name would bring her frown, he took joy from the way ferocity returned to her eyes before she ran back to the house.

Watching her go, Rhys knew he would kiss her again. She had returned his affection with more passion than he could have imagined. It should have doused the fires of his desire for her, yet he longed for more. Perhaps his plan was in error. First, he needed to find out why she disliked him so. Once she was out of sight, he strolled the cobbled path toward the house. He tried to remember a time when she hadn't regarded him with disgust, but other than a few moments earlier when they kissed, she had always thought him worse than dirt under her boot.

Try as he might, he could think of no reason for her to hate him. Other than always calling her Penelope, he'd never done anything to her that might cause a bad impression. In fact, in the six years of their acquaintance, tonight had been the first time in memory they had ever been alone together.

It shouldn't matter, but somehow it did. Finding out why Poppy had such a low opinion of him and changing it was his first order of business. When she saw him at George's, she would find him the most charming companion.

In the meantime, perhaps Breckenridge's foreign friend Geb was known around town. As soon as Faith and Poppy were in their carriage home, he would go to his club and ask a few discreet questions about the mysterious man with a map.

The ball was still horribly crowded when he returned. Lady Sottonfield was lamenting the early departure of the Duke of Breckenridge. Faith and Poppy stood with their heads together whispering. Poppy pointed to the tear on the hem of her gown while Faith inspected the dirt marring Poppy's glove. She must have fallen in her rush to get away from him. The Countess of Dornbury growled about the fact that Breckenridge had only taken two dances with Faith before disappearing into the gardens never to return.

Rhys made his way through the crowd toward Poppy and Faith and had almost reached them when his childhood friend, Garrett Winslow, stepped into his path. "Garrett, I thought you were out of the country?"

"I'm only in London for a few weeks. My mother forced me home for my cousin's wedding. I'm returning to the Continent as soon as possible." Garrett's easy smile was a reminder of simpler times. Though Garrett would one day be the Duke of Corbin, he was rarely stoic as most dukes were. He kept his hair overly long and tied back in a queue, his light brown eyes smiled, and the lines around his mouth proved the expression was meant for all to see. Even when Rhys was in a foul mood in their youth, Garrett always cheered him.

Searching over his friend's shoulder, Rhys caught a flash of lavender as Poppy exited to the foyer. He would have to wait for George's to see her again. He must be losing his mind to be suddenly consumed with any woman, let alone Poppy. Turning his attention back to Garrett, he said, "It's good to see you. I'm heading to White's. Would you care to join me? You can tell me of all your adventures while I've languished here in London."

Garrett crossed his arms, causing the fabric to stretch over muscular arms. "From the way you were looking at the pretty brunette in the purple gown, I'd say you have done a bit more than suffer."

Shanking off the comment as a joke, Rhys slapped Garrett on the back. "Just one of Aurora's friends. I'm always making sure those girls stay out of trouble."

"It looked like more to me." Garrett's gaze followed where the ladies had exited the archway. When he turned back, a sad cast clouded his expression. "How is your sister? I heard her husband died."

"She's as well as can be expected. Let's get out of this crush." Hoping to catch one last glimpse of Poppy as she left, he charged for the exit. Disappointed to only see the carriage rolling away, he returned to claim his overcoat.

Eyebrows raised, Garrett held back a laugh. "Yes, now I see you are just looking out for your sister's friends. That is very clear."

"Shut up, Garrett."

Garrett chuckled until they were seated in Rhys's carriage. "Who is the friend of Aurora's who has your attention so fully?"

"It's a long story." Rhys searched a sea of carriages clogging the street.

"As it would seem we shall be here for some time, you may as well tell me. But, only if it's an entertaining tale." Garrett's toothy grin shone in the light from the house.

Having been immersed in the Wallflowers for too many days, a male perspective was tempting. "I am helping Aurora and her friends discover if the Duke of Breckenridge is a suitable match for Lady Faith Landon."

Mouth agape like a carp, Garrett stared. He opened and closed his mouth several times. "Why on earth would you do that? He's a duke; of course he's suitable."

A vise tightened around Rhys's heart. "Radcliff was an earl, and I have recently learned not at all good enough to marry my sister or anyone for that matter."

"What do you mean?" Garrett leaned forward, and worry etched lines around his usually happy eyes.

Taking a deep breath, Rhys pulled his rage under control. "It's not my place to tell Aurora's story. You have been friends with her long enough. Perhaps she would be persuaded to tell you." He shook away his hurt at being kept in the dark for three years. "I am inclined to like Breckenridge, but his behavior is strange."

A heavy silence hung between them. When Garrett finally spoke, his tone was preoccupied and pensive. "My interest is piqued. I thought all women wanted to marry exceedingly rich, titled men with land. I'm sorry to know Aurora's marriage was not what she might have wished. How is Breckenridge's behavior unusual?"

Rhys told him about the duke's clandestine meeting with Geb but left out the fact that Poppy had been tucked perfectly against him throughout their spying.

The carriage moved several feet and stopped. Garrett clutched the window frame as he was jerked about. "I don't know Breckenridge, but I have met a man named Geb Arafa. He's from Egypt and deals in rare artifacts and, I'm told, information as well. He has an estate just outside of London. I can't imagine there are many men named Geb in London."

Rhys was almost giddy with the tidbit of information, and his desire to tell Poppy at once nearly had him jumping from the carriage and running across town to find her at his sister's house. He steadied his heart. "That's good news. Perhaps if we can't cypher out Breckenridge directly, we can see what kind of company he keeps."

"Geb Arafa is not a man to be trifled with. You may want to tread carefully." Garrett poked his head out the window. "We will be an hour getting out of this mess."

Sighing, Rhys leaned back and tried to forget how perfect Poppy felt in his arms and how she tasted. Unfortunately, the kiss was unforgettable, as was the vision in lavender. Something had to be done about the way she made him feel, and exposing himself to more of her was not working. Now that he'd tied himself into this investigation, there would be no avoiding Poppy Arrington until they completed their task. "Tell me about your travels, Garrett. Where did you go?"

"Since when do you care about France and the Italian Peninsula?"

It was true, Rhys had never cared about travel. He found enough distraction in his own estates and the vistas in England. He laughed. "I'm in need of a distraction."

Garrett leaned forward and watched Rhys. "Have you gone and fallen in love?"

"No." Rhys sat up straight and forced his best frown.

"Are you certain?"

"Positive."

With a *humph* Garrett sat back against the cushion as the carriage finally moved down the road.

Chapter 5

George's teahouse was full of happy, chattering clientele. Poppy had brought both Faith and Aurora with her. She told herself it was to keep things proper for the sake of the ton, but she knew it was her own propriety needing a chaperone.

The white tablecloth gave her something to fuss with and saved the lace on her dress from being mauled to tatters. Tea had arrived with the most charming rose-patterned cups and saucers. Poppy had no appetite for the warm tea and had only taken one nibble of her biscuit. She loved sweets, but her stomach roiled at the thought.

She'd slept little; the kiss she'd shared with Rhys played over and over in her head. He'd explained why he had kissed her. However, for the life of her, she couldn't fathom why she'd kissed him back. Oh, but it had been wonderful. That was the problem—she didn't like Rhys Draper, had never liked him. He was the epitome of what she thought wrong with all rich gentlemen. Yet his kiss had been sweet and more a question than a demand. Perhaps Rhys was the answer to a thought that had probed at her for some time. She had decided against marriage after the first month of Aurora's disastrous match, but the idea of never knowing what it was like to lie with a man niggled at her. Perhaps a rake like Rhys, who she need not fear would hurt her, was the answer.

Twice before she'd been kissed, and neither could be compared with the exquisite moments in Rhys's arms. The thought of more shot a pleasant thrill through her. "Zeus's beard."

"What is wrong with you today, Poppy?" Faith frowned from across the table. "You have not listened to a word I've said about Breckenridge and now you're cursing at who knows what."

Good Lord, she was becoming a complete ninny. "Forgive me. I am sorry, Faith. What were you saying?"

Faith took a long inhale as if she would say it all again.

Closing her eyes, Aurora placed a hand on Faith's arm. "Perhaps we can relive your assessment of the Duke of Breckenridge later, Faith. I'm curious as to why you're so distracted, Poppy."

"It's nothing." She spoke too loud and too fast. "I mean, I'm just thinking about what I already told you I saw in the garden last night."

The door opened and Poppy jumped. But it was only a lady and her maid, and Poppy regained her breath.

Narrowing her gaze, Aurora said, "Are you certain? You're jumpy and out of sorts."

"I'm fine." The door opened again, and Poppy forced herself to remain calm and didn't even look to see who entered.

Aurora smoothed her black mourning dress. "If you say so." She looked past Poppy. "Hello, Rhys."

Annoyed by her own reaction to his arrival, Poppy let anger fill her rather than acknowledging her heated cheeks and racing heart.

"Good afternoon, ladies. I didn't know I would be seeing all three of you today." His golden hair gleamed in the light coming through the windows, and somehow, he looked taller.

Poppy knew it wasn't possible for him to have gotten better looking, but why was her stomach all aflutter?

Faith said, "I wanted to hear what news you bring, and Aurora needed some time outside the house."

He bowed. "It is a pleasure to see you all."

Poppy couldn't bring herself to make eye contact. If he smirked, she might scratch out his eyes. Of course he would be pleased with himself after her wanton behavior. Kissing a rake, what had she been thinking? Fiddling with the white linen napkin in her lap, Poppy said, "I have told Aurora and Faith about what we saw in the garden last night."

His silence forced her gaze up. She thought she detected concern etched in the lines around his blue eyes and full mouth. It couldn't be he was worried over her feelings. No. It had to be something else.

Rhys cleared his throat and turned to Faith. "I have some further news about the man whom your intended met with."

Progress meant Poppy was a step closer to being rid of Rhys. That should make her happy…then why did she feel lost? "What did you learn?"

His gaze met hers and sent a thrill through her. "Geb Arafa is an Egyptian living in England. He has a home outside London and deals openly in rare artifacts and privately in information."

Faith placed her teacup in the saucer with a click. "Then perhaps His Grace is a collector and nothing is amiss."

"That is possible," Rhys said. "Shall we dispense with our investigation, Faith? Are you satisfied Breckenridge is suitable?"

Poppy's heart stopped. Was Breckenridge a good man? Would he treat her friend with respect? Yet to bully Faith into continuing would be no better than what her parents attempted with their high-handed arrangements.

Staring down into her cup, Faith patted her neat hair back. "Even if his dealings are aboveboard, it does not mean he is a nice man. I would still prefer to know what he was doing so long in France and gather a bit more assurance of his character."

Poppy let out her breath. "Perhaps Mr. Arafa would be willing to give him a character witness. If he is an information dealer, he must have knowledge to spare."

"I have the location of his home. Shall we pay him a call?" Rhys directed the question to Poppy.

"I cannot leave London with you without a chaperone." Even so, the idea sent a thrill through Poppy.

"Shall I come along?" Aurora asked.

Rhys's expression softened when he spoke to his sister. "If you are up to a day out, I would not object, Rora. However, paying a call while in mourning might raise some eyebrows in town."

"Must anyone know?" Poppy asked.

Rhys cocked his head and watched her. "I don't see how we would hide it."

Faith giggled. "You obviously don't know the Wallflowers of West Lane."

Forcing a stern look, Poppy said, "All we need do is use an unmarked covered carriage. No one need know who is inside or for what purpose. Carriages go in and out of London unnoticed all the time."

"That's rather sneaky, Lady Penelope." He failed in his efforts to hide a smile.

"Oh, Rhys," Aurora said, "how do you think we got away with so much?"

His smile faded. "As I recall, your antics got the lot of you sent away for three years."

"Worth every moment." Poppy fondly recalled all the fun she'd had before being sent away and the wonderful years at Miss Agatha's school.

"So, you would have me blacken the family crest on my carriage?"

Aurora sighed, but there was fire in her voice. "No need. I have a carriage and I'm happy to blot out the crest."

After a long pause, Rhys said, "I see. Then perhaps you ladies would collect me tomorrow and we will make an afternoon of it."

"Faith, I'm sorry to say it, but I don't think you should be involved." Aurora frowned, making her appear even more forlorn.

"I suppose it would be better if I remained at home. If I do marry His Grace, it would be better not to be too involved in investigating him. But I do hate being left out of an adventure." Faith popped a piece of biscuit in her mouth.

Poppy wished she could stay home and let Faith go. Being so close to Rhys for an entire day was a terrible idea. "How are your plans for a house party coming?"

Joy spread across Faith's face, and her eyes lit with excitement. She clapped. "Mother is enthralled with the idea. She has already made a guest list. I hope you don't mind, my lord, but I've had you added to her list. I thought, considering our mission, you might like to attend."

He bowed his head. "I am honored. Thank you."

A war raged inside Poppy between excitement and dread over spending a fortnight in the same house with Rhys and his mind-scrambling kisses. His woodsy scent filled her with the memory of being in his arms and wanting more of him.

She had to get away. She stood, forcing him to stand as well. "Well, that's settled, then. I have errands to run."

Rhys bowed. "I will see you tomorrow, Lady Penelope."

With a quick curtsy she studied her friends.

"I suppose we're leaving, then." Aurora stood and narrowed her gaze again. She paused for a moment in front of her brother. "See you tomorrow, Rhys."

Faith threaded her arm through Poppy's, and they left. Once on the street, she leaned in. "What was the hurry, Poppy? There were still biscuits."

"I noticed Poppy didn't eat a single sweet." Aurora took her other arm.

"I'm not hungry." Her stomach growled as if commanded to disobey her.

"Did something happen between you and Rhys?" Aurora was far too observant.

"No. He and I are still at odds, just as we always were. We danced and bickered before watching Faith's intended in the garden. I fell on the way back to the house, and Mother returned me to West Lane. Faith was there."

Faith fiddled with the lace on her sleeve. "They appeared very cozy dancing, but the rest is true enough. It was a shame you ruined the gown. It suited you very well."

"I see," Aurora said. "Shall we go home and have the carriage painted?"

Thankful for the change of subject, Poppy stepped into the vehicle and pushed her thoughts of Rhys to the back of her mind. She had more important worries. She had a Wallflower to protect.

* * * *

Poppy arrived outside Rhys's townhouse alone. She stayed inside the unmarked carriage while the driver went to the front door. Hands gripped in her lap, she forced herself to relax. It was only Rhys. She'd known him for years, and while she didn't like him, he was not dangerous. All would be well, and they would save Faith if she needed saving.

The carriage door burst open and Rhys jumped in. Wide eyed, he scanned the interior. His blond hair flopped over sky-blue eyes, and he brushed it back. "Where is Rora?"

"She said she did not feel well enough to travel today. Since we have an unmarked carriage, I didn't see any reason to delay. After all, we'll be back this evening and no one will be the wiser." Pleased with the staid tone of her voice, Poppy smiled as he sat across from her.

He removed his hat and grinned. "You have me all to yourself, then, Penelope. What will you do?"

Stunned to silence as the carriage rolled down the streets of London, Poppy recovered. "Are you trying to make me angry, Rhys Draper? I will not be baited into such childishness."

Grabbing his chest, he sighed. "That is a terrible shame. I dearly love to see you in a temper."

She crossed her arms over her chest and pretended to ignore him.

A light drizzle increased to a steady rain by the time they left the city. The sky darkened, and thunder boomed in the distance. After an hour Poppy's silence seemed petty compared to the situation. "I did not think Mr. Arafa's home was so far."

"Nor did I." All humor gone from Rhys, he pounded on the front side of the carriage.

A moment later they rolled to a stop. John had been Aurora's driver for three years. He opened the door. "I'm sorry, sir, madam. I cannot find the house in the directions."

A knot formed in Poppy's throat. "Are we lost, John?"

Sopping wet, John shrugged. "Not in that we couldn't get back to London, my lady. I just can't seem to find the house, and we've gone rather far off the beaten path. The roads have turned to mud. It would be best if we found some nearby shelter until the storm's passed."

Rhys's shoulders stiffened, and he frowned. "See what you can find, John. Perhaps my information was in error. I don't want to throw a wheel and land Lady Penelope in the mud."

"Yes, my lord. There must be some shelter to be found." John shut the door, and the carriage rocked as he jumped back up to the driver's seat and called to the horses.

A chill filled the carriage as they slogged through the mud. Poppy struggled to keep her teeth from chattering.

Rhys tugged off his coat and, easing forward, tucked it around her. "I'm very sorry about this, Poppy."

The sound of her preferred name on his lips warmed her even more than the lovely gesture of his coat. "It isn't your fault it rained."

"I should have double-checked the directions." Worry creased his brow.

"Without the bad weather it would be no more than a slight inconvenience. Besides, in good weather perhaps the house would be more easily seen."

The carriage turned suddenly, and she gripped the window frame to keep her seat. In keeping with her normal state, she was unsuccessful and flew to the other side of the carriage, arms and legs flailing.

Scooping her up, Rhys chuckled before settling her upright on the cushion. He didn't immediately release her.

It was perfect in his warm embrace, and the way his gaze shifted from her eyes to her lips, she thought he might kiss her. Fairly sure she would not stop him, her heart pounded and her attention was drawn to his mouth. She really was becoming a fool.

With a shake of his head, he released her. "John must have found something. Don't worry. We'll be fine."

"I'm dry and safe in the carriage, Rhys. Thus far, I have no grave concerns. You seem more fretful, to be honest."

The carriage rumbled over a bridge then onto smooth road.

When he turned back from the window, relief eased the lines around his mouth. That kissable mouth.

"There is a house," he said on a sigh.

Leaning forward, she studied him. "You really were worried."

"You are in my care. I would not forgive myself if you were harmed."

Shocked at his obvious fears, she didn't know what to say.

Rhys smiled. "Besides, Rora would never forgive me if anything happened to you."

John pulled up to the front door, and several footmen rushed down the steps with umbrellas.

"It seems we are saved." Poppy wanted to lighten the mood. A serious and caring Rhys struck her as far more dangerous than the lighthearted rogue she was accustomed to.

A very tall butler with dark hair and a mustache pulled open the door. "Madam, sir, please come inside before we are all drowned." His rich accent was similar to Geb's.

"Thank you." Poppy accepted his offered hand and stepped under the umbrellas.

Once they were inside, a woman with the keys of the housekeeper hanging from her waist and a bright red turban on her head ran toward them. "My word, what a time to be caught on the road. Welcome to Aaru. Our master is not in, but he would wish you to be given the utmost hospitality."

"You are very kind." Rhys bowed and smiled.

The butler said, "I am Kosey. Your driver and horses will be cared for. Mrs. Bastian will bring you some tea to warm you."

Rhys handed Kosey his hat. "I am Rhys Draper, Earl of Marsden, and this is Lady Penelope Arrington. We were looking for the home of Mr. Arafa when this sudden storm drove us off the road."

"Yes. This can happen. You are most welcome here, my lord and lady."

They were all very kind, and Poppy hated to break into their warm welcome. "Forgive me, but is this the home of Mr. Geb Arafa?"

Mrs. Bastian grinned, and Kosey gave a slow nod. He said, "I'm afraid the master is not at home, as Mrs. Bastian said. We do expect him for supper. Perhaps you might join him for the meal."

"That is very kind. Thank you." Poppy followed the housekeeper from the foyer and its polished wood-and-crystal chandelier into a large parlor adorned with massive lamps, overstuffed furniture, and foreign items she'd never seen before.

"What an unusual room," Rhys said.

"It is the master's favorite room in the house. All the items here are from his home in Egypt. I'll just go and order the tea. Feel free to explore." Mrs. Bastian slipped from the room and closed the door behind her.

"It would seem we have found Geb's home." Rhys picked up a stone statue depicting a bare-chested man holding a scroll and wearing a turban. The nose of the statue was missing, and the base had strange pictures carved all the way around.

An enormous round divan filled the center of the room. The burgundy material shone like silk, and it was strewn with a dozen pillows in every color.

Poppy sank into the soft, decadent seat. "Good Lord, I may never leave this spot. Rhys, you must try this. It is positively the most wanton divan every made. Like sitting on a cloud."

He touched another statue of some scaled beast with a long snout and sharp teeth. "This is remarkable."

Gold, silver, and bronze statues, trinkets, and relics filled every hard surface. The walls were draped in rich fabrics depicting Egyptian scenes of war, love, and daily life. It was impossible to sit up straight on the fluffy furniture, so she leaned back on her elbows. "I've never seen anything like it."

Crossing to where she sat, he beamed down at her. "You look quite at home there."

His smile faded, and some emotion she couldn't pinpoint crossed his face and made him look angry for an instant.

"You should try it."

Rhys leaned over her and placed one hand above her shoulder. As the cushion gave, it brought him closer to her until his knees touched hers and his mouth was mere inches from devouring her. "I do not know if I could join you there and not regret my actions, Poppy. Surely you would regret them, and I couldn't bear it."

"Are you teasing me?"

His gaze dipped to her body beneath his. "Myself, I think. When did you get so beautiful?"

Footsteps at the door startled her to sitting, and she whacked her head against his. "Ouch!" She held her bruised forehead.

Laughing and touching his own battered head, he stepped away. "A sign much needed."

There was no time to ask what he'd meant by a sign. Had he intended to kiss her? She shouldn't be disappointed by the arrival of the housekeeper, but her heart sank as she stood up and lamented the sore spot and bad timing.

Mrs. Bastian stepped in with a heavily laden tray. She placed it on a round table near the window. "Come and warm yourself with some tea. I'll have a maid come and build a fire. When the master is away, we don't warm this room, but you'll be comfortable here for a time."

Poppy sat at the table. "Thank you, Mrs. Bastian. You are very kind, and that cake looks delicious."

"Our cook is quite proud of her sweets. Shall I pour or will you, my lady?"

"Don't trouble yourself. I will pour. You have already done enough," Poppy said as she took the lily-painted teapot in hand and poured two cups.

Alone again with Rhys, perhaps she should have found an excuse for the housekeeper to remain.

When she put the pot down, Rhys let out a breath before sitting across from her. "Not even a drip on the linen."

There was the Rhys she'd grown accustomed to with his judgments and sarcasm. "I realize you think me a vacuous fool, but I can pour tea."

Those fine blue eyes she couldn't help but admire softened in their regard of her. His lips thinned, and he studied his tea before returning his gaze to her. "You are quite wrong, and I am very sorry to have given that impression."

Thunder boomed, stopping his admission. A maid, soaked through, rushed in. "Sir, Kosey asks if you might assist. A tree has fallen on the barn and several horses are trapped."

"Hades's breath." Poppy rose, heart pounding.

Rhys ran for the door. "Show me the way."

Poppy followed into the storm. There must be something she could do to help.

The entire front of the stone barn was crushed by an enormous old oak. The roof had been struck, and wood stuck out in all directions. Several footmen in white livery and Kosey were attempting to move the thick trunk to no avail.

Kosey hacked away at bits of raw wood with a large ax.

Soaked through in an instant, Poppy gripped her skirts and ran around to the back of the barn. The front would take hours to clear, and the storm made it impossible. One side step to avoid a tree limb and she fell hard in the mud. Picking herself up, she continued around the barn. On the opposite side, there was only a small door meant for a man's use. It would not be big enough for the horses to pass. Inside, two black and two white giants kicked and danced, ready to burst their stalls. Their eyes wide with panic, they brayed and kicked the walls. "Hush now. It's going to be fine." Approaching the closest stall, she cooed to the largest of the beasts.

"You're going to have to calm yourself or things will go very badly."

The whites of his eyes showing, he kicked the wall, sending the other three into fits. Thunder shook the battered walls, and bits of wood toppled to the floor.

Covering her head, she cringed until the dust settled.

The way he was kicking and rising on his back legs, the stallion would soon damage himself.

"That will do," she whispered and put her hand on the top of the door. "None of this will help your situation. If you injure yourself, then what a pickle that would be. The men will find a way to get you out."

He finally settled on his hooves and pointed his ears in her direction. A sign he was listening.

"Poppy, the barn is not safe. Come away." Rhys spoke softly from the door where she'd entered.

Glad Rhys had the sense to stay calm with the horses in such a state, Poppy swallowed her own worry. "Perhaps you might use the back of the ax to widen the door. I'll keep them calm, and we'll all leave together."

Black as night, the stallion pressed his nose against her fingers.

She petted his soft snout. "There now. That's better."

The other three calmed as well.

Rain poured through the roof, and lightning brightened the barn with each strike. Poppy formed a trust with the largest animal and petted his soft face while cooing to him. "There's going to be some noise and fuss, but I'll stay with you, my friend." Turning to Rhys, she gave him a nod. "I think you can open the wall now."

Kosey towered over Rhys. His turban gone his black hair hung to midchest. He surveyed the scene, and then the two men banged away at the stone around the doorway.

When the wall was wide open, grooms and footmen rushed in.

Poppy stepped back. "Be easy with them. They've had a scare."

Rhys's wet warm hand slid into hers. "Time you were out of here too."

They ran through the rain to the house. Keeping hold of her hand, Rhys steadied her on two slick spots.

In the foyer, Kosey said, "You are a fine woman with the horses, my lady."

Heat filled Poppy's cheeks. "Having little skills with people, I've always had a way with animals. I'm glad I could keep them from injuring themselves."

"I thank you both for your help." Kosey retreated into the stormy afternoon.

Soaked through, covered in mud, and exhausted, Poppy tried to smile.

Mrs. Bastian ran in. "I've had rooms made up for both of you. Thank goodness it was the barn and not the house. We still have places for all to rest. You'll not get back to London tonight. You can dry off and rest. I don't think the master will make it home either. This storm…"

It was an extraordinary household. Poppy wondered about the master of a house where the servants were so kind and generous.

Mrs. Bastian climbed the stairs. Poppy and Rhys followed. The storm and the danger passing left her washed out and inclined to do as she was told if it meant dry clothes and a warm bed for a few hours.

The fireplace was already lit, and a fresh-faced maid smiled from inside a doorway, holding a stack of towels and several dry clothing options.

Stopping her with a gentle touch on her shoulder, Rhys asked, "Will you be all right?"

Warmed by his touch, she wished she could step into his embrace, but that wasn't possible and it was only her exhaustion making her feel such nonsense. She moved away from him. "I will see you later. I just need to rest a moment."

"I have a room for you just down the hall, my lord." Mrs. Bastian stepped down the hall.

With his hand gripping the doorjamb, Rhys leaned in. "You were quite amazing out there, Poppy. I would not have thought you so brave."

As chilled as she was, his words warmed her from the inside out. "I do have some skills, my lord."

"It was entirely my mistake to think they were all with regard to your intellect." With a smile, he was gone.

Chapter 6

When the maid came downstairs to say Poppy was still asleep, Rhys decided to decline dinner as well. He read for a few hours in the remarkable parlor before his grumbling stomach forced him down to the kitchen.

The staff was most obliging with bread, cheese, and meats as well as a bottle of wine. They offered to bring the food up to his room, but he had other ideas and carried the culinary treasures upstairs himself.

He'd lost his mind. It was the only explanation. Yet suddenly, the idea that Poppy disliked him pained him more than anything else ever had. He always enjoyed their banter and how easily she was brought to anger. Perhaps it was just the kiss, the way she'd responded, or the way she gazed up from that ridiculous divan.

When he'd seen her calm those enormous horses, his heart had broken in two at the notion she might be hurt by either the beasts or the unstable building. Still, her magnificent bravery left him breathless. In such a turmoil of events she had the presence of mind to have them break through the back wall and save the animals.

He knocked lightly on her door.

Something bumped inside. "Ouch!"

Perfectly Poppy, she hopped on one foot when she opened the door. "My lord, is something wrong?"

Heavens, she was a sight in a voluminous white nightdress and cap with no more than an inch of skin showing. He didn't know when it happened, but he was sure he liked her more than he should and certainly more than she would ever like him.

"I've brought food. I'm sure you're as hungry as I."

"You didn't eat?"

It seemed foolish now, but he shrugged. "When you didn't come down, I didn't wish to inconvenience the staff. I thought perhaps a kind of picnic."

Lord, he'd become a complete imbecile.

Poppy stepped back and opened the door. "I am hungry, and there is a very plush rug in front of the fireplace."

The dying firelight wasn't enough to note any change in expression. However, she'd invited him in, and he couldn't ignore the charge of elation that shot through him. Placing the large tray on the rug, Rhys added a log to the fire and poked at the embers until it caught.

Poppy took two large yellow pillows from the chairs and placed them on the rug before sitting. Her nightgown billowed out around her like a rose in full bloom. "Why are you staring so? Have I something on my face?" She wiped her cheeks and chin.

Kneeling in front of her, he took her hands away and held them in his. "You are perfect."

"Hardly. I am in a giant gown belonging to a very large maid, and I'm still the clumsy dolt I have always been."

Her warm, fresh scent flooded him with a wave of desire. "Since when are you shy about your accomplishments? I have known you for six years, Penelope Arrington, and you have never been one to dwell on your flaws rather than your attributes. It is not as if anyone is without fault."

Pulling her hands back, she searched the rug and the fireplace before finally looking at him again. "Shall I be completely honest?"

A knot formed in the center of Rhys's chest. Yet to deny her would be the end to this evening, and he was not ready to leave her. "Of course."

She put her hands on her hips. "I hope to think neither have I boasted my gifts nor have I hidden my flaws. I am clumsy and tend to not care what society thinks. I always say the wrong things and will probably spill something on my dress or tear my hem on any given day. Your sudden attention makes me think it's time I remind you of these things. I couldn't care less what society thinks of me, but I know these things are important to you."

Rhys poured the wine from the decanter and handed her a glass. "I know all of these things about you, Poppy. I also know they do not define your character, only some habits."

Biting her bottom lip, she drew a breath then took a long sip of wine. "Habits you find intolerable."

Unable to deny some of her mishaps had annoyed him over the years, he shrugged. "Somehow knowing you better this past week, those little faux pas do not seem relevant."

"Because I calmed a few horses? I'm still the same girl you've fought with for years."

He tore a piece of bread from the small round loaf then placed it on a plate with some meat and cheese. Handing it to her, he wished he could turn back time and behaved better toward her in the past. "If we had not bickered, I would have sorely missed it. I did not lie when I told you I dearly love to see you in a temper."

She ate the bread and drank the wine, watching him through narrowed eyes. "I don't believe you. Your sudden attention toward me can only be for one reason, and perhaps this is a good time to remind you that I am a lady, *my lord*."

Stunned, he sucked wine down his windpipe and nearly drowned himself. When he'd coughed enough to clear the wine, he found her with her arms crossed over her chest, frowning. His own temper flared. "If you thought my intentions so base, my lady, why did you let me in here?"

Brow furrowed, her gaze fell from his. Her cheeks were on fire. "I was hungry and perhaps a bit curious. Not that many men have shown interest in me...at least none with intelligence enough to be interesting."

"At least you consider me intelligent."

"There are a great many smart rogues, my lord. You are not so rare. Only your interest in a social pariah makes you different."

If she hadn't been so adorable in her powder puff of a nightdress, he might have been offended. Instead, something twisted inside him. "Why is your opinion of me so low?"

She ate and focused anywhere but at him. "My opinions are none of your business."

"You have insulted me, won't look me in the eye, yet you refuse to tell me in what way I could have offended you."

"I am not offended." She met his gaze. "You are the same as my father and all the other wealthy men in England. I want nothing to do with any of you or your society. I go to balls to appease my mother in the hope that in a few years, she will give up on my marrying and leave me in peace. Now that I can live at West Lane with Aurora and the other Wallflowers, I need not be a burden on my family. Perhaps they will give me control of a portion of my dowry and I can live a contented life without having to wonder if my idiotic husband is making a fool of me with a dozen mistresses around town."

Something was coming into focus about Poppy, and Rhys wasn't ready to let it go. He needed the full picture. "Is it a foregone conclusion this fictitious husband will take a mistress?"

"Of course."

"Because all men are inclined to lie and cheat?" He leaned back against the chair with his legs toward the fire.

She pushed her plate away and rose to her knees. "Are you going to try to tell me you will be a faithful husband when you take a bride?"

"There is no sense in telling you anything, Penelope. You have decided my character is flawed and there is no defense. I understand your opinion of me in general and admit your father has shown some rather bad judgment, but I do wonder why you think particularly ill of me."

She huffed and lowered to one side. Her little pink toes poked out from under the gown, and every muscle in his body wanted to touch those feet and every inch above them. Deciding it best to keep his reaction to himself, he asked again, "Why do you think me so base?"

A single tear trailed down her cheek. "You will not remember. Of course you don't."

Searching his memory for some offense he might have given, he drew a blank. "Remember what, Poppy?"

"When I came to your country home before Aurora and I were sent away to school." She leveled her gaze on him.

He'd been just back from school himself. Most of that time he'd spent arguing with his father to keep Rora home. "I recall you stayed a week or so before leaving for Lucerne."

Nodding, she smiled. "Your mother was inclined to give long speeches about how to be a proper young lady and why your sister and I had failed our families."

"That must have been unbearable." He had been on the receiving end of some of Mother's sermons and imagined the girls had been bored to tears.

She plucked her wine from the small table and sipped before putting it back and gripping her fingers together. "It was terrible. One day, to avoid another berating, I took a long walk around the property."

Suddenly the image of a young woman from the village and Poppy's appearance that day flashed in his mind. Heat filled his cheeks. "I see. I do remember now. You think because as a young man I took advantage of the offers of a girl from town, I am of the same ilk as the other men in your life."

"I know what I saw." She blushed bright red and took up her wine again.

"And you believe any interest I might have in you can only be dishonorable." It took a force of will to hold his temper, but as it was his own foolish actions that had caused her low opinion, hold it he did.

Poppy put the wine aside and stood. She wrapped her arms around her middle and peered into the fire. Her kind eyes danced in the firelight. "It makes no difference what you intend. If you wish to have a tumble with a woman you think will have you, I am not she. Perhaps you are honorable and wish to marry me for my dowry. I don't know, but I will not have a husband who I already know will break my heart or my spirit."

Fury rushed to his head and he shot to his feet. "Break your spirit?" He took several long breaths. "I will not apologize for actions taken when I was still young and foolish. I am sorry that day changed the course of our friendship, and I will endeavor to change your opinion of me."

"Why?" She tipped her chin to the side and watched him.

Stepping close enough so she had to crane her neck to meet his eyes, he ran his fingers along her long, dark braid where it lay against her shoulder. "Oh, Poppy. I wish I could answer that question. However, until you think better of me, there is no point. I will just say, I cannot live with the notion you think me a cad."

"Are you saying you have no lovers?" Her pretty lips twisted with sarcasm.

Her scent left him drunk with desire and something more, which he dared not think about. "Are you certain you want the answer to that question? Beware, I'll never lie to you."

Whenever she was deep in thought her gaze shifted as it did in that moment; then she stared into his eyes. "I want the answer."

Sorrow pressed against the inside of his chest. "I have had lovers. Though, not so many as you seem to think. For most of my adult life I had one mistress."

"And now?" Her voice trembled.

"About a year ago, I gave her up."

"Why?" Her throat bobbed with a long swallow.

Rhys longed to run his lips along the curve of her throat and taste her skin. He settled for a chaste kiss on her forehead. "I realized I would soon inherit and it was time to grow up."

When she made no reaction, he stepped toward the door.

"What of the woman?" Poppy asked.

Stopping, he took him a moment to realize she was concerned for a woman she didn't know and whose position in life was quite far beneath hers. "Poppy Arrington, you are a rare thing. Her name is Melissa; she is an actress. I gave her a pension in case she wished to retire to the country. I've heard since she's befriended a young viscount."

"Are you jealous?" With her back to the fire and her arms wrapped around her middle, she looked like an angel. Perhaps she was exactly that. Her shapely legs shone in shadows of the firelight.

Rhys closed his eyes. "I wish Melissa happiness. No. I harbor no jealousy as I was not in love with her."

"Then why offer her retirement if you didn't wish her to never take another lover?"

"This conversation has taken the strangest turn."

"You said you would never lie to me?" She raised her chin as if daring him to go back on his word.

"All right, Poppy. Melissa was very good to me. She was a good friend and a good companion for several years. I thought I owed her whatever options she wished for her life. It was not my place to make any decisions for her, nor would I have wanted that responsibility. I thought it was the right thing to do."

"I don't know what to make of you now."

It was the best he could have hoped for. "Perhaps you might think I am not the terrible person you'd believed me to be."

When she remained silent, he went to the door. "Good night, Poppy."

"Thank you for the meal. It was very thoughtful." She turned away and walked to the bed.

Despite the fact she was not looking, he bowed. "It was my honor, my lady."

* * * *

Rhys poked at the sausage and coddled eggs on his plate. He'd slept very little after learning the source of Poppy's low opinion of him. It had never occurred to him that the folly of his youth would come back to haunt him one day.

He couldn't change the past. The best he could do was prove to her he was not that boy anymore, nor was he like her father. It was important she think better of him. He would need to sort out why it was vital she like him, but he shook away the thought.

Kosey bowed toward the door as Poppy entered wearing the same white day dress as she'd worn the day before. It was clean and dry and looked as fresh as the lady herself. "Good morning, my lady. Shall I make you a plate?"

"Good morning. Thank you, Kosey, but I will do it." Poppy took a dish and filled it from the sideboard before joining him at the table.

He stood. "I didn't know if you would join me this morning or break your fast above stairs."

She was suited to the finery around her. At Aaru even the breakfast room was ornate with gilded trim around the large window. No curtains blocked the light filtering through as day had fully broken. The tablecloth was hemmed in red and sewn with gold thread.

Sitting, she forced a smile. "I have never cared for the habit of avoiding the mornings with others. Besides, taking one's morning meal in bed is for married ladies."

"I don't think anyone would fault you here. The staff is half in love with you after what you did for the horses." It was the perfect opportunity to discuss his feelings, but Rhys kept silent on the matter since his mind and heart were in such a jumble.

"I did nothing so grand but coo at them until they could be rescued." She nibbled a bit of bread.

"That is not what I heard." Geb Arafa strode into the breakfast room as grand as the decor itself. Wearing a morning coat of burgundy and a crisp white cravat, he beamed at them both. His olive skin and rich accent was welcoming.

Rhys stood and bowed. "Sir. Forgive us for intruding. Your staff has been most hospitable. I am Rhys Draper, Earl of Marsden, and this is Lady Penelope Arrington." Poppy stood, and Rhys hesitated. "We had planned to pay you a call yesterday but were detained by the weather."

Waving off the apology, Geb bowed then took Poppy's hand and bowed over it. "You are most welcome. I heard you saved my best horses from serious injury. Kosey related the entire story this morning. He is not given to exaggeration, so I am sure the lady is being modest. Running into a damaged barn with hysterical beasts is a remarkable act of bravery."

Blushing, Poppy resumed her seat. "I'm glad the animals survived unharmed, sir."

Geb sat and accepted a plate made up by Kosey. "It was fortunate for me you were detained or I might have lost them and I would not have the pleasure of meeting you."

It was incredible, but Rhys had all but forgotten the reason they'd come. The storm and everything that followed had clouded his purpose. "We came for some enlightenment, sir."

"I am intrigued, my lord." Geb raised an eyebrow and shoveled eggs into his mouth.

"We just have a few questions." Poppy's blush had not faded.

Rhys didn't like a shy Poppy, and he wasn't sure if she was embarrassed by all the praise for her actions or if she liked the look of their host. Perhaps she was thinking of the picnic in her bedroom. Whatever it was, he preferred her boldness to this meek version of the girl he'd come to know.

"The rain finally stopped early this morning. I'm afraid my small bridge is under water. I got through on horseback, but your carriage will not manage the path. As you are somewhat trapped here, we can walk in the garden after your appetites are satisfied and you can ask your questions."

Poppy stood, forcing both men to rise. "I am quite done. Your staff has been very gracious in providing me dry clothes to wear, sir. I will just get a shawl and meet you gentlemen in the garden."

They watched her go before sitting again. Geb pointed with his fork toward the door. "Remarkable girl. My horse, Pharaoh, is a fierce beast. Kosey told me she calmed him as if he were a lamb."

"It seems the lady has a way with animals."

"Has she tamed you as well, my lord?"

Shocked by the question, Rhys took in his host.

Geb laughed. "Forgive me. It is none of my business and we are strangers. It is rather unusual for a lady of her standing to travel alone with a gentleman. I would think she risks her reputation embarking on such a journey. She must hold you in very high regard."

Pushing back his plate, Rhys's appetite fled. "She made the journey for her friend, not for me. It was meant to be a short trip, which would go unnoticed by society. Hopefully we will return today and no one will care about our absence."

"An unusual arrangement, my lord. It has been my experience that you English care a great deal about such things." Geb signaled with a wave to Kosey, who poured him more coffee.

Annoyed by the truth of what Geb said, Rhys stood and bowed. "I will see you in the garden, sir. Thank you for your very fine hospitality."

Still holding his fork, Geb waved off the thanks. "It was a blessing you and your lady were here last night. I owe you a great debt."

"It was our pleasure to be of service in your absence, Mr. Arafa." With another brief bow, Rhys left the breakfast room and barreled through the house until he reached the back garden.

The summer brought much of the ornate garden to bloom while the heavy rains of the previous night left the walkways strewn with pink and white petals. The air was fresh with only a slight breeze carrying the earthy soil and florals. Only fluffy white clouds remained from the torrents, and the sun shone through, warming Rhys's face.

It was lovely, but Geb's words haunted Rhys. He had no idea what their return to London would bring. Poppy's reputation might well be ruined. Only the fact that she lived with Aurora and not her parents might save them.

"It is a spectacular garden, isn't it?" Poppy stood several yards away on the path below the veranda.

To join her, he trotted down the stairs. "It is very nice. I have always loved the world after a good rain."

She fell into step beside him, and they walked around a maze of low shrubs dotted with fountains, flowers, and dwarf trees. "Yes. It is as if the rain has washed away life's dust and left everything new again."

Geb strode toward them from the path to the right. "I'm glad you enjoy the grounds. My staff works very hard to keep it in the English tradition."

"Are the gardens of your country so different?" Poppy asked.

Closing his eyes and raising his face to the sun, Geb smiled. "They have more trees, and in a wealthy man's home, there would likely be built a small pond with fish in the center. The climate is quite different, my lady."

They walked along the path to where the quaint garden opened up to a field. At the far end a small fenced area held the horses from the night before. "I see they are pleased with their new arrangements." Rhys pointed toward the paddock.

"Ah yes. A temporary arrangement until the barn can be repaired." Geb turned the corner of the path and walked along the edge of the garden. "You have questions for me, my friends?"

Rhys said, "It is with regard to the Duke of Breckenridge. I don't know how to say this except to be blunt. What can you tell us about his character?"

The lightheartedness fled Geb's expression. "His Grace is a great friend of mine. I'll not speak about him to you or anyone else. It would be a breach of our relationship."

"You don't know us, sir." Wide eyed, Poppy shook her head. She clutched her hands in front of her. "Forgive us for asking. I can see how it would not be proper for you to give details about His Grace to people whose motives are a mystery."

"I am pleased you understand, my lady." Geb's expression softened as he offered her a warm smile.

Poppy's smile would have melted any man's heart. "It's only that he is to marry my dear friend and we have no knowledge of his character. You can understand our desire to see a friend safe."

"Why would you think her unsafe with His Grace?" Geb cocked his head.

"Men have not proven themselves to our small group in the past." Poppy avoided a direct answer, but her clear gaze remained on Geb's.

Geb's quick frown was replaced with a neutral nod. "I see, but I'm afraid I will never betray my friend by speaking of him without his knowledge."

"I see. Forgive my impertinence, sir." Poppy curtsied and kicked at a pebble in the path.

Perhaps Rhys should have let Poppy handle the questions. She seemed to have Geb half in love with her already, which grated on his last nerve. The fact that he had no rights to those feelings annoyed him even more.

Chapter 7

The bridge was still impassable, and Poppy needed something to do. She walked along the field behind the gardens toward the fenced area. The day had warmed up nicely, and she was back in her own dress.

The entire trip had not only been a failure, but a complete disaster. They had offended their host, Breckenridge would likely hear of the visit to his friend, and she could only imagine what worry they had caused Aurora and Faith.

Thank goodness they had traveled in an unmarked carriage.

As she approached the paddock, the large black horse she now knew was called Pharaoh trotted to the fence to greet her. "You look fine. No worse for your harrowing experience," she said to the horse.

"He's happy to see you." She hadn't noticed Geb standing in the shade of a large oak on the far side of the enclosure.

Poppy petted his soft nose. "I'm pleased to see him as well."

Walking toward her, he might have been an Egyptian king in white pants and a long white tunic. Far different from the traditional English dress she'd seen him in before. "I've been thinking about your request, my lady."

Gut twisting, Poppy's face burned. "I am so sorry we asked too much of you, sir."

"Perhaps if you told me why you wished to know Nicholas's character flaws, I would be more inclined to help." He leaned his arms across the top of the fence and placed one booted foot on the bottom rail. It was a rough paddock for a stately home, but it would keep the beasts safe while repairs were made.

Whether or not Geb Arafa could be trusted was debatable, but he had been a good host and his staff, though unusual, was very kind. "I was sent away to school when I was fifteen, Mr. Arafa."

His dark eyes widened. "Is this normal for the English to send their female children away?"

"No." Her gut twisted in the way it always did when she thought about her parents' disappointment in her. "I was not an obedient child, and my parents sent me to Switzerland in hopes of teaching me to be a proper lady."

A kind smile tugged at his lips. "And was that an effective punishment?"

Considering her traveling alone with a man who was not her husband to a stranger's home, it was all quite humorous. "As you may have guessed, my parents did not get the desired result, though for me it was the best thing. You see, while my friend and I were away at school, we met two other miscreants who would become our closest friends. I would do anything for them, and they would do the same for me."

"I see. Friendship is very important to me as well, Lady Penelope."

"My friends were all keen on finding husbands after school, though I have never wanted that kind of life. When we came home from school one of our quartet was married off to a man none of us knew. He did not turn out to be a nice man. Luckily, his death came before he could cause any irrevocable damage." Poppy watched Geb to see if she might get some sense of his feelings on the treatment of women.

He sighed. "To injure someone who is yours to care for is abominable."

Pharaoh nudged her shoulder with his large snout.

Laughing, she turned and petted him. "Indeed, but he is dead and they tell me I shouldn't speak ill of the dead."

"I suppose because they are not available to defend themselves. However, you are not prohibited from remembering their true nature." Geb scratched Pharaoh behind his ear as the horse had put his head between the two, demanding attention.

"Thank you for that, sir."

"If I may say, this experience of your friend's might have colored your own opinions on marrying?" His kind voice cut to the core of the matter.

Poppy shrugged off the nauseating feelings she associated with marriage. "My own experience sullied any desire to marry long before the incident we're speaking about."

"It is a great shame as you are a remarkable lady and would make someone a fine wife."

Blushing, Poppy focused on Pharaoh. "Thank you. However, it is not my own life I'm concerned for. Another of my friends from school is about to be engaged to a man we know nothing about."

"Ah. Nicholas, I presume." Geb nodded.

There was a war of dragons inside Poppy's stomach. She forced a smile she hoped appeared kind and sincere. "So, you see, we came because we knew of your association with His Grace and hoped you might be able to shed some light on his character."

"Why not go directly to Nicholas?"

The other black horse trotted by, and Pharaoh ran off to play.

They walked together toward the house as a light drizzle started. "Unfortunately; His Grace is less than forthcoming."

"I don't see that I can tell you about him without betraying my friendship with Nicholas."

They reached the gardens and took the path to the veranda. "I understand."

At the doors, Geb stopped. "I will tell you this, my lady. If Nicholas wanted to marry my sister, I would be filled with joy at the prospect."

A bubble of delight mixed with the lifting of a heavy burden inside Poppy. "That is a great relief to me, sir."

He opened the door and allowed her to enter first. "I would suggest you speak to Nicholas and get to know him. In my opinion, you will find him worthy of your friend."

Rhys stepped down the stairs just as they entered the foyer.

"Thank you, Mr. Arafa. Our talk has been very enlightening. And thank you for your hospitality as well."

"Your being here last night was fate. The house and grounds are at your disposal now and always." Geb bowed and smiled at them both before stepping through the door to his study.

"Where were you?" Rhys demanded.

There it was. There was what all men thought was their right. "I do not answer to you, Lord Marsden."

"You don't answer to anyone for anything you do. It is what has always gotten you into trouble. I fear you will end very badly, Penelope."

Pulling her shoulders back, she raised her chin. "And I was just starting to think you were not the ass I had always believed you were. It seems my first instinct was indeed correct."

She stormed down the hall and pulled open the farthest door. Having no idea where it led, she grabbed her skirts and stomped down the stairs.

Footsteps followed her down.

At the bottom, a damp basement lit only by small windows near the ceiling was not the escape she had hoped for. When the fury cleared from her vision, she gawked at a long table. It ran down the windowed side of the cellar, and every inch of space held some strange treasure.

Poppy stepped through the opening of what must have once been a dungeon's cell, but the door had long since been removed. Perhaps it had rotted away in the dank cellar.

"You cannot just trespass into someone's cellar."

Standing among the crowns, statues, gold coins, vases, and other treasures, Poppy turned.

Rhys stared wide eyed. "I'll go up and see if I can find a lamp." He ran back up the stairs.

Geb had said they had full run of the estate, but with all these treasures, she felt she was intruding on some secret world.

Poppy ran her hand along the smooth marble surface of a statue depicting an Egyptian queen. Her golden headdress had been inlaid with black stones forming a striped pattern. She only stood about two feet tall, yet even in her stone form she was a formidable queen.

A strange lion with a man's head stood next to the queen, made in a rough beige stone.

Dozens of scrolls lay piled at the center of the table, and a box of silver and jewels shone in the light as Rhys returned with a lit candelabra.

"What a remarkable collection. Some of these look as if they are genuine. Not the faked door knockers everyone is so thrilled with these days." Rhys placed the light on an empty bit of table and explored with her.

"Perhaps he deals in these things. I imagine if Geb were collecting bits of his homeland, he would display them more prominently than a rough table in the old cellars." She brushed dust from an intricately inlaid table. Different-colored woods had been carved into the piece to create a stunning mosaic of a woman and child in a garden.

"That is a reasonable assumption. It is also possible these items were obtained in a less than lawful way and he keeps them out of public sight."

Poppy fondled treasure after treasure as they made their way to the end of the table. A dark hallway continued on.

Rhys retrieved the light. "We have snooped this far; shall we see what other treasures hide in the darkness?"

Excitement bubbled inside Poppy. She loved an adventure, and the last twenty-four hours had certainly been a break from her normal life. "I have never been in a dungeon before. We attempted to get into the one at school, but we never got past the locks."

He laughed. "You four Wallflowers really were incorrigible."

The walls were damp, and the floor squished under her light boots. "If we had been boys, no one would have thought us odd. We would have been called spirited and hailed for our adventurous spirits."

"I suppose that is true." He was close enough that his breath tickled the back of her neck as the hallway opened up into a cavernous room carved into the ground beneath the house.

Poppy rushed forward to put distance between herself and Rhys while she turned to get a better look at the remarkable stone construction.

The mushy floor turned to mud. Poppy's foot slipped. One second she was avoiding the lovely tickle of Rhys's breath on her skin and the next she was flat on her back in three inches of mud and who knew what else. "Oh, Satan's beard!"

Reaching down, Rhys took her flailing hand. "There is the Poppy I know."

Heart in her throat, she wished she could bury herself in the mud and disappear. "I suppose you will now berate me on all my flaws and how unladylike I am."

He cocked his head. "I was thinking how perfectly adorable you look." With ease, he lifted her to her feet, bringing her chest tight to his.

Breathing was difficult with him so close and his sweet smile just for her. "You're lying. I'm a clown to most of the ton."

"Only to those who don't know you, Poppy." His lips were only inches from hers.

Poppy couldn't take her eyes away from his mouth. She knew she should push away, but his sweet words held her as much as his strong arms. "And you know me, Rhys?"

He smiled and brushed his lips against hers like a promise. "I think I do. It seems my eyes were clouded for all these years and in the last few days you have become clearer to me."

"But you don't like me and your father hated me." She wished her voice wouldn't tremble, but her heart was beating so hard she couldn't catch her breath. In such a short time, the feelings she'd masked with disdain for Rhys were fighting to the surface. It was terrifying and exciting.

"My father was wrong about a great many things. I have been mistaken where you are concerned." He kissed her again, but with the same gentle touch.

A soft sigh escaped her, and she longed for more from him. She made a weak attempt to hold her ground. "I have never liked you."

"I know." He deepened the kiss, melding his lips to hers. Making love to her mouth as if she were the most precious treasure.

Low in her belly, a tightness tugged at her. A voice in the back of her mind told her to pull back and maybe even slap his face, but it was too delicious to want to stop. She touched the soft tendrils of hair at the back of his neck and slid her hand along his broad shoulders.

She had to stay in control. Losing herself in the affections of a man was not what she wanted for her life. She jolted with fear and pushed back, breaking the kiss. His eyes asked questions she didn't know the answers to. "If you know I don't like you, why are you kissing me?"

He took her hand and the candelabra and started back toward the stairs. "You should get cleaned up. That mud must be very uncomfortable."

Of course, he was right. Her boots had not staved off the wet and muck, and her dress was ruined once again. Covered in mud from ankle to midback, she should have just agreed and let the conversation die. "You'll not answer me?"

At the bottom of the steps he stopped and lifted her chin with his finger. "I know my opinions of you have been irrevocably altered in the last week, and I suspect you have changed your mind as well."

"And these changes prompted you to kiss me?"

"You did not stop me, Poppy." His smile was at once sweet and wicked.

"No. I suppose I didn't. It is all very confusing." She went up the stairs Rhys followed close behind. "I will give it some thought. You are not exactly as I have believed these six years."

"I shall take that as a compliment." At the top of the stairs, he stopped Mrs. Bastian crossing the foyer. "Madam, can you find a few maids to help Lady Penelope? She's had a bit of a mishap."

Mrs. Bastian took one look at Poppy, and her eyes went wide. "Good gracious, my dear girl. You've been in the pit. The master uses it for storage, but I avoid that dark, damp place. It would seem some of the past day's rain made its way inside. Oh dear. I'll have a bath drawn in no time and we'll get you cleaned up."

Poppy was ushered up to her room before she could ask Rhys any more questions about the kiss. It was just as well. What more could she ask? He hadn't declared his love. But he had indicated that his regard for her had changed since this most recent association.

What she wanted to know was why.

He was a rake to be sure, but some said those who reformed made the best husbands. Good Lord, where had that thought come from? It was only a kiss. Most gentlemen would take advantage of such a situation with an unprotected lady. Except it hadn't felt like he'd done anything untoward. She really had no idea how to manage a sweet and affectionate Rhys Draper.

Two footmen came with a tub, followed by a constant chain of them carrying buckets to fill the vessel, then a long line of maids with hot water in pitchers.

Sitting on a stool in the corner, she spotted Rhys down in the garden, his attention fixated on the landscape and his hands clasped behind his back. His blond hair fell to his shoulders and fluttered in the breeze. Not overly tall, he still struck a fine figure in his fawn breeches and boots. Had he always been so broad in the back and chest? If so, she'd never noticed until recently.

"My lady, the footmen have gone. Would you care to bathe now? I'll help you out of your dress and have it cleaned." Mrs. Bastian straightened her royal-blue turban and wore a kind smile as if guests fell in the muddy cellar all the time.

"Thank you. I apologize for my constant need for a laundress." Standing, Poppy allowed Mrs. Bastian to help her out of her dress.

"Not at all. These things happen." Mrs. Bastian put the soiled clothing aside and helped Poppy into the deep tub.

The water was warm and scented with lavender. It soothed every ache, and she melted into relaxation. "They seem to happen to me with greater frequency than anyone else."

Poppy leaned forward to allow water to be poured out of a pitcher to wet her hair.

With both gentleness and strength, Mrs. Bastian washed her hair and massaged her scalp. "It just happens that way for some people. One of the reasons I don't go down into the cellar, my dear."

"Then we have that in common, madam. It is not looked upon favorably to be so clumsy when one's mother wishes to marry you off to a fop with a large pocketbook." The scent, the warm water, and the massage were putting her in a complete state of bliss. Poppy sighed out her contentment.

Mrs. Bastian giggled. "It is not a happy ailment for a maid either, my lady. In Egypt I was thrashed more than once for a burned garment or torn sheet."

Sitting up, Poppy wasn't sure what to say. "I'm sorry, but I hope you mean verbally and not otherwise."

With the same pitcher, Mrs. Bastian rinsed the soap from Poppy's hair. "I wish it were the case, but things were different there. It was not as if an English maid could leave her English employer and go looking elsewhere for work."

Relieved it had not been Geb who abused poor Mrs. Bastian, Poppy's curiosity would not let her abandon the topic. "How did you come to work for Mr. Arafa, then?"

Handing Poppy a washcloth and soap, Mrs. Bastian smiled. "This was all a very long time ago, mind you. Geb Arafa was quite young and the son of a wealthy man. He had dealings with my master and came to the house often. I had fallen in the garden while hanging laundry. My knee was cut open and my elbow was badly bruised. My dress had torn, and both me and my lady's gown were covered in mud.

"It was unfortunate that my master crossed the foyer at the exact time I had come in to get a bandage and wash the dress again. When he saw me, he went into a rage and tossed me across the hall. I hit the wall very hard and collapsed in a heap."

Poppy gasped before she could cover her mouth and hide her horror.

"Mr. Arafa arrived and, having heard the commotion, let himself in. Appalled by my treatment, he commanded my employment be terminated. He carried me out of the house and took me to his father's home. I was cared for there as if I were a member of the family."

Mrs. Bastian gathered the soiled things in her arms. "The master planned a journey to England and asked if I would like to come and be his housekeeper."

"And then you came here?" Poppy already liked Geb, but his kindness to a stranger from another land solidified her opinion.

Nodding, Mrs. Bastian walked to the door. "Kosey, the master, and I sailed west a week later. I have been very happy ever since."

"Does Mr. Arafa require you to wear the turban?" She blurted it out before she could check herself.

Mrs. Bastian burst into laughter. "Oh, you are a treat. So different from the stoic or indifferent ladies of the ton."

"I have offended you. Please forgive me. My mouth is as clumsy as the rest of me." Poppy thought she might slide under the water and drown herself. Why couldn't she act more like Faith in these situations and always say the right thing?

"Not at all," Mrs. Bastian said. "I wear turbans because I like them, and here, I can do as I please as long as the house is in order. Mr. Arafa is a different kind of man both here and in Egypt. He enjoys all manner of people and lives without judgment. Besides, ladies don't wear turbans even in Egypt. I think it gives an old housekeeper a bit of interest, don't you?"

Poppy wished she could stay forever in a place without the world looking down upon her. "It suits you very well."

"Thank you, my lady. I'll just take these things to be cleaned. You enjoy your bath and I'll return with something for you to wear."

Pruney skin and tepid water were what finally dragged Poppy from the tub. She wrapped herself in the oversized towel and curled up near the fire with a borrowed comb.

Everything she'd learned about Geb Arafa told her he was a good and trustworthy man. If he considered Breckenridge a friend, did that mean Nicholas was the kind of man worthy of Faith?

Perhaps it did.

If she really thought about it, she'd liked Nicholas at their one and only meeting. He was hiding something, to be sure, but did it mean he was a bad choice for a Wallflower to marry?

She sighed.

To know, she would have to find out what he'd been up to in France and why he didn't want to share that information.

Maybe she wasn't the best person for this assignment. After all, she'd thought Rhys a complete ass and a fiend with regard to women. Yet when he kissed her it had been an invitation and not a demand. His kindness had made her uneasy as if he were up to something, but it seemed he liked her.

The real problem was, she liked him too. It had happened so quickly; she'd hardly caught her breath before she was in the middle of it. The kiss had put her over the edge. Determined not to turn into a ninny, Poppy told herself to focus on Faith and Nicholas and leave Rhys to his own life.

Hair damp and mind in the clouds, Poppy startled when Mrs. Bastian returned with a gown.

"Sorry to disturb you, my lady. Mr. Arafa sent this gown for you to wear to dinner. He was horrified to hear of the mishap in the cellar and hoped this would be accepted as his apology."

Poppy examined the light green confection. Lace over satin, it was far more daring than anything her mother would let her wear. "There is nothing to forgive. This is beautiful."

Mrs. Bastian beamed. "I'm so glad you like it. Mary is coming up to do your hair and help you dress. I've heard there will be music after dinner. Kosey is a very talented musician."

"Thank you, Mrs. Bastian. You and Mr. Arafa are very kind." Her heart sped up at Rhys seeing her in such gown meant for a married lady rather than a debutante. Poppy touched the soft fabric and dreamt of Rhys touching her in such a gown.

"It is the least we can do after all you did to save those horses the master loves so much and our neglect in the cellar. We will get your dress cleaned though, don't you worry, my lady." Mrs. Bastian thought Poppy was worried about an old day dress, when the gown before her was exquisite beyond words.

"It is nothing," Poppy said. She had danced with Rhys before, but somehow, now, it was different.

Chapter 8

Rhys couldn't get the kiss out of his head.

Geb had been speaking to him for several minutes about the difficulties of transporting rare artifacts from the East into England, but Rhys's mind was elsewhere.

A great deal of what Poppy believed about him was true. He had dallied with several girls in his youth and taken a mistress as an adult. He had enjoyed some of the local ladies at his family's country estate when he was young. The kiss in the muddy cellar had been far from his first, yet he felt like a neophyte.

The sound of her sigh and the scent of her lingered with him until he'd lost track of the day. He'd walked for hours in the gardens, hoping to return to his commitment of shedding Poppy from his thoughts. He believed if he persuaded her to like him, his interest would wane.

She had kissed him back and looked at him like he was the sun to her world, and still he wanted more Poppy. If he were honest, he wanted all Poppy all the time.

Everything was turned upside down with a few simple kisses, and he didn't know what he was going to do about it.

Geb whispered something that caught on the breeze, and Rhys couldn't make out the words.

Poppy stood in the doorway flanked by two impeccable footmen all in white. The moss-green gown dipped low, showing off the swell of her breasts. Like a goddess, her dark tresses were curled and braided on top of her head with only the most tempting curls resting along her neck.

Her blue eyes were somehow bluer as she watched Rhys through those dark lashes. "I hope I haven't kept you waiting too long."

Geb rushed forward and bowed over her hand. "You have not, but such a stunning vision would be worth any length of time."

"Thank you for sending the gown. I'm sorry to be such a burden." She curtsied.

"No trouble at all. It is one of many items I have stored in this house. I think it must belong to you now. No one else could do it justice after seeing you in it." Geb escorted Poppy inside the parlor and waited until she was seated on the ridiculous round cushion before he sat next to her.

Geb's smile was beginning to annoy Rhys, who sat across from them. "You look very lovely, Lady Penelope."

"Thank you. I've had a most relaxing afternoon."

He'd seen the footmen toting water up to her room. The thought of Poppy submerged in a warm bath had been the thing that had sent him out of the house. The realization that he'd have given anything to join her in the tub both excited and terrified him. "I'm glad. I walked in the garden."

"You had fine weather for a walk." She tugged on the lace around her gloved wrists.

Geb cleared his throat. "The good weather should mean you can cross the bridge tomorrow."

A knot tightened in Rhys's chest. They would return to London with little news and a lot to answer for.

Poppy bit her bottom lip and stared at the carpet.

Looking from one to the other, Geb said, "Of course, you are both invited to stay as long as you like. I just assumed you wanted to go home once it is safe to cross the river."

Poppy drew a breath so deep her breasts swelled. "Of course, we must go back to town. It is only that here I have had more fun and been more helpful than in my usual day."

"I am certain you are a great joy to those around you each and every day, my lady." Geb stood.

Kosey entered. "Dinner is served."

The meal, while sumptuous, was painfully slow. Poppy sat across from him, and Rhys wanted to touch her more than he wanted roasted duck, no matter how good the food was.

The more she spoke of weather and fashion with Geb, the more crazed Rhys's desire became. The dining room was too hot, and his cravat rubbed. He made several attempts to adjust the neck cloth, but to no avail. It was torture.

All the while Poppy and Geb continued their happy chatter.

When the final course was cleared away, Geb studied Rhys. "It is a bit warm in here. Perhaps we should take our cake in the parlor. I've asked Kosey to play for us. He's quite talented."

"Yes. Good." Rhys blurted out the monosyllables before he could stop himself.

Poppy said, "That would be very nice. Thank you, Mr. Arafa."

"Do you play, my lady?" Geb asked.

The footman held her chair, and she shrugged. "Not very well. I'm afraid I do not excel at any of the charming occupations that make a fine lady accomplished."

Something about the apology in her tone set his blood boiling. Had he been one of the people in Poppy's life who had made her feel less than spectacular? "You have a great many talents, Lady Penelope. I have heard you play and was well entertained. I also happen to know you enjoy reading a good deal, which is a fine way to improve one's mind."

Geb offered his arm, which she took. "And modesty is a fine attribute as well."

Vexed with Geb for being so charming and angry with himself for his behavior over the last six years, Rhys lagged behind, giving himself a moment to rein in his madness. Whatever was happening to him, he hardly recognized himself, and he didn't like it.

Notes from the pianoforte in the other room drifted in. A minuet filled the house.

Rhys swallowed down his raging emotions and went to the parlor, where he found Poppy dancing with Geb. She was laughing and happier than he'd ever seen her. Geb was a rich man with a lot to offer any woman. Perhaps Poppy was falling in love and Rhys should stay only as her protector.

A footman offered him a brandy. Rhys was happy for the distraction, though no amount of alcohol would dull his senses where Poppy was concerned. It would only impede his good judgment. After one sip, he left the glass on one of the tables that had been moved aside to allow dancing.

She had never been graceful, but she danced with ease and joy. His jealousy abated when she caught his eye and blushed the most stunning pink. She had not blushed when Geb admired her. Contented to watch her throughout the minuet, he realized the flaw in his plan.

Denying it would do no good.

He had fallen in love with Poppy Arrington.

Somehow admitting it, if only to himself, lifted a heavy burden from inside Rhys. His heart tripped, and joy filled the space where anger and resentment had come to reside. The doubts his father pounded into him all his life didn't matter anymore. His only worry was if she'd have him.

The minuet ended. Geb and Poppy joined him and accepted cake from the footman.

"Would you care for a brandy or sherry, Lady Penelope?" Geb asked.

Her nose scrunched up in the most adorable expression of doubt. "I have never tried brandy."

Geb laughed. "Here you need not worry over gossips and society's rules. Any personal choices you make shall remain our secret."

She giggled and accepted the glass. Sipping carefully then cocking her head, she drew one eyebrow up before sipping again. "It's quite interesting. Nothing like wine or sherry. I like the bit of burn as it goes down."

"Excellent." Geb grinned and drank down his entire glass.

Genuine happiness rippled through Rhys while watching her experience something new. It was like tasting brandy again for the first time himself.

Kosey played a waltz.

Rhys stepped closer. "Poppy, will you dance with me?"

Staring up at him, she blinked several times and swallowed before responding. "I would be delighted."

At some point, words spoken by her had become powerful to him. He hoped she meant her delight, not just a phrase used in company for politeness. No. This was Poppy. She wasn't inclined to false praise or courtliness. He ordered himself to stop overthinking every word.

Taking her in his arms, he whirled her around the small dancing area in time with the music. "That gown suits you."

"Mr. Arafa sent it with an apology for the mud in the cellar." Poppy missed a step but kept her feet.

Rhys tightened his grip to make sure she would not fall no matter how often she might stumble. "He has my thanks. You are a vision."

"Mother would not approve of such a daring gown." Poppy sighed. "Nor would she have allowed this impromptu visit to a stranger."

It wasn't possible to deny that their delayed return could cause a scandal, but he couldn't regret any of it. He was tempted to make up some additional reasons why they couldn't return to London in the morning. "Perhaps it is best to leave your good mother out of this. We came to help Faith. Only she and Aurora know we made this journey, and they will conceal your unavailability if need be. I think Mr. Arafa can be trusted to keep this visit to himself."

She tipped her chin up and studied him. "I would have thought you would disapprove of this type of departure from the rules of society, Rhys."

Leaning in close to her ear, he breathed in lavender and Poppy. His body's reaction was both alarming and wonderful. "Perhaps you don't know everything about me, Poppy."

"I have known you for many years, and you have never missed an opportunity to remind me of how inept I am at conforming." On cue, she missed a step.

Righting her, he pulled her against his chest. "I have been a blind ass, and I beg your forgiveness for my ignorant behavior."

No longer dancing, they stood in plain view staring and holding each other. Poppy's blue eyes filled with pain and broke his heart. "I don't know what to believe, Rhys. You and I have been at odds for so long, how can I trust any of this?"

The music stopped.

A low shuffle of people leaving the room filtered through his concentration. They were alone.

All the years of bickering melted away, and there was only Poppy and how much he wanted her to like him. Pain burned in his chest dull and constant with the knowledge of her low opinion. "Oh, Poppy, how do I make up for disappointing you? Tell me and I will do it."

Reaching up, she touched his hair and ran her soft fingers along his face to his jaw. "I am not disappointed. I want to believe you. I want…"

His heart raced. "Yes? What do you want?"

Pink cheeked and with worry in her eyes, she soldiered on. The woman feared nothing. "I am not an expert on kissing. In fact, yours was only my third kiss. However, it did seem rather special to me."

Dangerous ground crumbled beneath his feet. He should hold back, but he tumbled into the abyss. "It was more than special. Kissing you was a revelation."

"What could it have revealed to you? I am still the same Poppy Arrington who always says the wrong thing and stumbles during the dance." Unwavering, she met his gaze, and mixed with the familiar mistrust, he imagined a glimmer of hope.

Comforting her was all he wanted. He kissed her cheek; soft and warm, she was everything temptation. "I find myself happy to hold you up when you misstep and looking forward to the next inappropriate comment. I don't know how it happened, but I suspect all my angst with regard to you has been building to our current situation."

"What is our situation?"

"Don't you know?"

"Tell me."

"I want you, Penelope Arrington. I've never desired anyone as I do you, now, in this place." He waited for her to slap his face, but the strike never came.

Her nose scrunched up as it did whenever she gave something a lot of thought. "Then you do not hate me."

Holding in a laugh that would have given away how uncomfortable he was with his behavior over the last six years, his shame swelled in his chest. "I have never hated you, Poppy. I have always thought you a beautiful, smart, incorrigible woman. I won't deny that your antics and attitude toward me have inspired behavior I am not proud of."

Those sweet lips that set his blood on fire pulled down, and a crease formed between her eyes. "I have long thought you were off bedding everything in a skirt you could catch."

"I am not a saint. However, your assessment was a vast exaggeration."

She stepped back like an emerald in a room filled with every other color. Poppy shined the brightest in a room filled with jewels. "Do you remember our first meeting at George's when you escorted me home and said you hoped I would someday tell you my wants in life?"

While he wanted her back in his arms, he respected her personal space. The moment she spoke of had changed his presumptions about her. "I remember."

She toyed with the fringe on one of dozens of pillows tossed haphazardly on an oversized red chaise. All the furniture might fit nicely in a sheik's harem. Sitting, she sighed. "I want to have a different kind of life."

Following her, he sat close. "Tell me about the life you dream of."

"My dreams do not include a husband to boss me about and keep me at his convenience." An angry edge laced her words.

"Is that what all husbands do?"

The way she glared at him, he might have had three heads. "A husband owns his wife in the same way he owns a house or a dog. How is he to do anything else when the world commands he use his wife as he would any possession?"

"You maintain a very harsh idea of men and marriage, Poppy." A knife twisted in his gut.

"Odin's wolves, Rhys, I know what I've seen, and every marriage I know of favors the husband rather than the wife in every way. Children are the only thing to recommend the institution." She crossed her arms over her chest.

Shaking off the distraction of the low-cut gown, Rhys asked, "Do you want to have children of your own?"

Looking him in the eye, she bit her lip. "Not enough to be under any man's thumb."

"Then you will not marry?"

"I will not." Her lifted chin and pert nose were meant as a sign of finality, but she was adorable, and he longed to kiss the look off her face.

"Are there no circumstances that might change your mind? Perhaps you might meet a man, fall in love, and believe he will be different."

She faced him, her lips twisted as if he'd spoken the most ridiculous notion. "Men are men. However, I don't wish to remain as I am either."

"I don't understand."

"Well, you don't want to marry, and you said you want me. If I give my virginity to you, I won't risk you ever telling anyone. I shall learn what all the fuss is about and there will be no consequences."

While his body was on fire at the prospect of making love with Poppy, what she said was soul crushing. "Good Lord, Poppy, you always say the most outrageous things."

She jumped up and put space between them. "You don't want to bed me?"

Following, he touched her elbow to stop her retreat. "That is not the point. You offering up your virginity as if it's one of George's pastries is beyond the pale."

"Perhaps, but it is also a burden I no longer wish to carry about. You would not harm me physically; therefore, you are a logical choice. I like you more than I expected. It seems to me, everyone would gain something they wanted. Is it not better to be honest in these situations?"

Leaning in, he kissed her nose and ran his knuckles along her soft jaw. "If you had any idea what you were offering, I would not hesitate."

Wide blue eyes blinked up at him, and her mouth parted. "Then show me what I do not know."

Uncomfortably rigid, he pulled her hard against him. "A stronger man would walk away. A better man would tell you to go to bed and not mention this conversation to anyone."

Making tiny circles on his neck and curling her fingers into his hair, she drove him near to madness. "Is it possible you are making more of this than is necessary, Rhys? Can coupling be such a monumental notion as to punish yourself for wanting?"

The candles guttered in the late hour. The parlor dimmed by degrees as each light went with a puff of smoke. The fire flickered to embers. Only its dim glow and the moon cast them in sensuous shadow.

Powerless, he would challenge her assumptions later. His decision unavoidable, he stepped from her arms and bolted the parlor door.

Returning to her, he cupped her cheek. "If you change your mind, you must tell me."

With a shrug she smiled, but worry filled those eyes he'd long admired. "I will not change my mind."

Nothing was how he imagined with this extraordinary woman. She could instill passion and frustration all in one breath. "Penelope, I want you very much in more ways than you're desirous to hear. If at any moment you become unsure, you may stop."

Placing her hands on his shoulders, she bit her lip. "You mean I can ask you to stop."

"No, my dearest. If you stop, I will as well. This is not something I am doing to you. That is where you have been misled. We will make love together."

Her lips parted, and her gaze flitted from his eyes to his mouth. Lips never touching, their breath mingled. Rhys closed his eyes, wanting no distractions.

She kissed him, forcing his eyes open. Her long, dark lashes rested against her creamy skin. Glowing in the moonlit room, her beauty took his breath away. "You are the most stunning creature, Poppy."

Eyes opened, she frowned. "I think I prefer when you call me Penelope."

He chuckled. "I thought you didn't like that name."

Toying with the ends of his hair, she said, "Somehow it is different when you say it."

"Penelope, then." He kissed her forehead. "Penelope, my darling." He kissed her cheek. "Penelope, brave, Penelope." He kissed her nose.

She giggled. "I thought you wanted to bed me."

"Lovemaking is not about jumping on top of you and taking my pleasure. Are you enjoying standing here kissing?" He nibbled the side of her neck.

"Oh yes." It was more sighed than spoken.

"Good, because we have all night. I suspect we will not be disturbed." He tugged at the fastenings on the back of her gown.

She turned, giving him her back and permission to untie the gown and stays beneath. Both fell to the floor, leaving her in just the long white underdress. The silk was very fine and nearly transparent.

Turning, she faced him. Suddenly shy, she averted her eyes to the carpet.

"You are beautiful, Penelope. Please don't be afraid of me."

Raising her head, her eyes pierced him. "I know you would never harm me. It is only that you might not like what you see and change your mind. Mother says I'm not lithe in a way that is appealing to men."

Lifting her in his arms, Rhys wished his body wanted to go as slowly as his mind. He carried her to the large round cushion. "You are perfect. Whatever your mother has filled your head with has no place or meaning between us. Where she found flaws, I see only where I want to worship you with my mouth and hands."

"Do you always talk so pretty in such times?"

"I promised you I would never lie to you, and I have not broken my word." He removed his coat and cravat and knelt beside the pillow. Her calves were firm from the long walks she liked to take. He kissed her knee, rolled her stocking down, feeling the soft skin as he went, and removed the green slipper. He did the same with the other leg.

All the while she watched, her bright blue eyes glowing. There was no fear, only excitement and curiosity. "Will you remove your clothes as well?"

"I don't want to frighten you."

Rising to her elbows, she ran her foot along his thigh. "Are you disfigured in some way since the last time I saw you shirtless?"

"Was I shirtless?" He remembered the incident that had caused their six-year rift. Perhaps they would have come to this point sooner if Poppy hadn't taken a walk that day or he hadn't been so reckless. Perhaps they never would have. Without their constant bickering they might have found nothing interesting in each other.

"You were not terrible to look at. Of course, you were much younger then. Perhaps you have gone soft in the years since," she teased.

He pulled his shirt up over his head and tossed it to the floor. "I have not gone soft in any way, Penelope."

"Clearly not." Wide eyed, she turned the most alluring shade of pink.

Chapter 9

Poppy must have lost her mind, but she wanted him. Everything she'd said had been the complete truth. She had never wanted to marry, but she did not wish to die a virgin.

Watching his muscles bulge and ripple under taut, tanned flesh, she longed to touch him. Sitting up, her own body clearly visible through the sheath, she ran her hand down his chest. The smattering of gold-blond hair tickled her fingers as she traced the path past his navel to where it disappeared into his breeches. "You are very beautiful, Rhys."

"That is something I have never been called before." He relaxed alongside her, allowing her to explore his partial nudity.

"Really? One would think all your women would mention it." She skimmed her palm along his ribs, feeling each bone and muscle.

Snatching up her hand, he held it a moment before lifting her fingers to his lips. "I do not have women. I only have you."

It would only ruin a perfect moment to point out that tomorrow he would move on to some mistress and she would never see him like this again. Rather than risk ending the evening too soon, she kept her thoughts to herself. "And what will you do with me?"

Leaning over, he braced on his hands and hovered. His long hair shrouded the sharp contours of his face. "I'm going to show you how a pairing can be mutual rather than a dictatorship. I'm going to teach you about making love, if you'll allow me."

She tucked his hair behind one ear, ran her hand behind his neck, and pulled him down for a kiss. His silky warm tongue met hers and sent a shock through her. It settled in anticipation between her legs and teetered between pleasure and pain.

He pulled her bottom lip between his and then the top. Unpracticed, she struggled to keep up, but desire raced through her and she wanted more. His hand seared the skin of her hip, which she lifted to gain more contact. Kissing was too small a word for the magic he made as their lips danced together.

Their breath mingled, and maybe a bit of her soul joined with his. The world narrowed to just them in the parlor together on the odd cushion. Rhys pressed kisses along her cheek and jaw. His mouth on her ear and neck made her long to touch her most private places. Unable to resist, she reached between her legs and pressed her fingers against the ache, hoping for some kind of relief.

Rhys stilled and shifted to one side before covering her hand with his. "Do you pleasure yourself, sweetheart?"

"I have never ached like this before. Have I done something wrong?"

Tightening her grip but without moving her hand away, he kissed her neck and down her chest before sucking her nipple through the silk shift.

As if connected by an invisible cord, his attention increased her ache. "Hades's blood."

"Nothing you want or need is wrong. Shall I ease your ache or would you prefer to do it yourself?"

Hating the barriers between them, she tugged her hand free and pulled the shift over her head before tossing it aside. "I would not mind if you touched me."

"Good Lord, Penelope, you do drive me mad." He took her hand and pressed it to his shaft.

Through his breeches, he was big and hard against her palm. The idea she had done this to him was heady and tightened her own throbbing. "I'm glad I'm not alone."

Rhys slid his hand along the inside of her calf, lifted her knee to an angle, and then slid his hand up her thigh.

Raising up for more, her body seemed to have taken over as her mind was spinning with sensations. When he touched her most private spot, his fingers slid through her wetness and spikes of delight shot through her.

He swallowed her cries of passion in kisses while easing his fingers over her sensitive bud again and again.

The ache inside her built and tightened. She clutched at his shoulders and bucked against his hand, wanting more yet not knowing what more was until her world exploded in a million lights. She throbbed and whirled in ecstasy. Unable to catch her breath, she gasped. "Rhys."

Holding her close, he caressed her back and kissed her hair until the waves subsided and she was limp in his arms. "I never dreamed anything could be so beautiful as seeing your pleasure. I know nothing will ever thrill me as completely, sweetheart."

"I didn't know it would be so…so…good." She couldn't make her mind find words to describe something so total and all-encompassing.

He pulled her against him and rolled so she was on top. "There is so much more."

It wasn't possible. "How can that be?"

"Because when two people are perfect for each other, lovemaking is extraordinary."

No small thing to be well matched…she wondered at the rareness. For all she knew, he said that to all the women he bedded, but she didn't think so. She didn't want to think so. For tonight she wanted to be special. His shaft pressed hard between them, and already she longed to know more of him, be one with him, touch him as he'd touched her. She ground her hips against him. "I would like to give you pleasure, Rhys."

He spread his arms out, his smile wicked. "I am yours to do with as you please."

Easing to one side, she studied the full length of his muscular form. Touching him from neck to waist, she watched how his body tightened as she skimmed his nipples. Emboldened, she licked the hard pebble.

His arm wrapped around her back, and his fingers traced a path from the top of her buttocks to her shoulder blades.

Again, her body pulsed with desire. Kissing her way down, she dipped her tongue in his navel.

A tight moan issued from his mouth along with her name.

She loosened the fall of his breeches and slid her hand inside. He was hard, big in her hand, yet the softest skin she'd ever felt. She trailed her fingers along the ridge from base to tip, and the fabric fell away.

He let out a long breath. "Sweet Penelope, you will be my undoing."

Unsure but driven by desire, she kissed the tip of his shaft.

It jumped, and he groaned.

She pulled it inside her mouth and let it slide out.

"Dear God. If you keep doing that, this will be over before we've even begun."

She skimmed a wisp of a touch around his shaft. "Then you like this?" She did the same with her tongue.

He gripped her hands and pulled her up until she straddled him. "I like it, more than I can ever explain with mere words."

His shaft rested between her nether lips, and she slid forward and back, creating the most delicious friction. It was as much torture for her as she saw on his face, but the power of controlling their pleasure was heady. Rolling her hips shot delight from her core.

Expression taut, Rhys rested his hands on her thighs. "You look pleased with yourself, Penelope."

Poppy leaned forward until her chest pressed to his, and she devoured his lips. The kiss was as erotic as the way he still rested between her legs. "I never dreamed this would be so empowering."

He adjusted his hips so the tip of his shaft perched at her opening. "Becoming part of a pair does not have to mean giving up who you are."

"That is not what I've been led to believe." She eased back until she felt resistance and stopped.

Expression soft, he threaded his fingers through her fallen hair. "I feel I should apologize for the pain this first time, but I cannot regret being the first so I will thank you for this gift, sweetheart."

So sweet and thoughtful, Rhys was nothing like she expected. Aurora had told them about sex. She said it was embarrassing and painful, but this was neither. She thrust down and thought she'd ripped herself in two.

His arms wrapped around her.

Tears squeezed from her lids. "Hell's fire."

"Relax, love. Just stay with me for a moment," he murmured lovingly in her ear while caressing her back.

The pain eased, and she adjusted to his size. "I think it's better."

His shaft moved inside her, and pleasure replaced the pain. Poppy moved her hips, sending more delight through her. "Oh, yes," she said.

"You will tell me if I should stop, Penelope?" Worry and strain gave his voice an edge she hadn't heard before.

Stop? Was he mad? She pressed down, bringing him deeper. "Don't you dare."

A long groan pushed from his lips, and he kissed her ear. Rolling her over onto her back, Rhys took control of the pace, but there was no sense of being trapped or oppressed.

Pleasure built inside her, tightening and thrilling in ways she had never dreamed.

Rhys cooed loving words to her. He called her beautiful and wonderful. His voice was as erotic as their joining.

She moved with him, heightening the building rapture. She wanted to tell him how good it felt, but no words would form, only sighs and moans.

Everything inside her tensed at once, taking her over some unseen cliff, and she exploded over the precipice.

Rhys groaned and clutched her tightly but then suddenly pulled out, spilling his seed across her lower belly. "You are magnificent."

Confused about a few things, the first embarrassment niggled at her as the pleasure subsided. "May I ask you some questions?"

He chuckled. "I would expect nothing else. Stay here a moment, though. There is a bit of cleanup to be done, sweetheart."

Staring at the heavens painted on the ceiling, she missed the weight of him holding her. A moment later, he used his handkerchief to clean her from stomach to between her legs. It was the most intimate she had ever been with any person. Sex was one thing, but to care for her so tenderly was more than she could have expected from anyone, let alone a man she believed coarse and lustful.

Before lying beside her, he pulled on his breeches and tossed the ruined cloth in the fireplace. "What do you want to know?"

She allowed him to help her back into her gown without corset or sheath, both of which he collected with their other garments and placed in a neat pile. "Why didn't you spill your seed inside me?"

"To lessen the chances of a child coming from this night." He was as blunt as she, but tenderness filled his eyes as he smoothed her hair.

"That was very thoughtful." She turned so he could fasten her gown. "I didn't expect to enjoy this."

"Why not?" He kissed the back of her neck, creating the most delightful flush of sensitivity across her skin.

"I thought I would feel demeaned."

Holding her shoulders, he eased her around to face him. The lines around his mouth spoke of a man who smiled often, though now his concerned expression warmed her. "Then why did you wish to make love?"

"To know what it was like. I told you. Virginity is a burden." She backed away and stepped into her slippers.

Pain etched on his face, he picked up the pile of clothes. "Who told you this night would be ugly?"

"She probably thought it would be my wedding night. Though Aurora knows me well enough to know, I never wanted to marry and end up bitter or unhappy like Mother."

The sorrow filling his eyes broke her heart. He dropped the clothing and went to the window. Hand gripping the frame, he leaned his forehead against the wood. "Rora."

His pain seared through her. "I'm an insensitive idiot." She ran to him and wrapped her arms around him from behind. "I didn't think. I'm sorry, Rhys."

He turned into her embrace. Cheek pressed to the top of her head, he said, "It's not your fault, Poppy. I should have protected her and I failed. All our lives, I kept Father from hurting her when she'd go off on wild tangents. Then he sent her away and I failed her then. All my arguments to Father fell on deaf ears, so I did what I could from afar. I visited whenever Father allowed it, and she seemed happy with you and the other Wallflowers."

"She was happy, Rhys. We all were. We loved being at Miss Agatha's." She wanted to ease his pain. The only people she'd ever ached for like this were the Wallflowers. She kissed his bare chest.

"If I had known about that animal, I'd have killed him." It was a vow he had repeated several times now.

"Which is why Aurora made us promise to never tell you. And believe me, I wanted to tell you on more than one occasion."

He turned and wrapped his arms around her. "I wonder if you would consider allowing me to spend the night with you, Penelope. I would very much like to hold you for as long as I can."

Staying in his arms in the comfort of a bed was dangerous and too tempting to refuse. "I would like that."

On a long release of breath, his body relaxed as if he'd been holding his breath for her answer. His kiss was gentle but filled with need. "Thank you."

Oddly shy, she scooped up her clothes, unbolted the door, and rushed up the stairs. When she stumbled halfway up, Rhys was there with a strong hand on her elbow. Perhaps there was more to a relationship between a man and a woman than she'd been led to believe.

In her room, he took the clothes from her arms, helped her out of the gown, and carried her to the bed. Lying naked in his embrace was perfection and somehow right. "Why haven't you married, Rhys?"

He traced circles on her arm. "I hadn't met anyone I wanted to make a life with."

"I thought you would say you liked your rakish life too much," she teased.

He gave her a squeeze. "Perhaps a bit of that too."

Outside frogs sang to each other. The moon gave a glow through the open window. "Since you told me you imagined sex as a terrible degrading thing, I've been thinking you showed a great deal of trust in me."

"I didn't realize the act could be more than one way. I feel a bit foolish knowing how glorious it is."

"I'm truly honored by your trust and so happy to have shown you the truth."

Poppy rolled toward him. "What truth?"

"That not every joining has to be one sided." His lips met hers with utter tenderness.

In the parlor she'd been satiated, yet now she met his kisses with renewed passion. "I want you, Rhys."

"You're very tender from earlier." He ran his hand down her side and lifted her leg over his so they touched intimately.

"I don't care."

Kissing his way down her neck to her chest, he whispered, "I care."

One inch at a time, he covered her with kisses. Rather than risk hurting her, he made love to her with his mouth. Poppy's mind soared as her body writhed under his ministrations. As rapture took her, she knew everything she ever believed about Rhys and men in general was flawed.

Falling asleep in his embrace, she'd never been happier or felt more alive.

* * * *

Rhys's gentle snores woke Poppy just as the sun came up. She slipped out of bed, pulled on her own dress, which had been left hanging in the wardrobe the night before, and slipped out of the room.

She needed to think, and she couldn't with his beautiful, naked form lying beside her. Nothing of the previous night was what she expected. Even the pain, bookmarked by such ecstasy, was a faint moment that drifted out of memory.

The garden was cool and quiet at the dawn hour.

Geb knelt on a small woven mat facing the sunrise. He was all in white with long pants and a tunic.

Stopping, Poppy watched, not wishing to interrupt his prayer. She found a bench and closed her eyes, listening to the foreign sound and letting her worries lift away.

The sun warmed her face, and the breeze rustled the leaves. If she were planning an escape from her life, it would be in just such a place. No prying eyes, no gossip…it was perfection.

"Am I disturbing you, Lady Penelope?" Geb broke into her daydream.

With the sun behind him, he glowed like an angel. She shaded her eyes. "Not at all. I was just enjoying the morning."

"If I may say, you look like someone with a dilemma." He sat at the other end of the bench.

"What do you do when everything you know to be true is questioned in your own mind?" Never expecting an answer, she let her attention drift to a passing cloud.

"In such an instance, one must be willing to change his own truth." Geb's voice was filled with questions he was too polite to ask.

"Can there be more than one truth?"

He angled to face her. "We each have our own truths. One might believe he can run as fast as a lion. Perhaps he can, but if he believes the lion is faster, then that is his truth. Not a very pleasant truth if being chased by the beast."

Confused, Poppy considered the idea. "Are you saying whatever I believe is the truth?"

His white teeth shone when he smiled. "I'm saying it is your truth and you are the only one who has the power to change what is true to you."

Mind racing, she imagined a life different from anything she'd ever believed possible for her. "Then if I decide what I want, I can create a truth that makes it possible." It was too simple and yet unbelievably complex.

He clapped his hands together and wore a huge smile. "What a brilliant mind you have, my lady."

"You are too kind. No one has ever thought such a thing about me."

He leaned closer. "Then those people were not seeing you or keeping their truth to themselves."

"Thank you." Poppy lowered her head and smiled, acknowledging his compliment even if she wasn't comfortable accepting it.

"You and his lordship will return to London today?"

"Yes. We have troubled you long enough." She stood just as Rhys rounded the corner and strode toward them.

Geb rose and bowed to her. "Your visit has been a pleasure. I hope you shall come and see me in the future. I am happy to have new friends."

Rhys said, "I wish we could stay longer. This place is a piece of paradise."

His gaze fell on her, and she drew a tight breath. Hera's crown, what was happening? She was no blushing ninny who swooned at the sight of a man, yet it filled her with joy seeing him happy and beautiful in the morning light of the garden. "We should prepare to leave, my lord."

"Of course," Rhys said. "Thank you for your hospitality, Mr. Arafa. This unscheduled stay has been remarkable."

The men shook hands before Geb kissed her hand. "I hope we will meet again without a storm to hold us." He rushed toward the house and disappeared around a row of trees.

Once again alone with Rhys, Poppy wasn't sure what to say. "I suppose if I were a more worldly woman, I would act aloof and give you the impression last night meant nothing to me. Though, in truth, a proper lady would never have found herself without a chaperone."

"I hope you shall not pretend to be anything you are not, Penelope." He offered his arm, and they strolled back the way he'd come.

"I think I may have been mistaken about sexual congress. However, at this time, my ultimate desires for the future have not changed." There, she sounded reasonable and calm.

He lifted her hand to his lips. "It is lucky, then, that no one outside of Aaru and West Lane knows of our delay."

Why such a simple gesture should make her insides melt, she didn't know. "I'm glad you agree. No need to burden anyone with our newfound friendship."

One of those expressive brows lifted. "Then you will keep our night of passion a secret from your friends?"

She couldn't decide if he sounded relieved or disappointed. Resolving that it must be the former, she swallowed down the unease building inside her. She had never kept anything from the Wallflowers. "I think it best if last night remain between the two of us. I am trusting you will not run off to brag to your rakish friends."

He stilled, clenched his jaw, and then turned to face her. "No matter what you think of me, I am not some child ready to run and gossip about my exploits. For me, last night was private and wonderful. You may assume the worst of me, Penelope, but I am a gentleman."

As he stepped away, she clung to his hand. "Forgive me. I know you would never risk my reputation in such a vile way. I sometimes say terrible things in order to drive people away, and while it has served me with my parents and some unkind students at Miss Agatha's, I should not treat you with so little respect. You have become a good friend in these last few weeks, and I shall hold the memory of last night sacred for the rest of my life."

Her throat closed on the last word. Poppy kissed his hand and ran to the house. She needed a moment to get herself under control for the ride back to London. Her own feelings aside, they had much to report to Faith and Aurora. It wouldn't do to let her own dramatics interfere with the job at hand.

Chapter 10

After a very quiet ride back to London, they arrived at Aurora's West Lane home. Rhys had dozens of things he wanted to say to her, but her decision to be strong and not change her mind about a life that included marriage kept him silent.

He would never order her about since doing so would contradict the kind of woman he wanted. Poppy would have to choose him. Nothing less would please either of them.

Aurora, blond hair gleaming, stormed across the foyer. "Where have the two of you been? We thought you'd been killed in the storm."

Rhys kissed his sister's cheek. "We were delayed and had to seek shelter. A flooded bridge kept us away a second day and made it impossible to send word. I'm sorry if you worried over Poppy, but I would never let any harm come to her."

Head cocked, Aurora narrowed her eyes. "Poppy, is everything all right?"

The two embraced. "Of course. We have much to tell you and Faith. Is she at home?"

Aurora looked from him back to Poppy before nodding toward the parlor. "She and I were about to have tea. Perhaps you can join us and tell us all about your adventure."

In the parlor, Faith leaped to her feet and rushed over to hug Poppy. "Are you hurt? We were so worried. We couldn't tell anyone for fear of ruining your reputation. It was an impossible situation. One more day and we'd have called out the Bow Street Runners."

He had made some very good friends at Eton, but even his friendship with Garrett could not rival the bond between these Wallflowers.

Poppy's joy-filled laughter filled the room. "I'm fine. We had to find shelter when the storm hit, and as luck would have it, we landed at Geb Arafa's home."

"He was not there," Rhys offered.

"And a tree fell on the barn," Poppy said.

"Poppy brilliantly soothed four horses and kept them safe," he said.

"It was the next morning we met Mr. Arafa."

They continued with the story, each adding bits and pieces without ever stumbling over one another.

He loved the excitement in Poppy's voice when she told Faith that Mr. Arafa highly recommended Nicholas. Even the way she apologized for not finding out what his business was in France made him long to hold her again.

Faith listened intently and sipped tea until the story brought them back to London. "It is good to know that someone you both seem to admire would allow his sister to marry Breckenridge. Still, it would help to know what he was up to and why he refused to talk about his past."

Aurora put her cup down. "Perhaps we'll learn more when he comes to the country."

Faith grinned. "My mother is making all the preparations for the house party. I might have suggested it to get to know Breckenridge better, but it was all Mother's idea." Her wink said otherwise.

"I see. And when do you leave?" A firm, steady voice gave away none of his inner turmoil.

"The invitations went out the day you two left," Faith said. "You should have yours when you get home, Rhys. I told Mother that Aurora needed time away from town and her brother was a big comfort to her. It is the truth, after all."

Flooded with relief, he swallowed down a whoop of elation. Even having been told he would be invited to join them, he worried they would leave town without him. The notion of being out of Poppy's company for a fortnight was unbearable. "I'm honored. I'm sure we will all get to know Breckenridge better after a few weeks in the country."

Poppy stared at her hands in her lap with her brow furrowed.

"I dearly hope so." Faith abandoned her teacup.

If he had been alone with Poppy, he'd have asked her if she preferred he not attend. He wanted to be close to her, but not to make her uncomfortable.

Maybe it was the wrong attitude. He needed time to convince Poppy she wanted him as much as he wanted her, if that was indeed true.

Gut clenching, he stood. "I had better get home. My staff will think I've turned up toes. Ladies, I will call in a day or two."

"I will walk you out," Aurora said.

In the foyer, she took his hat from the butler and waited until they were alone. "What is going on, Rhys?"

"Nothing."

"Are you certain of that?"

He kissed her cheek. "After six years, I have finally managed to make peace with your friend Poppy and now you are suspicious. She and I have been thrust together and have come to a friendly understanding."

"I suppose I should be happy. I've tried most of these past six years to keep the two of you from devouring each other. I'm glad you have formed an amicable friendship."

"As am I." He took his hat, feeling somewhat guilty for the lie of omission. However, if Poppy wasn't willing to discuss their night together with her friends, he certainly would not divulge the information. Besides, the night was more intimate if just the two of them knew of it. And intimacy with Poppy was what he wanted.

* * * *

The long weeks between their adventure and the Dornbury house party were interminable. Rhys sat back in his carriage and watched the rush of trees and countryside blur by.

It had been maddening, but every time he called on his sister, Poppy was out on some errand. He had tried on no less than six occasions to see her. He'd even attended a damned ball, but only Faith was there grumbling about her mother demanding she be seen in public.

Even sending a note was denied him as Aurora would become suspicious if he started corresponding with Poppy and not the rest of the Wallflowers.

His driver rounded the drive at Dornbury Manor and stopped at the front doors. Faith and her parents, with a line of servants, stood waiting at the steps. Wanting to seek out Poppy wouldn't change the fact that he had to be polite and waste an hour or so with the earl and countess before he would have his freedom.

Faith's parents were formal and dull. It was a miracle the girl had found time to be disobedient and get herself exiled to Switzerland.

He accepted tea in the parlor. "Have the other guests arrived yet?"

Lady Dornbury patted her tightly coiffed hair and pursed her lips. "Breckenridge has not yet arrived, but the other guests are resting above stairs."

"It was kind of you to invite my sister and me. She has needed a break from town these weeks."

Faith hid a grin behind her teacup.

Dornbury cleared his throat and ran his hand along his graying beard. "Not at all. We are happy to have you both. We have always liked Lady Radcliff even if some of Faith's other friends are questionable."

"Father!" Faith scolded.

Lady Dornbury said, "All of that is in the past. They are all fine young ladies who have learned their lessons well."

Rhys held his tongue. How had Faith listened to such nonsense her entire life? Even now, with her on the verge of marrying a duke, her parents couldn't contain their disappointment. "Lady Faith, would you show me the grounds? I have never had the pleasure of seeing the Dornbury Manor gardens, but I hear they are spectacular."

"It would be my pleasure, my lord. I believe we may even cross paths with your sister. Mother, Father, do you require anything?" Faith curtsied.

Lady Dornbury beamed. "See to our guests, my dear. You are going to make an excellent duchess."

Once in the hallway, Rhys couldn't hold it in anymore. "Are they always like that, Faith?"

She threaded her arm through his and sped their pace through the house. "I'm afraid so. I've grown used to it, but it's become such a habit for them, I don't even think they realize that in most company I would be embarrassed."

"But not with me?" He patted her hand.

"Of course not. You know me well enough to know all they say is just balderdash."

A footman dressed in yellow-and-white livery opened the door into the gardens, which stretched out into the lake district's magnificent vistas.

"Thank you, Joseph," Faith said.

"My pleasure, my lady." Joseph made a stiff-backed bow as they exited.

They rounded several large trees and followed the path. Faith walked with purpose.

"Faith, where are you taking me?" Rhys studied the way so he could get back to the house if this was some plot to lose him in the gardens. Wallflowers could be devious, and he'd fallen prey to their antics more than once over the years.

"To the others, of course."

"Should I be worried?"

She laughed. "You are one of us now, Rhys. I promise you will not be tortured any more than you deserve."

"Somehow, that does not make me feel any more secure when Wallflowers are involved. I remember very clearly the summer I came to visit Lucerne and the four of you tied me to a tree under the guise of some silly game. You left me there for hours while you ran off to do mischief." He rubbed his arm where the rope had cut into his coat and skin.

"We came back for you. Besides, you managed to free yourself."

"It took me an hour, and the four of you had gone on a shopping excursion of all things."

Faith stopped and put her fists on her hips. "If you had agreed to take us to town for a few hours, none of that would have befallen you."

He held up his hands. "I am well aware of my past mistakes."

A bright smile spread across her face. "And that is why you are one of us now."

Around the next bend a grove of five trees surrounded several benches where a gurgling stream meandered past. Poppy stood staring out toward the lake in the distance. If he were a painter, he would have found great pleasure in recreating the moment.

"Rhys, you're here!" Aurora called from the bench.

Mercy jumped up and took his arm. "We have been waiting for you."

"Really? I thought you Wallflowers preferred to be alone together." Rhys had always liked Mercedes. She was funny in spite of a rather difficult life where she was always called by the whim of a relative. Surviving when her parents had been killed in a terrible carriage accident, she'd never lost her sense of humor.

Her smile was infectious. "We have decided you are one of us. The first male Wallflower of West Lane. Not to mention, the only other person we've ever let into our quartet."

Dragged into the middle of the stand of trees, he bowed. "I am honored beyond words."

Poppy kept her gaze on the view and didn't join the rest of them.

Aurora said, "As you should be. Now, how do we find out what Breckenridge was up to in France?"

"Then you ladies have not given up on this investigation despite Poppy's accounts of Breckenridge's good character from a man she and I both found honorable?" He waited for Poppy to chime in, but she wouldn't look at him. His heart pounded at the sight of her, but she kept her gaze on the horizon. As lovely as ever and in a day dress not yet marred by a fall or accident of some kind, Rhys was tempted to turn her to face him.

It was untenable the way he longed for her attention. Forcing himself to respect her desire to remain apart from the group and him, he focused on the other three ladies.

Mercy fluffed her skirts and flounced onto the grass like a pink tulip. "We recognize you both liked Mr. Arafa and value his opinion. Some men will cover for others."

"You think Arafa lied to us? Poppy?" He waited, but she shrugged and then wrapped her arms around herself as if she might come apart at any moment.

Sitting next to him, Faith sighed. "Men do protect one another."

"So do women." Mercy winked.

Unable to keep his seat, Rhys made every effort to keep his voice level. Somewhere between their mistrust of Geb and Poppy's refusal to speak to him, his restraint had all but tattered. "Poppy?"

The bit of pleading in his tone must have been enough. Poppy turned. Eyes haunted and skin pale, she met his gaze with her chin up.

"Do you think Mr. Arafa was dishonest?"

The way she clutched herself around the waist pushed her breasts to the edge of her peach day dress. She glanced at the other ladies before coming back to him. "I believed Mr. Arafa. He is a good and honest man, but he also sells information, which is not necessarily an upstanding profession. He's a spy, Rhys. He could have been lying to us and be so skilled at it, we were fooled."

There was no disputing the assessment. "I see."

Faith touched his arm. "It is my life we are talking about, Rhys. It seems such a small thing for him to tell me what his life has been, yet he refused and skulked off into the gardens for some clandestine meeting."

Looking down into Faith's worried eyes, it was impossible to argue. He had known these women since they were girls. Making sure no further harm came to them was the least he could do. He'd failed Aurora for three years. It would not happen again. Taking Faith's hand, he bowed and kissed it. "I will never allow any of you to be harmed again. We shall ferret out what Breckenridge was up to and if need be, discard his proposal."

With a bounce, Faith hugged him. "Thank you. I knew you would help us."

She sat on the grass next to Mercy. Now a yellow tulip with her skirts fluffed around her.

Mercy snickered. "All is well again and you may remain a Wallflower."

Sitting, he watched the four of them. Four perfect little flowers and he like a nagging thorn among them. "I hadn't realized my new status was already in jeopardy."

Aurora smiled. "I wish we could stay just like this and not worry about the outside world. However, Breckenridge will arrive shortly and we need a plan. How do we find out what he's up to?"

"How many men will be here this week?" A spark of an idea had Rhys thinking.

"Including Father and Lord Mitchem, there is you, Breckenridge, and a friend he's bringing along; plus Mother met Garrett Winslow at the theater last week and invited him. She gushed about what a gentleman he was."

"Not to mention he'll be a duke one day," Mercy muttered under her breath.

Poppy giggled. "I'm sure that was more intriguing to your mother than his good manners."

Raising a warning finger, Aurora halted any insults. "Garrett has been a good friend to Rhys and me for most of our lives. Nothing bad is to be said about him."

"But Faith's mother is fair game." Mercy poked Faith in the ribs, and the two fell into gales of laughter.

Despite how adorable the four of them were together, Rhys stifled his smile. "Garrett is a good friend and might be helpful to our cause. He would not wish any harm to come to any lady and definitely not a friend of Rora's and mine."

Aurora's face turned ghost white. "Rhys, you haven't told Garrett about my past?"

He rushed to her side. "Of course not. I only told him your marriage was not a happy one. The details are yours to tell or not. However, Garrett cares very much about you and would make a good confidant, if ever you needed one."

Clutching him, she said, "I have enough confidants with you and the Wallflowers. Thank you for keeping my secret."

"You know, Aurora, if we told Breckenridge of your troubles and the fears they have instilled in the other ladies, he might be more willing to disclose his past." Rhys's stomach churned at the thought, but he felt it worth mentioning.

She shook her head. "Only as a last resort. My troubles are not for public amusement or gossip. I understand Poppy gave some information to Mr. Arafa in order to learn what we now know. As he doesn't know me and our paths are not likely to cross, it is harmless. Telling people we don't know and who are in our social circle would leave me exposed to their pity. The thought makes me sick to my stomach."

"I only thought I should give the option. I tend to agree the matter should be kept private within a close circle of friends." Rhys hugged her tighter.

"Why did you ask about the men?" Faith asked.

Keeping one arm around his sister, Rhys turned to the other three tulips in pink, yellow, and his Poppy in peach. "Often with a sizable concert of men, there is a hunting party. I might befriend Breckenridge more easily with time away from the ladies. Men sometimes divulge things about themselves to other men that they keep hidden when women are around."

Poppy stepped away, her attention back to the vistas. "Women do the same."

"I shall put the idea of a hunting party in Father's ear." Faith stood. "I have to meet with Mother to go over the seating for dinner."

Mercy rose as well. "I'll go with you. I brought some books my aunt disapproves of and I'm going to read to my heart's content now that I'm out from under her roof."

The color back in her cheeks, Aurora jumped up. "Oooh! New books. I'll go with you, Mercy. I might have a few treats in my trunk as well."

Expecting Poppy to run off too, he held his breath.

Once the others could no longer be heard giggling about books, she turned to him. "I had a thought you might not come this week."

"Did you want me to send my regrets?" The ache in his chest expanded.

She sighed, looked around her at anything but him, then sank onto the bench. "I don't know what I want. You are a puzzle I can't make out."

"Do you regret our time together, Penelope?"

"No. It was a beautiful night and I would not change anything." Her sad expression belied her words.

"Then why do you look as if your dog died?" She kept the space between them, and he didn't want to make her run for the house. Even this awkward time together was better than no time at all.

She stood, walked to the edge of the line of trees, and fussed with the lace on her bodice. "It is very strange to be around you now. I know it's childish, but I can't stand that you can have no respect for me now."

He rushed to her but did not touch her. "You could not be more wrong, Penelope. It is unfair for you to judge me as so shallow and uncaring. I don't deserve that. After all, it was you who requested we make love."

"I know." Tears slid down her cheeks and tightened her voice. "It's completely foolish. You have done nothing wrong. You were a kind and wonderful lover, though I have nothing to compare the experience to. You are a good friend, Rhys. I will find a way to overcome my own stupidity."

"Look at me, Penelope." He wanted to shake her, hold her, love her, and smother her all at once. No woman should sway his good sense as this one could.

Her eyes were red rimmed as she turned to him.

She never wanted to marry. He had been a tool to rid her of her virginity. He'd told himself this for days; yet looking at her now, it was hard to remember. Was it unfair of him to want more, knowing it would make her unhappy to be his wife? The fact that he could bring her only sorrow if he asked for what his heart desired crushed him. "I am at your service. We are friends if nothing else, and I will protect you as I will protect all the Wallflowers. You need never be ashamed of what happened between us. I'm going to say it again as it is very important."

He touched her chin, forcing her to look him in the eyes. "You need never be ashamed of the beautiful night we spent together. I will always be here for you no matter what you desire or need. Do you understand?"

With a nod, she said, "You are my friend."

It would have to do. "That's right. I shall always be your friend and keep you safe, no matter the situation."

"Thank you." Her tiny smile lifted his heart.

Pulling her into his embrace, he took in her warm scent and rubbed his chin against her soft hair. He could spend a lifetime in this paradise with only Poppy, but that was not what she wanted, so he'd have to settle for friendship and keeping her safe unless he could convince her otherwise. Rhys had never wanted to hear a woman tell him she loved or even liked him more.

He pressed his lips to her forehead then stepped away. There was no point in overwhelming her with his flood of emotions until she was sure of her own. "I will try to gather information from Breckenridge. You might convince Faith to spend some time with him. Perhaps she will like him."

"I will try, but she is quite stubborn regarding the subject. She's determined not to like him." She walked toward the field, away from the house.

Following, he let the warm sun fill the spaces left empty by Poppy's rejection. "I don't understand. He seems a nice fellow if a bit unconventional. I know she mistrusts his past, but that didn't stop you from liking him."

The grass was high, reaching to her hips. She ran her fingers along the tops, creating a wave in her wake and sending bugs and butterflies flitting from their hiding places.

Her hair was stretched into a bun, and he longed to pull it down and watch it flow in the breeze. If he wasn't careful, she'd turn him into a poet.

"It's a funny thing about Faith. She likes everything to appear perfect even as she's plotting to do something outrageous," she said. "Breckenridge would have been better off acting the part of a perfectly boring duke when they met." She put her finger close to a yellow butterfly that perched on a tall white blossom.

It stepped onto her finger with its wings slowly moving up and down. A moment later, it flew away and she laughed.

Rhys let out the breath he'd been holding. "Are you good with all creatures big and small?"

She shrugged. "I have some trouble with people."

Closing the gap, he tugged her hand, slowing her pace. "Not all people." She allowed her fingers to thread through his, and they walked together.

Skin to skin even in such a harmless way, heat infused him from head to toe. Someone might see them, and then she would be ruined and he would be obligated to marry her. He glanced back toward the house, but they were alone.

"It took us six years to become friends, Rhys. My ineptitude as a socialite is safe."

Unable to stop himself, he kissed the back of her hand. "It was my fault for not getting to know the real you. I was a fool to let a few torn hems and some minor incidents drive my beliefs about you. I knew you were smart and kind. I should have let that be enough."

Facing him, she cocked her head to one side and then the other. "You cannot take all the blame. You were always good to your sister, and yet your rakish reputation ruled my internal description of you."

"Internal description?" He laughed at the odd term.

"Yes. When I meet someone, I describe them to myself. Sometimes, I label them kind, stupid, pleasant, untrustworthy, or something of that nature."

"Poppy, do you think that's fair?" He'd never thought to label people.

Another shrug. "I think most people do the same thing. They just don't admit it. You meet a person, decide if you like them, don't like them, or need more time to decide and whether they are worth the time to be bothered. You have reasons for those assessments even if you don't put a name to it."

"I suppose that's true, but to plop a label on someone and stand by it is rather unforgiving on your part." Still holding her hand, he did not relinquish it when she gave a tug. "Do not run from me just because I don't agree with you."

Her eyes narrowed, and a small crease formed between them as she focused on their clasped hands. "Is that what I do?"

"What?" He eased her closer.

"Am I irreversibly judgmental? Do I run from anything that does not suit me?"

Leaving no space between them, he couldn't resist pressing a kiss to her lips.

She leaned in and wrapped her hand around his neck. Her mouth opened, allowing him in.

The world shrank to a space that only held the two of them. Everything else slipped away as their tongues met and he made love to her sweet mouth as he dreamed of more kisses and days like this one.

Pressing his forehead to hers, he caught his breath. "You run from me. I cannot say it is a chronic habit; only you can be the judge of that, Penelope."

With a long sigh, she laid her cheek on his chest and sank into his embrace. "I am flawed, hopelessly flawed."

Giving in to his desires, he pulled the pins holding her tresses firm and let the silky locks fall over his hand. "We are all flawed. We come to be this way by our upbringing."

She laughed, and it rumbled delightfully against him. "Are you saying it's not my fault I'm damaged?"

"It is only your fault if you stay that way, my sweet." He tipped her chin up for another kiss. "Now, we had better get back to the house before we are spotted and I am forced to marry you."

Wide horrified eyes gaped up at him before she pushed away. "Yes. We should get back."

"I was joking, Poppy." He reached for her hand, but she clutched both to her chest as if he might tempt her to her doom.

She looked like a cornered mouse searching for an escape. Twisting her hair up into a rough knot, she said, "I know. I know. You should not follow me directly. We wouldn't want anyone to get the wrong impression."

Unable to contain his hurt, he drew it in like a shield. "What impression is that?"

She stopped and stared at him with those deep blue eyes saturated with confusion, passion, and something he couldn't identify. "That we are anything more than old family friends."

"I see."

She put her hands on her hips and glared. "What's wrong? You don't want to marry me and I don't want to marry at all. Why do you suddenly look put out when it was you who mentioned being spotted out here?"

The last was a valid point. He didn't want to be forced into anything. Marriage should be a choice, not an accident; it was a bad way to start a life together. Hell. Calming his raging emotions, he forced a smile. "You're right, of course. Go find your friends. I'll see you at supper."

"Are we still friends?" Her voice suddenly small and unlike the boisterous Poppy, she sounded vulnerable.

Closing the distance, he opened his arms and let her in. Rhys kissed her hair, reveling in the softness and flowery soap mixing with the essence of Poppy. "We will always be friends and more, my sweet. I am here for you, whatever you need."

Her smile bright, she pulled away from him and ran toward the house. Rhys followed more slowly. How had he come to such a turn? Poppy Arrington would be the death of him; that much was certain.

Chapter 11

Why it should bother Poppy if Rhys had avoided being alone with her since their talk, she couldn't say. However, each time during the week of picnics, dinners, dancing, and card playing that he made an excuse to be out of her company, the ache in her chest grew more unbearable.

Even as the dinner party broke up and made their way into the grand parlor for dancing, Poppy noted how Rhys escorted Aurora rather than let Garrett Winslow take her in.

Keeping her chin up was not easy, but in this case, he was the wiser of the two of them. If they were seen too much in each other's company, people would begin to talk. Gossip of that kind would never do.

Poppy swallowed down the emotion forcing its way into her throat. She didn't want Rhys. He was her friend and had been a kind and thoughtful lover, nothing more. Keeping up her resolve was becoming harder and harder as the house party continued. Seeing him daily but not knowing his thoughts or hearing his laughter gnawed at her.

The parlor's stately furniture had been pushed aside and the rug rolled up to afford a large space for dancing. The dark wood on the walls and coffered ceiling gave the same formal feel as Faith's parents with no room for diversion.

Taking a seat behind the pianoforte, Mercy played a lively reel. Mercy had a knack for the ironic and had probably picked the country dance with the purpose of annoying the lord and lady of the house. It was delightful and inappropriate, and no one would say a word about it. She was quite brilliant.

Faith dragged Poppy to the center of the room and pushed her toward Rhys, who bowed as he consented to dance with Poppy while Faith danced with Garrett.

A.S. Fenichel

Garrett laughed. "I suppose we have our marching orders."

"It would seem so," Rhys said, offering Poppy his arm.

Garrett gave a mock bow. "Faith is by far the most charming general a man has had to take his commands from."

Blushing, Faith smacked his arm with her fan. "Stop teasing. The music is about to start."

They made the first pass, and Poppy bit her tongue.

On the second, Rhys broke the silence. "You have something on your mind, my lady?"

"You have been avoiding me." She wanted to sound aloof, but it came out petulant and hurt.

His step faltered. "I have done exactly what you asked."

Had she asked him to keep his distance? She'd wanted to avoid gossip. Oh Zeus, she'd become an imbecile after all her efforts to keep her head. "I supposed you did."

Nicholas leaned against the wall with a glass of brandy and watched. If he was jealous, he showed no signs; however, as soon as the reel was over, he strode over and claimed Faith for a waltz.

Poppy curtsied without looking into Rhys's eyes and turned to walk away.

He wrapped his hand around her wrist, halting her. "One more will not make the gossips in this small crowd crazed, Penelope."

Stepping into his arms was the worst kind of torture. "This is not wise, Rhys."

Leaning in just enough to allow for a whisper let his woodsy scent fill her. "I shall never regret any opportunity to hold you in my arms, whether wise or not."

"You are far too bold." Whirling around the parlor, she was safe in his arms. No mother to scold her and no father whose disappointment colored her life from birth to present. It was just the two of them, and he expertly guided them in his easy way. He even managed to keep her from stumbling around like a ninny.

One side of his mouth turned up. "You might dance the next with Breckenridge. I can see from Faith's expression she will glean no information."

Risking a glance, Poppy confirmed Rhys's assessment. Faith rolled her eyes at whatever Nicholas had said, keeping her expression bored, rude, and generally unpleasant. "Perhaps you're right."

"I have never seen Faith so set against someone." He turned them around Faith and Nicholas, who soon gave up on the dance and went to join Aurora on the couch. A bit lost but at the same time regal in her dark blue gown, Aurora chatted politely with Faith's parents.

It was a keen observation. Faith was rarely rude and disliked very few people. She was forgiving by nature. "Perhaps she really doesn't like him."

"Or perhaps she does." His voice rang with some insight that Poppy couldn't quite figure out.

Before she could ask him to clarify, the music ended and he escorted her to the pianoforte where Mercy grinned watching them.

Faith and Nicholas were already there, and Faith had not warmed. Nicolas sighed. "Lady Penelope, do you play?"

"A little, but not so well as Mercy." She'd always admired the ease with which Mercy could play any instrument she picked up.

"Then perhaps you would honor me with a dance before relieving Miss Heath of her bench?" Nicholas smiled warmly and offered his gloved hand.

It was far easier to gain a dance than she'd expected. With a grin she couldn't hold back, Poppy accepted his offer and avoided Rhys's gaze as she went back to the center of the room. Garrett had convinced Aurora to dance and joined them in the minuet.

Garrett's hair gleamed with a streak of red in the candlelit room. He spoke over the music. "It's good to see all of you ladies again. It has been too long."

Aurora replied, "You've been off traveling for almost as long as we've been home from Lucerne. I thought you might never come home."

Unsure why Aurora was churlish, Poppy cleared her throat on the next pass. "I think it was our last year at Miss Agatha's when you came to visit with Rhys."

Garrett gave Aurora an apologetic smile, squared his wide shoulders, and let the mirth return to his light brown eyes. They always shone with amusement. "Indeed. You were all thriving there."

Poppy agreed, liking Garrett Winslow more and more.

When they broke apart and she was relatively alone with Nicholas, his calm expression changed and his blue eyes burned with displeasure. The angular bones of his cheeks and jaw seemed more pronounced. "Why does Lady Faith appear to dislike me so vehemently?"

The dance didn't allow her to respond right away, and she was relieved to have a moment to gather her wits and decide how to answer. This would not be a good time to bumble in her usual clumsy fashion. "I doubt very much she dislikes you. Perhaps only the fact she might be forced to marry someone she doesn't know."

"All my attempts to get to know her have been ignored." A lock of dark brown hair flopped on his forehead, and he pushed it back.

Once again, they were silenced by the dance coming together in a foursome. It was difficult to have a conversation of any value while interacting with the dance.

Poppy waited for the last pass to bring them together. She curtsied and met Nicholas's regard. "Perhaps you are only trying to know her without divulging anything about yourself."

His eyes widened. "I told her about my schooling and my home in the country."

"Anything recent or just your distant past?"

"I don't understand." He rubbed his temple.

"I believe you corresponded with Faith's mother for many months prior to your meeting. I'm certain that you know all about Faith's life, likes, and dislikes from those letters. Not once did you address mail directly to Faith and make an effort to know her." Poppy waited for a reaction.

Nicholas stared at his feet before regaining his impressive height. "I suppose that's true. It would have been highly irregular to write to a young woman without an introduction. I was also quite busy at the time of those letters."

"Busy with what?" Finally, the opportunity she'd been waiting for.

He sputtered for a moment. "I have business in France."

"What kind of business? Do you own land or ships, perhaps?"

Rather than loosen his lips, the prompt shut him down. His eyes narrowed and grew hard. "I'm afraid those things are private, Lady Penelope."

Holding back her sigh, she faked a smile. "Of course. And please call me Poppy." There was no point in pushing the issue. "You know, I met a friend of yours, Mr. Arafa. He is an extraordinary person. He speaks very highly of you."

Before he could mask his expression, shock registered on his handsome face. "How did you meet Geb Arafa? I can't imagine your life brings you into his circle."

"And that is a pity. I was caught in a storm outside of London. His home was the closest shelter, and he and his servants were kind enough to afford me shelter for two nights."

"Interesting." Nicholas rubbed his chin.

"You find it odd a lady would take shelter in a stranger's home?" She studied him, noting the way his eyes shifted but did not meet hers for some seconds. He must be considering all the possibilities. Perhaps he worried Geb had exposed him in some way. Poppy wished that were true.

"I gather you liked Mr. Arafa?" he finally asked.

"Oh, very much. He is such a fine gentleman."

Nicholas raised a brow. "He is, but most people of the ton cannot see past his exotic looks. I'm pleased to know that type of prejudice does not extend to Lady Faith's friends."

The thing Poppy hated almost as much as being forced into a life not of her choosing was to be lumped in with the rest of the snobs in London's upper crust. "I can assure you none of the Wallflowers judge people by anything but their own flaws or merits. We know quite a lot about being judged by assumption rather than facts."

"If that is true, Lady Faith believes it a fact I am not suitable for her." His frown deepened, and he ran his hand through his hair, loosening the queue and giving him a rather wild look.

"Perhaps you might spend some private time with Faith. She only knows she was not consulted. You and her mother made an arrangement without her knowledge and then she was tossed some letters after the fact." Poppy held her breath. She'd given away more than Faith might have wanted, but someone had to be honest in this mess.

Eyes wide, Nicholas took a step back. "Her mother didn't share the letters until after the initial agreement was made?"

"I'm afraid not."

He stammered then regained his composure. "I was not aware of that. I assumed Lady Faith was privy to the odd courtship from the start and her mother was keeping things proper by acting as correspondent. To be honest, if you read the letters, you would have assumed the same thing. Even though they were addressed from the Countess of Dornbury, some were quite personal. It seems I have made an incorrect assumption if you are in Lady Faith's confidence."

Could this be true? Had Lady Dornbury been so overzealous she wrote love letters rather than business correspondence? "I only know Faith knew nothing about you until a week before your return to England. At that point she was given leave to read your letters. And to be frank, she knows little more now."

"I...I..." He took a deep breath and fisted his hands at his side. "This is a surprise. I will give the matter some thought."

"And perhaps speak to Faith about the entire situation." Poppy tipped her head to one side and affected a playful smile to lighten the mood but still get her point across about communication.

"Of course." He bowed.

Poppy turned and went to the pianoforte where she relieved Mercy of her duties and muddled through a piece of music. Her mind spun with everything she had learned. The desire to pull the Wallflowers out of the party and tell them everything was strong. That would not go over well with the rest of the guests, though. If most of the eligible female dance partners left the room, there would be little point in continuing the dancing.

It would have to wait. She sighed into one of three tunes she knew how to play.

* * * *

It was close to midnight when the knock came on her door. Poppy knew the three raps, a pause, and one more meant a Wallflower wished to enter.

Jumping from the bed, she didn't bother with her wrap.

Faith pushed through before the door was fully opened. A moment later Mercy and Aurora tiptoed in as well.

They all piled onto the bed.

Poppy hopped in as well. "Is this an official meeting or could none of you sleep?"

"I couldn't sleep," Faith said. "I went to Mercy's room and found her awake as well. We thought it might be nice if we all could chat like old times, so we gathered Aurora and here we are."

"It is splendid to sit like this." Poppy's heart filled with love for the friendships she shared with these wonderful women.

Mercy leaned back on her elbows, and her green eyes flashed. "I miss these days."

"But now we are all at the West Lane house." Faith crossed her ankles, and her billowy white nightgown puffed around her.

They probably looked like four meringues sitting on the bed.

Aurora sighed. "Not for long. Soon each of you will marry and I'll be left in that big house alone."

Confused, Poppy said, "Why would you worry over something that might take years to happen? Besides, I have no interest in marriage. If I can find a way to avoid the ominous prospect, I intend to do so."

Mercy laughed, but there was something hollow about the sound. "It's not likely I'll ever marry. I have no dowry and am far too tall."

"That is your aunt talking," Faith scolded. "You are smart, lovely, and funny. You will marry if it is what you want. Besides, you're the same one and twenty as the rest of us."

"That brings me to an important point, Faith." Poppy leaned forward. "Why are you so rude to Breckenridge? Aside from the secret keeping, he is charming and handsome."

Throwing her arms up and letting them fall and deflate her nightgown, Faith whined. "I don't know. Something about him brings out the worst in me. He talks of farms and houses, and I want to jump out the window."

"What do you want him to speak of?" Mercy cocked her head and lifted her chin. Her spectacles dipped down her nose, and she pulled them off.

"I don't know. Books and theater maybe. Something that gives me a clue about him."

"Why don't you bring up those subjects instead of rolling your eyes and dancing as if someone has sewn your lips shut?" Poppy waited for a reply while Faith gazed into the corner.

Faith sighed and flopped her arms down around her skirts, which had ballooned up around her. "I suppose I could try a bit harder."

"Or at all," Mercy put in, popping her glasses back on to give Faith a stern look.

Faith pulled a face. "You spent a long time talking to him tonight. Did he say anything that might give a clue what he was doing in France?"

It was hard to determine the line between gossip and information gathering in this journey they were on. Poppy had to say something. "Did you ever read any of the letters your mother sent to Breckenridge, Faith?"

Tucking her dainty fist under her chin, she leaned on her knees and frowned. "No. Only the ones he'd sent her. Is that significant?"

Aurora sat forward, eyes wide. "What did you learn, Poppy?"

"He said the way the letters were written he believed Faith had written them and Lady Dornbury had posted them in her name for propriety's sake. He had no idea you knew nothing of the arrangement over the course of the months your mother and he were corresponding."

Mercy gasped. "I wonder what Lady Dornbury wrote. You believed he was telling the truth?"

Poppy shrugged. "Before he could put on the indifferent mask he wears, he looked genuinely surprised and appalled."

"It is interesting, and Mother can be rather sneaky. I will give the matter some thought." Faith focused on nothing in the corner while she did as she said.

"On a similar yet different subject, what is going on with you and my brother, Poppy?" Aurora raised one slim eyebrow and patted her silken gold hair into place.

Mercy sat up and leaned in. Her green eyes caught the firelight and flashed with golds and browns. A wicked smile curled her lips. "Oh yes, there does seem to be some heat there."

Hades's breath, if they had all noticed, she was doing a poor job of hiding things. "Nothing is going on. We have become friends is all. You are so used to us being at each other's throats, you are imagining more than there is."

Mercy narrowed her eyes and crossed her long legs under her mound of skirts. "The way he looks at you when he thinks no one is watching tells a different story."

"Mercy." Poppy's warning meant very little in this group, but she didn't know how to stop the questions and didn't want to lie to her dearest friends. Even avoiding the subject seemed dishonest.

"You would be a countess." Faith grinned in a way that said she was happy to join the fun and abandon her own problems.

"If you care about such things," Aurora added, teasing.

Temper flaring, Poppy narrowed her gaze on each of her closest friends. "As you well know, I do not care about a title. I leave those concerns to my parents. I also have no desire to marry. If by some miracle I changed my mind, it would be due to a love that couldn't be denied. The kind of love that doesn't exist in our experience."

"Oh Poppy, you're no fun." Mercy pushed up her spectacles and turned her attention toward Aurora. "I danced with Garrett Winslow tonight. He spoke of nothing but you."

Aurora flushed and hugged her bent knees. "What do you mean? Why would he speak of me?"

"He asked me about you too," Faith said. "He wanted to know how you were and if you needed anything."

A deep crease formed between Aurora's eyes. "He's an old family friend who knows nothing of my marriage. He's just concerned."

Aurora reacted with worry and maybe embarrassment. Aurora, who never cared what anyone thought for as long as Poppy had known her.

Poppy leaned back on her pillow. "I suppose it's of little consequence anyway. He leaves in a few weeks for Spain or Portugal. I can't remember which. He didn't give an exact date, though, and I had the impression as long as he's enjoying England, he'll be in no hurry to leave. Strange man, but I like him."

There was a half a second where sorrow filled Aurora's eyes before she masked the emotion. "There you have it. He's always wandering from one country to the next."

"One day he will be the Duke of Corbin. Perhaps then he will be more appealing to you, Aurora." Faith studied her fingernails.

"You might like to marry again one day," Mercy said.

Aurora sat up straight and propped her fists on her hips. "Never. Not even for a duke."

* * * *

When her friends finally left, the clock had struck two bells. Poppy tried to rest, but her mind would not quiet with regard to the Wallflowers' suspicions. Her affair with Rhys was the only thing she had kept from them in six years, and somehow it made a beautiful night seem sordid.

A deep sorrow settled over her that she couldn't dismiss. It was ridiculous. She was a grown woman who had made her own choices and had the most splendid night of her life.

Poppy threw back her covers and pulled on her slippers. She walked to the door, grabbing her wrap as she went. In the hallway she tugged on the silky lavender confection.

The house was drafty, and she pulled her wrap tighter as a shiver wracked her body just as her misery racked her mind.

There were several identical doors along the hallway, but Poppy knew where to stop. She had made her own investigation earlier in the day to learn which room was Rhys's. Another thing she would have to keep to herself. More tears poured down her cheeks.

She knocked.

A shuffling from within made it clear she had gotten his attention. Oh Zeus, what if he'd wasn't alone? She shouldn't have come.

The door opened on a sleepy-eyed Rhys. Delicious in every way. He'd pulled his breeches from the evening back on, but his chest was bare, as were his calves. She'd seen him naked, yet somehow this was far more devastating.

"Penelope, what is it? Are you hurt?" His sleepy state gone in an instant, he touched her shoulder.

The heat of his hand scorched her through her nightclothes. Stepping inside his room was an act of madness, but she'd come this far. "I'm deeply unhappy."

"You're freezing. Come by the fire. I'll add some logs." He wrapped an arm around her waist. It was possessive and comforting.

She refused to look at the large bed with dark drapes or his blouse draped over a chair in the corner. The shadowy room gave away little of its content, and Poppy focused on the way his hand warmed her from head to toe. She shouldn't have allowed it, but his touch felt too good to pull away. Sitting in one of two chairs near the hearth, she watched as a half-naked Rhys coaxed the fire higher.

When he'd created a blaze, he knelt before her. The kindness and warmth of his expression made her admission even worse, and more tears pushed out. He thumbed one away. "Now, tell me why you are unhappy."

"I'm trapped with no one to talk to." She covered her face and folded to her lap.

Combing his fingers through her hair, he whispered, "You can tell me anything, sweetheart."

She looked up, captured by his startling eyes. "Don't you see? I can't speak to you about you."

Anguish reflected in those eyes she'd just admired. He took her hands and kissed them one at a time. "Then you do regret our night together."

"Yes. No." Her mind was muddled with his closeness and the swirling emotions tormenting her. How to explain such a thing? He was all she had, so she forged forward. "I do not regret anything we shared together."

The red that had infused his neck eased back to a normal pink. Rhys tucked wayward strands behind her ear, leaned in, and kissed her cheek. "Then what is it, Penelope?"

He might as well have branded her the way the heat of his lips seared her skin and filled her body with desire. "For more than six years, I have had the Wallflowers to tell all my secrets to. I have never kept any confidences from them. Suddenly, I'm hiding something." She pulled her hands away and covered her face again. "I sound like a complete ninny."

With only a tiny chuckle, he eased her hands away from her eyes. "You are not a ninny. Why do you feel you cannot speak of our relationship with your friends?"

"We have no relationship, Rhys. We had one night of…of… You know what it was. I can't tell Aurora I've been ruined by her brother. As enlightened as the Wallflowers are, they would want you to marry me. I'm not trapping either of us into a life of misery." She drew a long breath.

"And marrying me could only lead to misery." There was an odd sorrow in his statement. He closed his eyes and took a deep breath. When he spoke again, the warmth was back in his voice. "You can always speak to me, Poppy. I am your friend, but I think you underestimate the ladies. They would never want you to be unhappy no matter the circumstance."

It was true the Wallflowers loved her very much. Perhaps Rhys was right and she should trust them. She couldn't look at him and kept her focus on her hands. He was too tempting. "You may be right. I will think about telling them."

"May I say something?" His usually assured and strong voice shook with some emotion she'd never heard before. It might have been anger, but she didn't think so. Fear?

"Of course. I am your friend as well." Whatever was troubling him, she wanted to help. Seeing him distraught churned something ugly in her belly. She didn't like it. Sliding from the chair, she knelt on the rug with him.

Rhys closed his eyes and took a breath. She watched his throat bob several times before he opened his eyes. "The idea you consider yourself ruined because of a night that was, for me, the most wonderful of my life, is untenable. I know popular opinion is women must be virgins to have value, but your worth is not determined by your virginal status. When you begin to think like that, the only way is down. You are a beautiful and wonderful woman, and I consider that night a great gift. Please don't sully it with regrets. You not wanting to marry is your choice, Poppy. I would…"

He left the sentence hanging, and Poppy was not brave enough to ask what he would do. Leaning forward, she hugged him. "That is very kind of you to say."

His caress started at her shoulders and eased down to her bottom. "I would never lie to you."

"No. You never have." Unable to stop herself, she relaxed into his arms. It was so safe and warm, she wished she could stay like this forever.

Wait. No. That wasn't what she wanted, was it? Still, she couldn't bring herself to push away.

"Penelope?" His voice was low with a rasp.

"Yes, Rhys?"

"Despite our being friends, I am only human. If we remain intimate like this much longer, I shall want more from you."

It should have been shocking. Yet his consistent honesty prompted her own. "Me too."

He broke the tight embrace just enough to look her in the eye. "Do you want to stay with me for a while?"

Her face was on fire, and she was sure her blush was the same shade as the russet drapes. She cupped his cheek and ran the pads of her fingers over his day-old beard. "I wouldn't mind. Do you think me a complete wanton?"

Leaning in, he tugged her bottom lip between his. The tender kiss sped her pulse until she thought she might lose her senses. "I think you are magnificent, sweetheart. It is all I will ever think."

He pulled a fur blanket from a small stool where it had been draped and lay on the floor in front of the fire. Easing her to her back, his smile rang with desire, delight with just a hint of worry marring his eyes.

Poppy longed to ask him what worried him, but his fingers traced a path up her leg and she couldn't think at all. It would be another night she would have to keep secret. The invading worry shot fear through her. "Rhys, I think this is a mistake."

His hand stilled. "You want to leave?"

Pulling back, she had to avoid the longing in his eyes lest she be pulled back into the lovemaking. "I cannot continue to create moments that must be kept secret."

"I have not asked you to keep anything secret." He stood and offered his hand to help her rise.

Even his gentlemanly touch shot her full with desire. Perhaps she really was a wanton destined to be some man's mistress. Shaking off the notion, she removed her hand from his. "No, but I cannot tell my friends about the intimate nature of our relationship. It is too embarrassing and unacceptable. I will have to learn to live with keeping the secret, but I'll not create more."

He closed the gap between them, forcing her to crane her neck to keep eye contact. There was something dangerous in his eyes. They rang out some warning that Poppy didn't heed as she stayed close.

Easing his knuckles down her cheek to her jaw, the hardness in his gaze melted. "We could solve all of these problems by marrying."

It took her a full beat to realize what he had said. It wasn't possible. "I…I told you I never want to be the property of a man."

"Must a marriage be so?" He dropped his hand away.

Everything was confused. The loss of his touch left an emptiness in her soul while her brain screamed warnings over the idea of marriage. Images of her parents' contentious life together streamed through her head along with Aurora's various states of battery over the last three years. "I wish it were different, but this is how life is, Rhys."

"You don't trust me." Devastation rang in his voice.

It was important she make him understand. The notion of him coming to despise her gnawed in her gut, though she saw no way around it. "If we married, you would realize sooner or later I was yours to do with as you wish.

No one can resist that kind of power. The government has decreed a wife is the property of her husband, and men use that fact to their advantage."

"You have given this a lot of thought."

Raising her chin and meeting those steel eyes, she held his stare. She could not waver no matter how attractive he was or how kind he appeared. "I have."

"Is it not possible your knowledge of marriage is limited to those who were forced to marry people whom they didn't have affection for beforehand?"

There was truth to his assessment, but it didn't matter. "It is the way of our society. Marriages are to lift people's place either in society or financially. Love is beside the point. The other two factors always win out."

He kept his eyes averted and his fists clenched at his sides. "It is pointless to argue with you. If you change your mind, my offer stands."

"That is very generous." She went to the door.

"It's not generosity, Penelope." Fire danced in his eyes with an intensity that shot to her heart.

Afraid to ask what he meant, she curtsied and ran from the room.

Chapter 12

Rhys spent the rest of the night tossing and turning before rising early to go hunting with the men. He paced the yard long before the others arrived. The area between the house and the barn was grass but cut low for easy passage between the two. It was a large space that took Rhys five or more minutes to traverse in each direction. Either side was lined with trees, giving him a feeling of privacy.

She'd rejected him. He'd offered her marriage and she'd told him no. He was an earl. Women didn't reject earls. Yet Poppy was no ordinary woman. He enjoyed a private smile. No, Poppy was special, though misguided about marriage. Not that she was entirely wrong. His parents' marriage, as an example, was as she described. Mother was a pawn following Father's direction until he died; however, the arrangement seemed to suit both of them. Mother never complained or seemed unhappy, that is, except on the day Aurora was sent away. That day, Mother had cried.

His friends Walter and Marie Stratton were different. They had the kind of marriage he wanted. They had married for love and ran their home and properties together. Perhaps there was a way to show Poppy it didn't have to be like his parents or hers.

Rhys was on his third pass across the wide yard and deep in his own thoughts.

"You look like a man with a problem." Garrett walked toward him. Friends since Eton, Rhys was usually happy to see him. Unfortunately, Garrett was also the one person who always saw through any attempt to hide his emotions.

The crisp morning left a haze on the fields. Footmen appeared out of the mist from the house with guns, cloaks, ammunition, and anything else gentlemen might need during a morning hunt.

Rhys shook off his reverie. He had to protect Poppy, not to mention the teasing he'd be in for if Garrett knew too much. "I have no problems. Just thinking about the week and all the fine entertainment we've had."

"And all the lovely ladies." Garrett wagged his eyebrows comically. His easy smile was wide, and his eyes shone with familiar mischief.

"And the ladies as well. When did you become such an old dog?" It was good to see his oldest friend back in England. He'd been gone too long.

"I've done a lot of traveling, and women are always a fine distraction. Remember the time we went to Bath and wooed all the girls in town. I admit, I miss those innocent days. Soon we'll have to marry and be done with such nonsense."

"I'm already done with it. Dim women in gaudy ballrooms have little interest for me anymore." Only one woman interested Rhys, and he saw no end to that situation.

Garrett crossed his arms over his chest and stopped before taking long strides to close the gap between them. His normally reddish hair looked brown in the foggy morning, but his eyes narrowed suspiciously. He lowered his voice. "I have not heard a word about that mistress you wrote me regarding. Is all well there?" Garrett accepted a weapon and waved to the other men joining them.

They walked along a path and headed for a field Dornbury claimed had some fine shooting. Rhys and Garrett kept apart from the rest as they talked, and Breckenridge walked farther ahead, keeping his distance from the group.

Speaking softly so only Garrett could hear him, Rhys said, "I gave her up last year. When my father's health began to fail, I had little time for her, and she was unhappy with the arrangement."

Garrett clapped him on the back. "Sorry to hear it. I know you liked that one."

Shrugging, Rhys struggled to remember what color Melissa's eyes were or how tall she was. His heart was full of a certain brunette with eyes like the sea, and there was no room for any other women. "It's of little consequence. She was a lovely distraction, but nothing more."

"And you are taken with the Arrington girl." Garrett's smile was annoying.

"Perhaps, but it is not something I wish to discuss with you here, or anywhere for that matter," Rhys ground out. A full denial would have sent

Garrett on a different kind of hunt, and Rhys didn't want to provoke him. They had been friends so long that he knew how Garrett's mind worked.

Luckily the others were far enough ahead there was little possibility anyone had heard. Poppy needed to find her own way to him, and a buzz of gossip would send her running in the other direction.

Garrett raised a brow but said nothing more.

Faith's father, the Earl of Dornbury, said, "Why don't you three stay here." He pointed to Garrett, Rhys, and Breckenridge. "You should find some fine coveys in those thickets. Don't shoot my footmen. They're damned hard to replace." He chuckled to himself and strode off with the rest of the party and several footmen.

Two of the aforementioned footmen stayed back to flush the coveys for them. Rhys turned to the one who had brought cloaks. He'd learned earlier in the week the footman's name was James and he had two sons and a wife in the village. "James, does that ever bother you?"

James's grin revealed a missing front tooth and a cheerful disposition. "It's best to have either very good or very bad hearing as the duty requires, my lord. Once we get this table and the ammunition in place, Levi and I will flush those birds for you gentlemen."

"Thank you, James." Rhys studied the brambles that likely held their quarry. The morning cool did little to release his lethargy. He'd wanted to shake Poppy until she realized she was being silly, but that was not how to win her. He'd held his tongue and would bide his time.

A day away from her was what he needed. He turned to the other distraction this week. "Breckenridge, this must be a good amusement after so much time in France. Are you enjoying all that town and the English countryside have to offer?"

With one arm, Nicholas cradled his gun. The other was perched on his hip. He took a deep breath, looking out over the vista. Dornbury had a pretty piece of property. "It's good to be back. My time in France was difficult."

Garrett looked down the barrel of his shotgun. "I had to flee France when a few battles came to close. Wanted to go to Portugal, but I understand Bonaparte has made a mess of the place."

"Yes. Quite a mess. I was lucky not to get caught up in that end of things." Nicholas checked his weapon.

"You did some business for the Crown?" Garrett readied his weapon.

James and Levi rounded the brambles where they suspected coveys. Quail flew.

Breckenridge and Garrett both aimed and fired, felling two birds.

Caught up in finally learning something about the duke, Rhys never lifted his weapon.

Inwardly, he cursed the timing of the footmen.

"I took care of a few things for the regent on behalf of the king. A small commission to keep my country safe. It lasted quite a few years longer than expected. The one-year assignment turned into four." Breckenridge reloaded.

John ran the quail back to the table. "These will make a fine start for the dinner, my lords."

"Good work, James. Do we have another covey to roust?" Garrett asked.

"Yes, sir. Give us just a moment and we'll lead the way." James trotted back into the field.

When James waved, they took up their guns and walked through the field. The mist still hung near the ground, but the rising sun would burn it off soon enough. The leaves rustled from the wood line to the left. The breaking day left shadows across the grasses, and the birds chirped wildly.

Not wanting to seem too eager, Rhys waited until they were halfway across the field. "Well, that's all behind you now, Breckenridge. You've made it home safely."

Nicholas sighed. "It's a difficult line of work to break free of. As a duke I suppose I could have cried off, but that didn't seem right. My father's death was no excuse for not finishing what I was sent there for."

"But you managed to complete your duty?" Rhys should have found a better way, one that didn't sound so pushy.

Oblivious, Nicholas shrugged. "I did all I could, and the prince regent decided my home and lands needed me back."

Garrett patted him on the back. "Now you're ready to find a bride and make an heir, I presume. Faith is a lovely girl."

"She is lovely." Nicolas frowned.

They walked on until James signaled them to stop. Lifting their guns, they waited.

A still moment held the day as if time itself had stopped moving forward. A slew of pheasant flew.

They all shot. Three birds fell.

"Thank you both for the company today. It's been some time since I had gentlemen to confide in. It might sound like a small thing, but once lost, its value increases." Nicholas gave them each a nod.

Guilt seeped inside Rhys. Those women had him thinking like one of them. Looking for something wrong with Breckenridge when his instincts told him otherwise. Shaking off all things Wallflowers, he enjoyed the rest of the sport and much-needed male company.

* * * *

It was better to face them sooner rather than later, Rhys thought as he approached the stand of trees where his sister and her friends liked to gather. He wanted to see Poppy. He longed to know if she was still his friend or if all hope was lost. There was an emptiness when she was far from him.

It was another fine day. The weather had been remarkable. The late day sun cast shadows of the trees across the lawn, giving them shade on a warm day.

They were all sitting on the grass in various shades of pastel dresses. Four flowers, waiting for their thorn. He wished he could just admire them for a few minutes, but he'd been spotted. "You ladies look lovely."

"How was your hunting, Rhys?" Aurora smiled up at him. Each time he saw her, she seemed more relaxed and less the woman Radcliff had made her.

"I am happy to report we shall have quail for supper." He joined them on the grass.

Faith clapped. "Well done!"

"I aim to please, though I was not alone. It was a fine day to be out in nature. What have the four of you done all day?"

Mercy rolled her eyes. "We were forced to sit for hours with her ladyship and stitch bits of cloth and put ribbons on bonnets."

Laughing at Mercy's drama, Poppy said, "It really was ghastly, but there were sweets."

"Poppy loves her sweets." Faith grinned and tugged at the ribbons on the bonnet she held. It was covered in lavender and pink with no room to spare. "Now I'll have to pull all of this."

"Why did you put them on?" Rhys tried to understand the inner workings of the life of a lady.

"Because if I didn't look busy, Mother would have started a lecture on how a lady must always have an occupation. It is my least favorite of her diatribes, and I'd rather poke my eyes out than hear it again. So, when she demands these little afternoons of sitting about doing womanly things, I comply in my own way. The hat is unwearable, but there was no sermon."

Rhys was confused by so much of this that he settled for asking, "If it is so distasteful to live at home, why don't you give marrying more thought?"

Faith cocked her head. The usual innocence gone from her face, she stared him in the eye. "I'm at West Lane now and while temporary, it is a great relief. Besides, I want to marry. I want a dozen children. What I don't want is to be forced to marry a man I cannot love."

"And you cannot love Breckenridge? He seems a good man to me."
Poppy's expression was an emotionless mask.

Aurora asked, "Did you learn something today, Rhys?"

Here it was, the moment when he had to choose sides in this ridiculous battle. "What I learned was in confidence. However, I am willing to say his activities in France were for king and country."

Poppy's eyes widened, and she turned red. "You are willing to say. You're on his side. You are protecting him. After all we have done as Wallflowers, you now have joined the club of men who protect each other regardless of the wishes of women."

His own anger rose to where he had to clench his fists to keep from raging at her. "I am not on his side, but when someone tells you something in confidence, you keep the confidence. Why is it after all we have been through together you can't trust my judgment? Do you think I would allow anything bad to happen to Faith?"

Poppy's eyes widened for a moment before her mouth twisted in an ugly sneer. "I think you are just like the rest of them with your private clubs and secrets."

Knowing how she felt about his sex, it cut him to the heart that she would lump him in with all men. "Are you angry at me or yourself, Poppy? Maybe your rage is at Faith for wanting marriage when you don't."

"I am not. You are twisting things." She jumped up and ran from the circle.

He watched her go before realizing the other three Wallflowers were staring at him with wide eyes and open mouths. "A bit of a temper."

"What on earth is going on?" Aurora was the first to recover. "And yes, when provoked, Poppy has a temper."

Faith scowled. "Poppy is not angry with me. Is she?"

"Of course not, Faith." Mercy shifted her weight and sat up on her knees, narrowing her eyes on Rhys. "I don't think that little display had anything to do with any of us. Nor do I think it was about His Grace."

"Would you ladies excuse my brother and me? We'll only be a little while, and then I'll be in to dress for dinner."

With a nod from each, Mercy and Faith walked toward the house arm in arm.

When they were well out of hearing, Aurora turned to him. "Are you in love with her?"

"Who?"

She gave him her best don't-toy-with-me look. "Don't be daft. Are you in love with my dearest friend, Poppy Arrington?"

"Yes, but the lady does not return my feelings." His heart contracted into a small stone in the center of his chest.

"Why do you say that?"

"I can no more disclose a conversation with Poppy than I could one with Breckenridge. She's your dearest friend; why don't you ask her?" His words dripped with sarcasm and disgust. He hated himself for not being the man Poppy wanted. She said there was no man, but he didn't believe that. She was a beautiful, smart, kind, and caring woman. Some man would win her.

If it were possible to hate a man who didn't yet exist, Rhys had found it. He longed to wrap his hands around the throat of that imaginary man.

Aurora's face fell in sorrow, but he wasn't sure if it was for him, for Poppy, or for herself. "Poppy would not tell me something so personal. At least, not until she admits it to herself. Clearly, that is not the case."

"Have I upset you, Rora?" Reaching out, he took her hand.

"No. I want all my friends and you to be happy." A tear slid down her pale cheek.

"And what of you? Don't you think you deserve to be happy too?"

Her smile was forced. "I will be happy. Give me some time. I love having my friends living at my house. I love that you and I are spending more time together. Mother is keeping her distance for the time being. I have nothing to complain about."

He squeezed her hand. "I suppose I was silly to think you could be the cheerful young girl I grew up with."

A long sigh pushed from her lips. "We can none of us go back in time, Rhys. No matter how much we wish we could, we must live in the present. I will see if I can help with Poppy, but try to see her perspective."

"I do. I understand. I just don't know how to overcome things that were not my doing, at least not entirely." It was frustrating on so many levels. Still, what he had learned about Poppy in the past few weeks was far more than he had in the six years prior. This was a complicated woman who knew what she wanted. The problem was, she had closed off the possibility of changing her mind.

Aurora patted his arm. "It will all work out."

* * * *

After the argument, he could not get Poppy alone to talk to her. The fortnight was coming to an end. They were seated next to each other at the final dinner.

Her attention was either on Garrett on her other side or her plate.

By the entree course, Rhys was bordering on lunacy. "Will you never speak to me?" he whispered.

She placed her fork on her plate, took up her wine, and sipped. Setting the glass back on the table, she angled her lowered chin toward him. "What would you have me say?"

"I would have you admit information given in confidence should not be shared."

She pinked. "I do not disagree. But this situation is not common, and it is quite serious."

A footman refilled his wineglass, keeping him from making an immediate reply.

"I understand your feelings, but still think you should trust my opinion in this matter." They were still speaking so low only she could hear him.

"Faith said as much. She has decided to give Breckenridge a chance. She has taken two walks with him and said he was very charming. With regard to your part, I am disappointed." Poppy went back to tearing bits of roast with her fork and pretending to eat.

"I am sorry to have caused you any pain." What needed to be said could not happen sitting at a public table and speaking in hushed tones. It would have to wait.

After dinner they all retired to the parlor where card tables had been set out for whist. He rounded out a foursome with Poppy, Aurora, and Garrett. "Rora, I didn't think you liked cards."

"I hate them, but I couldn't think of how to get out of the entertainment." She wore a brown gown that made her fade into the décor rather than gleam like the flower she was. Most days in the country she had rejected the darkest colors traditional to mourning.

Rhys could not wait for her bereavement period to be over.

"Why have you returned to such dark mourning clothes?" Garrett dealt the cards.

Aurora sighed. "It seems my lighter, more comfortable dresses were offensive to our hostess."

Poppy ground her teeth, making a crunching sound.

"She said that?" Rhys wanted to give that overbearing witch a piece of his mind.

"Not in those words, but the point was clear." Poppy examined her cards.

Garrett's jaw clenched and unclenched. "It is a miracle Faith became such a sweet woman."

"What did you say, Rora?" Rhys couldn't believe his sister would be silent after such an insult.

A giggle that reminded him of when Aurora was a girl escaped from behind her hand. "There was no need for my response. Poppy took care of the situation."

When they all turned to Poppy, there was a regal tilt to her chin. Shoulders back, expression serene, and lips pursed, she looked quite pleased with herself a she tossed out a card.

A grin broke out on Garrett's face. "What did you say, Poppy?"

She shrugged. "I merely pointed out a few of her ladyship's flaws."

"Such as…" Rhys's gut filled with a bubble of anticipation.

Poppy eyed him. "I know you will find this shocking, but our hostess slurps when she drinks tea; passes wind when she thinks she can blame one of those silly dogs of hers; wears gowns several years too young for her; pastes bits of hair into her own, creating a nest of ratting old hair; treats her lady's maid like a slave; and bullies her daughter, who is an angel on earth. I felt it my duty to point these and a few other things out while she was forcing us to listen to one of her sermons."

A loud bark of laughter flew from Garrett's lips, and he kept right on laughing. Taking Poppy's hand, he kissed it. "You are a treasure."

Aurora hid her smile. "Yes, but there is not likely to be any more invitations from this house."

"We shall find other means of entertainment," Poppy assured her.

Full of love and admiration, Rhys said, "Then you don't regret what you said?"

She shook her head. "For once in my life, I didn't stumble over any words or say the wrong thing at the wrong time. It was the one instance when my bad habit came in handy. She deserved every word."

A footman entered with a note on a silver tray. He approached Breckenridge. "Your Grace, this just came by special messenger."

Nicholas read the message, frowned, and stood. "Is the messenger still here?"

"Yes, Your Grace. He's below in the kitchen having something to eat."

Nodding, Nicholas said, "I'll have a letter for him to take on his return. Be sure to have him wait."

With a bow, the footman rushed from the room.

"I hope nothing is amiss, Your Grace." Lady Dornbury folded her cards and placed them on the table. She grinned like a woman enjoying the idea she would soon be the mother-in-law to a duke.

"Nothing to concern yourself with, madam. Some business in town needs my attention. However, I will have to depart tonight." Nicholas stepped back from the table and bowed.

Faith's eyes narrowed. "Tonight. But, Your Grace, we are all departing tomorrow. Surely this business of yours can wait a few hours, so you can join us for the trip."

It was bold for Faith to say so much in such a public setting. She tended toward demure in general society.

Nicholas grimaced. "I apologize, my lady, but I'm afraid I must leave almost immediately."

Most ladies in Faith's position would have smiled politely and wished him well. Faith was not most ladies. Without another glance at him, she studied her cards and pursed her lips. "Go then, if you wish."

Any progress the Duke of Breckenridge had made with his perspective bride had just been lost, and he perhaps slipped further from her grace.

Rhys felt for him, but what business could be so critical it couldn't wait until morning? Leaving in the dark of night to attend to something was highly unusual. Perhaps Rhys had been too quick to accept the vague explanations about Breckenridge's time in France for the Crown. Just because a man worked on the right side of a political line didn't mean he was a good fit for a friend. Strange as it was, these Wallflowers were his friends and family. He'd not let another of them suffer.

The host and hostess saw Nicholas to the door a short time later.

Poppy's eyebrows were raised in question as she gazed across the table at him. "That was interesting. Don't you think so?"

"I'm sure there is a very reasonable explanation." Rhys hated half-truths, but this was no place for a debate on the subject.

"I think I've had enough cards for one night." Poppy stood, disappointment burning in her eyes.

"We've hardly started," Garrett complained.

Aurora stood as well. "Let's take a turn around the room, Poppy."

The ladies strolled arm in arm around the perimeter of the room. They whispered their secrets too softly to be overheard.

Rhys missed being in their confidence and longed for the time they'd spent together at Geb Arafa's home, where they'd become friends.

"Well that's it for whist." Garrett scooped up the dealt cards and shuffled the deck. "I learned a quaint game for two in Spain, if you'd care to learn."

Shrugging, Rhys pulled his attention away from Poppy. "I suppose a new game is in order."

Garrett dealt the cards.

Chapter 13

Poppy did her best to ignore Rhys for the entire ride, which was not really possible. She was completely and annoyingly in tune to every sound and movement of the man. Faith had to ride with her parents, so it was Aurora, Mercy, and Poppy in Rhys's carriage for the two-day ride home.

They had stopped at a coaching inn for the night and had one more night of dinner together as a party. Luckily, she was able to sit at the other end of the table and not be forced into any kind of politeness when she wanted a fight.

How he could have turned to Breckenridge's side, she couldn't fathom. Men always took each other's part—that was true. But Rhys had seemed to really care about what happened to the Wallflowers right up until his loyalty was tested; then he wavered. She sighed and watched the passing buildings as they entered London.

Yet she could not deny that information given in confidence should be kept private. It was all very confusing.

"Poppy, what do you think?" Aurora startled her out of her thoughts.

"I'm afraid I was lost in thought. What were you saying?"

Mercy rolled her eyes. "We were speaking about meeting at George's tomorrow to determine what our next step should be."

It took an act of will not to look at Rhys. He watched as if he hung on her every word. It was maddening to both want and not want his attentions. "I'm happy to meet, but the decision must be Faith's. She seemed quite put out the other night. She may have decided irrevocably against Breckenridge."

"Perhaps, but I think she was beginning to like him." Aurora fisted her gloves in her lap and gestured with them as she spoke.

"It would be a shame if she had decided against him, but as you say, the decision must be Faith's. She must know what she wants or doesn't want." Rhys spoke as if the matter was not worrisome, but his gaze was fixed on Poppy.

The certainty he was speaking of more than the situation between her friend and Breckenridge stirred butterflies in Poppy's stomach. She refused to think about what she wanted. It was decided a long time ago marriage was not for her, and she couldn't waver at the first sign of masculine attention.

The thing was, it wasn't the first sign. In the last three years many men had shown interest in her title and her dowry. London never lacked for men hoping to increase their coffers through marriage, even if the lady was awkward and clumsy.

Rhys didn't need her dowry. He had far more than she and could have made a bid for her many years ago. It wasn't until they'd been intimate that he'd felt some obligation to ask for her hand. His sense of duty demanded he ask.

Imagine his relief at her refusal. However, he hadn't looked relieved. Sorrow and disappointment had cried out from his sunken expression the night she'd stolen into his room.

Her musings would have to wait as they pulled to a stop in front of the West Lane townhouse.

Rhys stepped down first then helped Mercy and Aurora down before turning into the carriage to capture her gaze. Worry creased his brow. "I believe your mother is here, Poppy."

Heart in her throat, she gasped. "Why, what, how do you know?"

Accepting his hand, she stepped down on shaking knees. Parked in front of them was her family carriage with the Merkwood crest emblazoned on the door. Poppy's stomach lurched, and her heart lodged in her throat. What on earth could her mother be doing at West Lane? This didn't bode well.

Aurora threaded her arm through hers, and they all climbed the stairs to the front door together.

As bad as this might be, at least she had her friends. Even Rhys's presence was a comfort. She would have thought he'd have dropped them off and gone to his own home, but as they entered the house, he stayed with them.

"Welcome home, ladies. The Countess of Merkwood is waiting in the parlor. She has been here for nearly an hour," Tipton, the butler, informed them.

"Thank you, Tipton. We'll go in directly." Aurora handed him her hat and gloves.

They all foisted their outerwear at Tipton, who balanced the mound without a word. His bushy eyebrow rose when Poppy thanked him.

The grand parlor was far different from the sanctuary where the Wallflowers had always met. This was a formal room to greet guests in the style of Radcliff. Dark woods, austere curtains pulled precisely halfway across floor-to-ceiling windows. The dark furniture and rug absorbed the light. Poppy had only been in the room a few times, and it always set her nerves on edge.

Gwendolyn Arrington, Countess of Merkwood, didn't bother to stand. Her dark hair had just a touch of gray above the temple where it was pulled into a loose bun. No curls were left out to soften the look. She was dressed in a dark blue day dress with a lace collar.

Mother's eyes narrowed on the foursome. "I have been waiting half the morning."

"If you had told someone you were coming," Poppy began, "or waited until we were at home, Mother, you would not have had to wait." Mother's sense of superiority set Poppy's nerves on edge.

"I will speak with my daughter alone." The command in her voice might have sent another party of ladies running, but her friends held their ground, waiting for more information.

"You can have nothing to say that my friends cannot hear, Mother." Poppy grasped for some safety net.

"Manners, Penelope. Is that anyway to greet your mother?" Her double standard had always miffed Poppy.

"As you didn't bother to say hello or greet the lady of this house, I saw no reason to bother with manners, Mother."

If daggers could have flown from Gwendolyn's eyes, they would all four be bleeding on the carpet. "Fine. I see your point. Lady Radcliff, it's a pleasure to see you again. Miss Heath, good to see you as well. Would the two of you mind excusing us? I have some very serious business to discuss with my daughter."

Mercy and Aurora were both wide eyed.

Rhys stood stoically watching.

Aurora recovered first. "Nice of you to pay a call, my lady."

With a round of curtsies, the ladies left. Each gave Poppy a sympathetic look as they abandoned her to her fate.

"My lord, you should stay." The show for the other ladies over, Mother studied her nails for a long moment. The hint of a grin tugged at her lips.

Rhys bowed. "Of course, madam."

Mother returned to the settee where she'd been when they arrived. Her eyebrows rose high on her forehead, and she ogled at Poppy as if she were a cat that just made off with the first course.

Waiting near a chair, Rhys couldn't sit until Poppy did, and Poppy was not sure she was willing to find out what it was that put her mother in a mood between furious and gleeful. Danger emanated from her, a beacon of destruction.

"Well?" Mother pointed toward the other chair facing the settee.

Unable to think of a way out of the room short of running and screaming like a maniac, Poppy trudged over and sat.

Rhys kept his gaze on Mother, and he sat as well.

Mother's attention shifted between the two of them, and though there was a glint in her eye, she forced a deep frown. "It has come to my attention the two of you spent two days and nights together without the benefit of a chaperone."

The world around Poppy started spinning too fast. Mother's words bounced around in her head like a wild horse bucking his saddle. "What are you talking about, Mother?"

"Do not toy with me, Penelope. I know you got in a carriage with this unmarried man and left the city. Some kind of weather kept you from returning, but that is of no consequence. The fact still remains you were two days and nights with a man unchaperoned. If word got around town, and it will, you would be ruined and your father and I shamed. We wouldn't be able to show our faces in good society again."

It was impossible for her mother to know this. No one knew. Could Geb have sent a letter to her mother? Why would he do such a thing? "Mother, you really are making more of this than is necessary."

"Am I?" She elongated the words.

"Yes. We planned to come directly back, but there was flooding and we couldn't return. There is no need for you to have come here with so much dramatics." Poppy liked the sound of that. She was a grown woman and could make her own decisions.

Rhys was strangely quiet. He fixated on the carpet as if he were not in the conversation.

Turning away from Poppy, Mother focused on Rhys. "What are you going to do about this situation, my lord?"

"I will marry her." His voice was even and his tone steady. He continued to look at the carpet.

"What!" Poppy's brain was close to exploding. She replayed the last few seconds, and no matter how she spun it, Rhys had agreed to do the very thing that she dreaded most.

"Well, fine then." Mother smiled as if all was well and nothing out of the ordinary had happened.

Whatever sense Poppy had come into the room with had flown right out that giant window with its horrid draperies. The walls of the room closed in on her, and her mother suddenly looked like some villain in a children's fable. It would come as no surprise if Gwendolyn Arrington grew horns and a tail before rising to forty feet tall and devouring them both.

At any moment sense would be made of this madness and Rhys would laugh and take his words back, but it didn't happen.

Poppy bit the inside of her cheek to keep from flying into a rage. "I will not be forced to marry you or anyone. You, my lord, should understand. How dare you make that offer knowing how I feel. How dare you take her side." She pointed at Mother. "She is a puppet led around by the strings held by a rich, horrible man who couldn't bother to come here himself."

Mother's expression remained calm, though she frowned at the pointing finger. "Your father knows nothing about this. Though I'm sure Lord Marsden will want to go and ask his permission to marry you."

"I will speak to his lordship today." Rhys's voice was strong and void of emotion.

Unable to continue, Poppy stood. Her heart raced. Her body shook and her knees were weak. "I will not marry you or anyone else."

Rhys rose as she did. He reached out a hand to steady her.

Poppy pulled away from his touch. She met his gaze.

Longing, regret, and something else she couldn't put a name to swam in those stunning eyes. "Penelope, please listen to me for just a few minutes."

Her full name had become an endearment for the first time in her life, and now even that was soiled. He was party to her demise along with her parents who had been plotting this her entire life. Perhaps she was the one being dramatic, but she didn't care. Something snapped inside her, and no amount of cheek biting would control it. "Don't you dare call me that. Don't you ever call me that."

She ran from the room but couldn't bear not knowing what would be said about her. Sneaking around through the servants' passage, she listened through the other door.

The rustle of skirts indicated Mother had risen. "Please pardon my daughter. Clearly she is overwrought by the excitement of becoming your wife."

"Clearly." Sarcasm dripped from his words.

"Then we will expect you at the house today." Satisfaction oozed from Mother's tone. She'd gotten what she'd always wanted from Poppy, marriage to a man of wealth and title. It was Poppy's own stupidity that had sealed her fate.

Tears rolled silently down her cheeks. She would have to run, but where? She had no family to run to, at least none who would take her in. She had little funds.

Rhys's voice rang out. "I will call on his lordship in an hour. I would like to speak to Lady Penelope before I speak to him."

"If you wish. At least there is a chaperone here. I suppose this is my own fault. I should never have let her leave home. But when a grown child tells you she's going to live with her recently widowed friend, it all sounds quite innocent." Mother's voice grew farther away.

"It was innocent, madam. May I see you to the door?" Rhys's voice faded as well.

"Not necessary. I found my way in, and I can get out the same way. I will see you in one hour, my lord."

Whatever Rhys replied was lost in the hallway outside the parlor.

Poppy slid down the wall and buried her face in her hands. How could he have agreed? And with no attempt to fight Mother. His lack of emotion on the subject showed him to be just like the rest. He might be doing this to save face rather than money, but it was all the same.

Yet for her it was not the same. She longed for him to be different somehow, to understand her needs and put them above these stupid rules of society. She'd thought he was her friend, someone she had gone to when she needed to talk. Now she felt like a fool having poured out her heart to him and given him information he could use to hurt her later. Husbands were a menace who used what they knew to keep their wives submissive and obedient.

A young maid, Patty, hummed as she walked through the narrow corridor. When she saw Poppy, she stopped. "Pardon me, my lady." She ran off toward the main hall.

* * * *

The wall sconces gave off little light and with no windows, Poppy didn't know how long she sat there weeping out her fury.

Faith's voice was soft. "Come, Poppy. Let's get you out of here."

Obeying, Poppy's legs ached from inactivity. She let Faith help her to stand before falling into a hug. Trembling, she asked, "Is he gone?"

"Rhys? Yes. He waited a good while trying to find you, but then had to go. He will return later this afternoon." Faith wrapped a hand around

Poppy's waist. They entered the main hall, crossed over, and entered the Wallflowers' parlor.

Poppy rested on the chaise but flung her arm over her eyes to block out the bright sun shining through the lightly draped windows. "You should have told him never to come back."

"He was very concerned for you."

Uncovering her eyes, Poppy sat up. "Did he tell you what happened?"

"Yes, of course. He said your mother heard about the unchaperoned trip and demanded he marry you, and he agreed." Faith said it as if it were an everyday occurrence.

"He knows full well that I don't want to marry. Not like that. He offered me up like the stuffed goose at Christmas without a word of protest. This is my worst nightmare come to pass." That was what hurt the most. He knew her wishes and let the dictates of a society he scoffed at force him into a marriage neither of them wanted.

Faith studied her for a long moment. Faith could act the part of a dim young woman in public, but not much actually got past her. Her scrutiny was unsettling. "Poppy, what is it you're really upset about? Do you not want to marry, or not want to marry Rhys? Because from what I've seen over the last few weeks, he appears to like you very much. He watches your every move and has been solicitous to your moods and needs. I think he agreed because he wants to marry you."

"I doubt that very much. He's a rake, Faith. A man who beds women for sport." Nausea made her a bit dizzy, and she reclined.

Brow furrowed, Faith continued her examination. "Perhaps in his youth he was, but I've not seen signs of that behavior in years and certainly not since he became an earl. Could it be you cannot get over a traumatic experience from more than six years ago? Perhaps you should just forgive him for one day so long ago and see if you could like the man he's become."

Hating it when Faith made so much sense, Poppy gritted her teeth. Until his agreement to marry her, she thought she had forgiven him. Lord, she hated it when Faith was right. "Zeus's beard, I have been set against being a man's chattel all my life, Faith. How can I become a piece of property never to have my own say again?"

Faith sat close and took her hand. "I wonder if it is the only possibility after marriage. My mother is difficult, but she does not cower to my father. She stands up for herself and even for me sometimes. Father is not a bad sort, just inconstant and moody. He usually gives my mother her way."

"You never told me that before." Poppy wiped her cheeks. She was not given to fits of hysteria, and the entire scene curdled her stomach.

Shrugging, Faith pulled a face. "I didn't want to be the only one with parents who got along. It seems silly now, but when we were fifteen, it made sense to just go along."

"But, Faith, we haven't been girls in a long time." It somehow made her feel better for keeping her secrets knowing sweet Faith had kept one all these years. Perhaps everyone kept secrets and it was just the way of things. Poppy's head throbbed.

Faith smiled and made no apology. "I know, but sometimes it's easier to just let a thing be rather than fighting all the time."

"I wouldn't know." Poppy giggled and Faith joined her.

After sharing a good chuckle, Faith sobered. "Do you love him, Poppy?"

The knot returned to Poppy's throat. "Why would you ask that? I have refused to marry him."

Faith's soulful eyes bore into Poppy's heart. "I have known you for a long time, and I can count on one hand the times I've seen you this out of sorts. And weeping, maybe twice in all these years."

"Could it not be I am upset over my mother's high-handedness and Rhys's easy agreement?" Poppy wanted to run from the room, but running from Faith made no sense. Faith was sent in when the others would not do the deed.

Mercy and Aurora were likely waiting to be called in when things had calmed down. When a Wallflower was very upset, they never all came at once as that could be overwhelming or confusing. The Wallflower best suited to the job would sort it out.

Not ready to be bombarded with questions from all three of them, Poppy was thankful to only have Faith in the room.

"I don't think that would make you cry. You might rant and rave, but these tears make it more personal. So, are you in love with him?" Faith patted Poppy's hand.

"I have decided to never marry." Her tears began again.

"No one would blame you if you had changed your mind. We Wallflowers change our minds all the time. We also stand together. So, if you don't want him, we will find a way to resolve the matter. It's Rhys. after all, He's not going to drag you by the hair and make you marry him."

She was right, of course. Rhys was a reasonable man, and even if he felt forced to say he would marry her, he would allow her to bow out at a later date. Perhaps he imagined she would go along with the process and save him the trouble of finding a wife elsewhere before returning to his mistress. Titled men must marry, after all. Her worries flipped from fear to jealousy in a heartbeat. Hades, she no longer knew her own mind. When had that happened? "I think it's safe for Mercy and Aurora to come in now."

The door burst open and her friends rushed in. They crowded around her, asking if she was all right.

"I'm better now. Faith was good counsel as always." Poppy smiled.

Aurora sat on the carpet at Poppy's feet. She stared down, not meeting Poppy's eyes. "You know Rhys would never hurt you physically. You would be safe with him."

Touching Aurora's shoulder, Poppy said, "Yes. I know. He is not a violent man. I just don't know how Mother could have found out about the stay at Mr. Arafa's home."

Shaking her head, Mercy huffed. "I suppose someone might have seen the two of you leave London together."

"Mother seemed to know more than a passing notice. She knew where we'd gone."

"It must have been Mr. Arafa who told your mother," Faith said.

Poppy hated the idea that Geb would have betrayed her but could think of nothing else.

Aurora fiddled with the lace on her gown but made no comment.

Mercy said, "There is cake in the kitchen. I think this would be a fine time to eat an entire cake and make no apologies."

"Cook will be furious," Faith warned.

Lord, how Poppy loved these women. "Let's go. Cook will get over her disappointment."

It was like being back at school again with the four of them raiding the kitchens, though those adventures generally happened in the middle of the night while all of Wormbattle's slept.

Halfway through the sweet treat, footsteps and banging above stairs drew them out of the kitchen.

"What on earth?" Aurora led the way.

Poppy's skin prickled with a sense of doom. "I have a bad feeling."

"Don't be silly. Probably one of the dogs from next door got in and is wreaking havoc." Faith took Poppy's hand as they ascended.

The familiar bark of orders sounded from the foyer. There was no mistaking the Earl of Merkwood's voice as he commanded footmen to do his bidding. "Go and gather her trunks. I want her back at Arrington House before the hour is out. I have better things to do than deal with a wayward wench who never deserved our attention to begin with."

Tears pricked the backs of Poppy's eyes. Her father's lack of regard had followed her all her life. It had never occurred to the earl it might have been his disappointment since her birth revealed her female that had made her so contrary. Perhaps if he'd had a son at some point, Poppy's existence might have disgusted him less.

Swallowing any show of emotion, Poppy pulled her shoulders back as they entered the foyer. "Father, what in the name of Zeus are you doing?"

Father stood just inside the front door as if fully entering might soil him in some fashion. He filled the opening with his imposing height and barrel chest. His scowl made it clear he wasn't happy to see his only child. He ran one hand lightly over his silver hair combed straight back from his handsome face. Even as Arthur Arrington aged and grew his sideburns long, he had not lost his looks and attracted the ladies wherever he went. Perhaps if those women knew what a fiend he was to live with, they would have kept their distance.

Tipton, the West Lane butler, pulled his pudgy form to full height and frowned a few feet to his right as if the earl might need his coat collected or a sound thrashing at any moment.

A deep frown creased Father's brow and caused lines around his mouth and between his sterling eyes. "What your mother should have done from the start of this. I'm taking you in hand. You will return to your family's home and be married from there ten days hence. The arrangements have already been made. You are damned lucky Marsden agreed to wed you, though I can't imagine why he would be bothered."

Mercy stepped forward. "You are insufferable."

He narrowed his eyes on her. "I do not hear words uttered by a nothing with dead parents and who has leeched off the goodwill of a relation most of her life."

Faith gasped.

"Not one of you is worth a damn halfpenny."

Aurora stepped out from behind Mercy. Fire flashed in her eyes, and her pert chin tipped up. "My lord, you are in my home, and I'll remind you I am a countess and the daughter of an earl. My rank is equal to yours. Now that you have behaved like an animal in my foyer, you may take yourself to the street."

"I have never been so rudely treated." He growled something else under his breath.

Poppy found her voice. "Perhaps that is why you think it your right to treat people with so little respect."

He stepped closer, raising his hands like claws.

Tipton raced around to block the path of the earl. Despite his lack of any rank other than servant, it was his job to keep the residents of West Lane safe, and he took it quite seriously from the fierce look on his face. "My lord, perhaps you might wait in your carriage while the packing is concluded."

Pure hatred burned in Father's eyes as he glared from Poppy to her friends then back to her. "I will return home. I expect you to be there within the hour, or I will hire henchmen to come and get you. They will be instructed to use whatever force necessary to drag you home. I'm sure you wouldn't want your friends to suffer the stain of such a scene. The neighborhood would talk of nothing else for years. I doubt any invitations would be forthcoming after such a spectacle. Especially when they are further instructed to call out about the whorehouse Lady Radcliff is running."

"You wouldn't dare." Poppy knew full well he would and he could do everything he said.

A filthy smirk tugged at his lips. "I think you know better, daughter."

The danger appearing to have passed, Tipton opened the front door for the earl to exit more quickly.

Father stormed down the front steps, and his carriage was soon on its way down West Lane.

Her entire life and everything she'd ever hated and feared had become her reality. Poppy collapsed on the floor. "I cannot bear this."

Faith, Aurora, and Mercy crowded around her on the floor.

Tipton hovered with concern. "Is Lady Penelope ill? Shall I send for the doctor?"

"No, Tipton," Aurora said. "She is fine. Please excuse us for a few minutes."

A moment later they were alone.

Aurora took her hands and kept them in hers until Poppy met her gaze. "You can bear it and you will. You will go to your parents' house while this gets sorted out. If you are that much opposed to marrying my brother, then we shall find another way to solve this." Her voice softened, but she didn't look as assured; her gaze shifted. "However, he truly loves you, Poppy. He would not have agreed to marry anyone he didn't have strong feelings for."

Once again tears stung her eyes. She'd not cried this much in all her life as she had in the last few weeks. Dashing them away, she said, "He was cornered and had no choice."

Mercy leaned in. "There is always a choice, Poppy. He could have stalled or hesitated. He did neither. Are you certain you and he could not be a good match?"

"I don't know anymore. I only know I feel like a mouse snared in a trap with a large house cat hovering in for the kill."

Pulling a disgusted face, Faith patted Poppy's knee. "Perhaps you might try to conjure up a less nauseating image when you think about a possible marriage."

A stifled giggle from Mercy made it hard to stay despondent. "I don't know; Poppy has always had a flair for the dramatic. If Rhys be the cat, maybe a strong trap is what she needs."

Taken aback, Poppy faced Mercy. "What do you mean by that?"

Standing, Mercy offered her hand to help Poppy up. When they were all on their feet, Mercy said, "You have always claimed you would never marry because you could not make such a pledge for money, power, or property. You have also said you would be no one's property."

Not knowing where she was going with this, Poppy's unease grew. "That's right."

"Well, Rhys does not need your dowry and will get no property. He's far more powerful than your blowhard father. All he gains in this bargain is you. Unless I'm mistaken. He must want you, or he would have immediately made demands on your mother in order to take your hand. He could have asked for a great many things to make the bargain advantageous for himself. Your father is rich and has many assets in England and abroad. Rhys asked for nothing but you."

Before Poppy could make a rebuttal, Mercy held up her hands to stop the torrent of denial.

"I'm not telling you to marry him. I'm only suggesting you have an open mind about the idea. Perhaps you might even ask the gentleman why he wants to marry you." Mercy raised a brow.

Confusion and a streak of panic rumbled around like a great war inside Poppy. Her head pounded, and her heart seemed determined to punch its way out of her body. Drawing in several deep breaths, she calmed herself. "I will give the matter some thought, but I don't want to see Rhys. At least not yet."

Aurora sighed. "Rhys will not like it, but he will respect your wishes if you make them clear. I'm afraid I don't see a way out of your going back to your parents' townhouse."

A fresh wave of anger washed over Poppy. "No. Father will make good on his threat and ruin all three of you. At the very least, Faith and Mercy would be doomed by such a horrible rumor. I will go back."

The foyer closed in as a door slammed inside Poppy. She was losing her freedom by degrees, and there was little she could do about it.

Chapter 14

The look on Poppy's face when she'd rushed from the room at his agreement to marry her would haunt Rhys for a long time. He didn't want a wife who hated him. The idea of living without Poppy in his life didn't make him feel any better. What he needed was to talk to her.

He jumped down from his carriage at his sister's West Lane home without waiting for the assistance of his footman. He'd tried to think of the right words on the ride over, but all he could think was that he'd beg her to understand. Again, the despair in her eyes when he said he'd marry her haunted him.

Before he reached the top step, Tipton opened the door. "My lord, so good to see you again so soon."

"I'm here to call on Lady Penelope, Tipton. Can you tell her I'm here?" He handed his hat to the butler.

Keeping the hat in his open palm, Tipton cocked his head. He cleared his throat just slightly. Perhaps a sign the stoic butler was uncomfortable. "I'm afraid, the lady is not here."

"When will she be back?" It might be a good thing. Rhys would have more time to think of what to say. He could go to Rora's study and write down a few points in his favor before he saw her again. He would wait as long as it took to see her and make her listen to him.

Tipton's expression turned dark for an instant before he pulled it back to the typical lack of expression worn by all good butlers. "She will not be returning, my lord. The Earl of Merkwood came and collected her. It was quite a scene, but the earl left her no choice, and she has left West Lane."

What did he mean, left her no choice? Poppy could have refused. It was not a question he could ask the butler as it would put the man in an awkward position. Telling tales was not something a good butler did, and Tipton was a very good butler. "I see. Thank you, Tipton. I will call at the Arrington townhouse." He took his hat back and rushed from the house.

"Good luck, my lord," Tipton said as he closed the door behind Rhys.

It was damned inconvenient to have to go through Poppy's parents to see her. How was he going to get her alone with Lady Merkwood hovering about? He called the new address up to his driver and settled into the carriage.

At the Arrington townhouse he was admitted with reluctance as it was his second call that day. He waited in the parlor for twenty minutes before Lady Merkwood entered.

"I'm afraid Penelope is exhausted from the events of the day and asks for you to come back another time." Her ladyship frowned, but no expression could be seen in her eyes.

Rhys had to bite his tongue to keep from saying something he'd regret. "I take it she was displeased with her orders to return to this house."

A slight shrug, which reminded him of a French coquette he'd met a long time ago, made her even more distasteful. "She is not a prisoner. This is her home and the proper place to be married from. She said she will see you and your sister tomorrow at George's."

"I see. I will say good day, then, my lady." He bowed and left without ceremony or waiting to be asked if he'd like tea. The last thing he wanted was to spend time with this manipulative woman. How could his sweet Poppy have come from this woman and the arrogant villain he'd asked for permission to marry? It was a mystery.

Rhys didn't know what to do. He needed to speak to her alone. George's would not offer him that opportunity. Not knowing what to do, he tramped across town on foot, telling his driver to go home. After an hour, he found himself in Garrett's study with a glass of very fine brandy and a splitting headache.

They hadn't spent much time in Garrett's home in London. His parents usually stayed in the country, so the townhouse was at their son's disposal. However, Garrett had bolted from London over three years ago and this was the first time he'd spent any time in England in all those years.

Sitting in one of four overstuffed chairs around a low round table, Garrett crossed his ankle over his knee and studied Rhys. "Are you going to tell me what happened, or do I have to get you good and drunk to find out?"

Sinking into a pit of drunken waste sounded better than it should. Instead, he focused on the tall window with its arched transom and dark blue drapes. He watched the day turn to dusk and avoided Garrett's gaze. "I'm in love with Poppy Arrington."

"And this has you in such a state you wander into my house at this odd hour? I don't understand. I knew you were in love with her months ago at that ball where you couldn't take your eyes off her. It's one of the reasons I didn't leave England as planned. I wouldn't want to run off and miss your wedding. If you love her, ask for her hand. It's not as if you don't have to marry at some point." Garrett smiled and sipped his drink.

"Well, you're in luck; the wedding is in ten days and then you're free to follow your wanderlust wherever it takes you," Rhys ground out and then downed the rest of his brandy. It burned on the way down, and he refilled the glass. Being cornered wasn't how he had imagined he would win Poppy. He'd wanted to show her how he felt before he told her. He wanted her to realize she loved him too.

Garrett sat up. "Ten days. Good Lord, what on earth happened?"

Rhys was unable to hold his tongue, so the entire story came pouring out. He only left out the night he'd made love to Poppy and the night she'd come to him for comfort. Those things would remain theirs alone.

When he came to the ending with Poppy refusing to see him earlier in the day, Rhys blew out a long breath. The tale was exhausting when it should be joyous, sad where it should be happy, and damning where it should be a new beginning. Nothing had turned out the way he'd hoped.

Blinking several times, Garrett gaped. "So, she's refused you twice yet you still intend to marry her because you were trapped by a rainstorm without a chaperone. The lady gives no indication of affection for you, yet you intend to saddle you both for the rest of your lives. Am I missing something?"

Pain emanated from the center of Rhys's chest. Put that way, he sounded like a fool and a bully no better than her father. "I think she loves me. I know she likes me. She's just so stubborn about rules she made for herself years ago and ideas she's had about me since we met."

"What ideas?"

"When I first met Poppy, she had been dropped at our door in the country for one week before she and Rora were shipped off to that school in Lucerne. She stumbled upon me and a girl from town in a rather embarrassing situation. I'm afraid she has never forgiven my bad behavior." Heat filled Rhys's neck and cheeks.

With a laugh, Garrett said, "Well, we all did stupid things as young men. I think she must see that is not behavior you still indulge in."

"Yes, well, I'm working on her seeing that. In the meantime, it is not going to happen unless I can speak to her alone, and that has not been possible since this entire thing blew up in my face this morning." Frustration and hopelessness made him want to go back to the Arrington townhouse and climb a trellis into her bedroom where he would force her to listen to him. Of course, that would be foolish and never work.

"What are you thinking? You have the most devious look on your face."

"Do men still do stupid things in the name of love, or is that reserved for those novels the ladies like to read?" An impossible plan began to form in the back of Rhys's mind.

Garrett poured more brandy. "What is going on in that head of yours?"

"That Poppy said no twice because I've been an ass and didn't tell her how I feel. Now, after all that has happened, she wouldn't believe me if I told her I love her." Excitement built inside Rhys as his plan started to take a realistic form.

"And?" Garrett sat with his elbows on his knees and his drink propped in both hands between. This room with all its warm woods and plush decor suited his friend. Despite his continued need to travel the world, he was well suited to life in London.

"And maybe if she understood, things would be different. I wish I could whisk her away and give her the option to toss me aside or marry me because she wants to."

"Then do it." Garrett finished his drink and placed the glass on the table. He put the topper on the decanter and stood, stretching his arms above his head.

"What, kidnap a lady of the realm and run away with her?" The idea had more appeal than it should for a sane man.

Garrett shrugged and pulled a cord. "Why not? Not kidnap, but ask her to run away with you. Give her a choice as opposed to what her parents have orchestrated."

A choice… That was it. That was why she was so angry. He'd betrayed her by taking away her choice. Good Lord, what an idiot he was. "Garrett, my dear friend, you are a genius. I may need some help."

A wide smile spread across Garrett's face, he spread his arms wide and gave a mock bow. "I am at your disposal."

When the butler appeared, Garrett told him they would be two for dinner. They had a lot to discuss.

* * * *

Rhys arrived at George's Patisserie and Tea Shop with a plan, which he seriously doubted would work, but he had no choice but to try. He sat at the largest table and waited.

The scent of sugar, fresh baked biscuits, and tea filled the small eatery. White linen covered the tables.

A waiter asked if he needed anything, and he ordered tea for five. There was no harm in being optimistic.

Within the quarter hour his sister arrived with Mercy and Faith. "Hello, Rhys. I wasn't sure you would come."

His heart sank when Poppy wasn't with them. "I made a commitment to the four of you. I will keep my word."

They smiled and sat just as the tea was served.

Mercy's smirk was caught between amusement and doubt. "We have some bad news, but I think we might wait until Poppy arrives before we speak about it."

"Are you certain it is bad news?" Aurora asked.

Faith blinked at her gloved hands in her lap.

"Has your intended found out about our prying?" Rhys spoke softly to Faith, who did not look at all like it pleased her. It didn't surprise him Geb Arafa would tell his friend of the strange encounter. If it had been one of his good friends, he would have done the same.

Eyes swimming, Faith said, "He sent a letter indicating my sneaky nature was perhaps more than he had bargained for. He said if I wanted to call it off, he would understand."

"And do you want to call it off?"

The bell on the door jingled. Rhys felt Poppy in the room before she approached the table. Still, he kept his attention on Faith.

"I don't know." Faith cried silent tears. "I was just starting to figure him out, which is his own fault for being so stingy with information." The last was full of reproach.

Without interrupting, Poppy took the last seat at the table and focused on Faith.

Rhys wanted to help, but if he had been investigated by the Wallflowers without knowing them and their nature, he might have the same reaction as Breckenridge. "May I speak freely, ladies?"

"Of course," Mercy and Faith said together.

Aurora raised a brow, and Poppy remained uncharacteristically solemn.

"I don't really blame Breckenridge. At least he didn't ruin you by calling off. He doesn't know you four or what you have been through as a group. Perhaps he needs a bit of time to sort it out. I suggest you write him a letter and explain everything. If you want to know him better, then tell him that as well. Then tell him where you'll be, so he knows how to reach you." Rhys waited while they thought it through.

Poppy cocked her head. It was the most adorable thing he'd ever seen. "Why would he not know where Faith would be?"

"Because I want the four of you to come with me to my friend Garrett's home in the Lowlands. I'd like for you to do so this afternoon, but perhaps first thing in the morning is more realistic." His heart was solidly lodged in his throat. This was the moment he needed her to trust him. If she refused, he didn't know what he'd do. Kidnapping was still an option. Though, perhaps counterproductive.

"Why on earth would we do that?" Poppy asked.

"Garrett has a home in Scotland?" This from Aurora.

Faith cleared her throat. "Forgive me, Poppy, I know this is a delicate subject." She turned toward Rhys. "Aren't you supposed to marry Poppy in just nine days? That's a long trip to return from in such a short time."

"I would like to not marry Poppy in London nine days from now. Not under the current circumstances."

"What?" Faith.

"You wouldn't." Aurora.

"You can't." Mercy.

The three of them gaped, and it was almost enough to make him laugh. They were like three fish devoid of water.

Poppy blushed bright red but said nothing and didn't look at him. She smelled of sunshine and roses. He could wrap himself in her scent and be content for all eternity if only she'd let him.

Save for them and the staff, the shop was empty. He turned to the other three Wallflowers. "Pardon me, ladies, but for the next few moments I'm going to pretend you are not here."

Rising, he took a deep breath, rounded the table, and knelt down next to Poppy. Despite his claim to ignore them, he felt their glares on him. "Please listen to me, Poppy. The last thing I want is to force you or anyone to marry me. However, I do want to marry you. I want to be very clear. Nothing would make me happier than to make you mine and to belong to you only."

She remained still and stared at the white tablecloth. Yet there were subtle changes. Her back stiffened, and her fingers stilled where they'd been fussing with the edge of the tablecloth.

Her lack of encouragement made his speech harder, but he was not going to give up. Not yet. "I propose to thwart your parents' high-handedness. We can go where they cannot influence us with society's ideas of right and wrong. You can leave a letter saying you have gone to the country to think about your situation and will return soon. Don't tell them where you're going or when you'll return, but tell them Rora is with you as a chaperone. They will be angry, but they'll not be panicked over your safety.

"If after the journey and arrival at Thwackmore you do not wish to marry me, you may release me from our engagement and no one need know or care about any of this. Your mother will never tell a soul about our trip to see Mr. Arafa. I don't even know how she found out, but she'll never divulge the information."

Now the hardest part. He took a deep breath. "Poppy, yesterday was a disaster, but I couldn't refuse to marry you. You must understand. If I had done so, your mother would have made a cad out of me. And while you felt trapped and angry, how would you have felt had I rejected you? You would have thought I didn't care for you."

Finally, she met his gaze. " I don't know what to think."

Not used to her voice being soft and full of doubt, he wanted to reassure her. The public place was all wrong for this, but he leaned in. "Forgive me. I was put in an awkward position, and I handled it with less grace than I ought. I would never betray you, Poppy. I'm asking for your trust and the trust of your closest friends."

When he returned his attention across the table, Faith was dabbing tears from her eyes with a napkin and Mercy grinned from ear to ear. Aurora would not make eye contact and fussed with her gloves. His sister's response confused him, but it made no difference.

He took her hand and kissed it. "Poppy, trust me. I'll not force you to marry me. You will always have a safe haven with Rora. I'll see to it you have whatever you need financially regardless of whether you marry me or not. You have my word. The choice will be yours."

Poppy looked across at her friends for a long moment before turning back to him. Doubt clouded her eyes, but she met his gaze like a warrior. "I will have my trunk placed at the back of my parents' garden tonight. In the morning I will tell Mother I am meeting you in the park for a walk. A maid will accompany me, but I will give her the letter to deliver to Mother. She will do as she's told. You can pick me up at West Lane with the others."

Relief washed over him. Bowing his head to her lap, he said, "Thank you."

There was the briefest touch of her hand in his hair before she pulled away. "I have only agreed to thwart my parents, Rhys. Beyond that, I've made no guarantees."

Standing, he adjusted his coat and smiled down at her. "You have shown me trust, and that is all I ask for the present, Poppy."

The jingle of the bell on the door indicated they were no longer alone. Rhys rounded the table and sat. He kept his voice low. "I have some arrangements to make with Garrett. We will need at least two carriages."

With her usual calm and slight smile, Mercy said, "We shall be ready at West Lane when you arrive. You will need another carriage for trunks, and we shall bring Gillian and Jane. You can't expect us to go away for an indefinite period without lady's maids."

Using all his control to keep from dancing with glee, Rhys allowed a small smile. "I shall see to a third carriage. I want all of you to be comfortable and happy."

"I must go and write to His Grace. Rhys made a fine point earlier. I shall take his advice." Faith's eyes were clear, and she stood, pulling on her gloves.

Aurora stood, and her expression remained guarded. Something wasn't right, but he had no time to find out what troubled his sister. "We have things to ready as well. Good day, Rhys."

Having stood with the ladies, Rhys bowed. His pulse pounded. "Thank you, ladies."

Poppy stopped before him. The line that appeared between her brows whenever she was worried was as deep as he'd ever seen it. He longed to smooth the wrinkle and ease her stress. "I am sorry for the things I shouted yesterday. I see now that I misjudged your intentions."

Stepping closer than was appropriate for a public place, he whispered, "You have nothing to be sorry for. I wish I had thought of a better way to handle the situation. I never wanted to hurt you."

"Thank you." She rushed away, dabbing the corners of her eyes.

Like the four flowers they were, they bustled down the street to where two carriages waited for them.

Rhys waited just outside George's until they were away before he climbed into his own carriage. He put his head in his hands and thanked all that was holy she'd agreed. It was an impossible gift for her to put aside the disaster of yesterday and still trust him.

No matter the cost, he would see Penelope Arrington happy. Even if it meant his own misery, he would see to her needs.

The carriage rolled down the street. Rhys was glad he'd have at least twenty minutes to gain control of his emotions before he met with Garrett. He hadn't realized how much of himself he'd had riding on her response. The idea she could have told him no and been done with it churned demons in his gut.

Most troubling of all was she might have married him just to satisfy her parents then never forgiven him. The notion was what sent him to George's with such an elaborate plan.

Poppy despising him while being tied to him kept him up all night. The only thing keeping him from falling asleep in the carriage was the thrill of excitement that came with spending time with Penelope Arrington. She must not hate him yet, if she agreed. She might doubt him, but she didn't hate him. It would have to be enough for the present.

The carriage rocked as they rounded the corner on Garrett's street. Rhys took several long breaths to clear his residual panic before they reached the townhouse.

Garrett stood at the top of the stairs, holding the door open.

His butler looked to be about to burst at the seams where he fussed from beside him. "I will attend the door, my lord. There is no need for you to receive guests like a farmer."

Garrett's good-natured laugh gave Rhys a sense it would all work out. "Quinn, you shall always be here to keep me in line."

"Hardly, my lord." Quinn waited for Rhys to enter then shooed them both from the threshold so he could close the door.

"How did it go?" Garrett's eyes were bright with enthusiasm. One might think it was *his* heart at stake.

Calming those demons still battling in his stomach, Rhys nodded. "As well as I could have hoped for. She and the other ladies have agreed to go to Thwackmore tomorrow morning."

Wide eyed, Garrett closed his mouth and shook his head. "She must like you a little at least. We have a lot of details to work out if you're to woo her properly, my friend."

And that was what Rhys planned to do. He followed Garrett into the study to get to work.

Chapter 15

Poppy woke early. Well, if truth be told, she'd hardly slept. After having a trusted footman place her trunk at the garden gate, she'd tried to rest. Staring up at the shimmering gold curtains surrounding her bed didn't actually qualify as rest. She didn't know if she was relieved or terrified by the prospect of running away to Scotland. The only thing she was sure of was, a large public wedding in London orchestrated by her parents a few days hence didn't appeal to her at all.

At dawn she got out of bed, washed, and got dressed in her light blue day dress. It was comfortable, and she could get into it herself. She donned boots for the walk over to West Lane. One last examination of the room where she'd spent most of her time in the last three years. It was sparse, as she never felt at home in the golds and staid browns her mother preferred. She'd once suggested a change to rose or cream, but Mother had scoffed at the notion. Not dramatic enough for an Arrington, she'd said.

Instead of making up an elaborate story to tell her mother, she put a letter on the mantel in her room and left before Mother woke. When her maid found the letter around ten, she would hold it until Mother came down at eleven. By that time, Poppy would be long out of London. Her parents would be furious, but they were unlikely to do more than rage about the house and lament their horrible daughter once again.

Poppy stepped onto the street and strode purposefully toward West Lane without looking back.

When she returned to London there would be a reckoning, but how it would go would depend on her and Rhys's status. She shook off the decision ahead of her. She'd agreed to Scotland to get away from her parents' bullying. Unsure about anything else, she wasn't immune to his sweet declarations at George's. There wasn't a woman alive who could be unfeeling when faced with such a declaration. No one had ever stirred her heart as Rhys had.

Despite her early arrival at Aurora's townhouse, three carriages lined the street when she stepped onto West Lane. Her trunk sat neatly on top of the last carriage, and Gillian was directing footmen for the packing and loading of the rest of the luggage.

The lady's maid gave Poppy a quick curtsy and a smile before scolding the young man in Marsden livery for putting a hatbox under a heavy trunk.

Poppy rushed past and up the stairs to the front door.

The door opened with Tipton checking the scene on the street. "Good morning, my lady. The ladies are finishing up above stairs, and the gentlemen are waiting in the parlor."

"Thank you, Tipton. You'll be happy to have things quiet for a while, I expect."

An unusual frown crossed the butler's face. "It is always a pleasure to have you ladies at home. I shall be sorry to see you go."

Warmth bloomed inside Poppy. She'd always thought the stoic butler indifferent, but clearly, she had been mistaken. "I will return in one manner or another, Tipton."

"I look forward to it, my lady." He returned to his mask of indifference and bowed.

Swallowing her instinct to run upstairs and hide out with the ladies, she raised her chin. "I will join the gentlemen."

Tipton rushed to the parlor door and opened it for her.

Thankful they were in the lady's parlor and not the grand parlor where the scene with her mother had taken place, she found Garrett Winslow lounging on the chaise. He jumped up when he saw her.

Rhys stood by the window, his back rigid and his expression suffused with worry. "You came."

After a quick curtsy, she sat on the couch. "I said I would."

Rounding the room, Rhys nodded. He stood behind the chair, his knuckles white on the chair's back. "Did you have any problems leaving the house?"

"Mother has not risen yet. I left a letter and walked out the front door. It will be hours before anyone notices I am gone, and by then my maid will have found the letter and delivered it to my mother. I hope we shall be long out of London by then."

Garrett smiled. "If the ladies ever finish fussing, we can leave immediately."

"How do you do, my lord?" She had not spent a great deal of time with Garrett Winslow. A little time at the house party and she knew he was a good friend of Rhys's. Aurora spoke highly of him as well, and he was in line for a dukedom of his own.

He was very tall as he bowed over her hand. In the sunlight streaming through the window, she noted streaks of red running through his brown hair. There was something in the way his eyes always smiled even when his mouth didn't that made Garrett likable. Here was another man who would one day be a duke but had none of the haughtiness that usually accompanied the title.

His smile was charming, though it did not create the quiver inside her that Rhys's always did. "I am well and happy to be on this journey with you all. I hope you will dispense with formality and call me Garrett."

Relaxing into the easy conversation, she said, "Then you must call me Poppy."

Faith burst through the open door. Out of breath and flushed, she shouted, "We are ready!"

"Thank goodness." Rhys threw up his hands. "I thought we'd never leave this house."

Aurora and Mercy tromped down the stairs and out the front door.

All arms and legs, Garrett ran to join the ladies.

Faith followed.

Holding open the door, Tipton looked in her direction still sitting in the parlor. He raised a brow.

Rhys blocked the view of the foyer with his broad chest in the threshold. "Second thoughts?" His voice was soft and filled with worry.

Poppy closed her eyes and took a deep breath before standing and brushing out her skirt. "No. I'll not lie, I'm a bit overwhelmed by the events of the last few days, but I'll not allow my parents to oppress me anymore."

Crossing to her, his mouth pulled into a wide smile. "There's my strong girl. I'd hate to think all of this has made you meek or broken your spirit."

No one besides the Wallflowers had ever cared for her strong will and independent nature. Taking his offered arm, she raised her gaze to his. "Be careful what you wish for, Rhys. You may come to despise my spirit."

His laughter filled the foyer and filled her with more delight than she imagined possible from another's joy. "I will risk it."

"As you wish." She couldn't help her own smile. They walked out. "Goodbye, Tipton. Thank you."

Tipton bowed and closed the door behind them.

Leaning down to her ear, Rhys whispered, "Will you ride with me, Poppy?"

Pulse racing, she shook her head. "Not yet."

He handed her up into the carriage holding the other three Wallflowers. "When you are ready, then. I shall wait for you."

It was a promise, but of exactly what, Poppy didn't know.

"This is exciting." Faith folded her hands in her lap.

Mercy took her hat off, letting her hair fall free, and leaned back against the ruby cushions. "Garrett told me Rhys was up half the night writing messages and sending out couriers. I think we are in for quite a treat."

Watching the city roll by her window, Poppy let the breeze cool her face. Whatever Rhys had planned, she would not let him bully her any more than she'd let her parents. Yet, at George's, he had given her a means to escape. He'd told her he would pay for her to live the rest of her life with Aurora if that was her choice. "Aurora, do you think he meant it?"

"Meant what, dearest?" Aurora took Poppy's hand.

"Do you think Rhys would let me beg off and live with you. Would he let me have the life I'd planned?"

Aurora squeezed her hand. "I think he loves you so much he wants you to be happy and if it means living with me or even marrying another, he will do what he can for you."

Scoffing, Poppy retrieved her hand gently. "He has never said he loves me. Men do not fall in love. They marry for other reasons and perhaps some find marriage agreeable, but more than that is not likely."

"Good lord, Poppy. I hope you're wrong about that." Aurora narrowed her eyes and shook her head. "My brother is not reckless. He would never go to this much trouble for someone who hadn't stolen his heart." Aurora's voice rang with sadness, and she turned and looked out her own window.

* * * *

They didn't stop until late afternoon. No chasing carriages sped to stop them. As Poppy suspected, her parents would not go to much trouble on her behalf, which suited her.

Climbing out of the carriage, Poppy stretched her legs in the neat yard of a very charming inn. It might have been a house from a fairy tale, all scalloped shingles and white shutters and doors.

A bulbous-nosed man stooped to get his enormous form out of the door. His dark hair stood out from his head wildly, and one of his eyes didn't quite look where the other did. He might have been terrifying if not for the wide, welcoming smile spread across his face. He called out with a strange accent. "Welcome, welcome. I've been worried you had a mishap as I expected you an hour ago."

Rhys shook the man's hand. "The ladies took a bit longer to get ready, and we stopped for a rest as well."

The man aimed a delighted grin at the women of the group before turning back to Rhys. "Of course. I have everything prepared as your note indicated. The Romani Bride is at your service." He pointed to the building.

Footmen unloaded the carriages, and stable boys saw to the horses. Poppy watched with interest, wondering what Rhys could be up to.

"Oslo, bring them in already. The ladies will be tired," said a woman who stood in the doorway. She had silky brown hair touched with gold, a narrow nose, and eyes the color of a spring sky. She was something out of a dream. No one could be that beautiful.

"Madelina, my wife," Oslo said to Rhys. "Come, everyone. You can settle into your rooms and rest before dinner."

As they entered, they were introduced to Oslo and Madelina formally. It wasn't like any inn Poppy had ever stayed at, and the owners were not your average innkeepers.

There was a refinement to the couple, which was not quite noble, but neither were they working class. They spoke beautifully with their rounded accents. From the name of the inn, Poppy guessed they were from Romania.

"What kind of inn is this, Rhys?" Aurora asked.

Madelina smiled. "We have a very small clientele, and when not requested, we are able to live here without guests."

Poppy had little knowledge of private inns. She had heard of boardinghouses closing themselves to new guests, but not an inn or hotel. Inside the common room was more parlor and dining. There was no bar with raucous locals drinking after a day's work. It was quiet. Someone played pianoforte in another room. The warm scent of beef cooking filled her senses with anticipation.

It was no wonder Rhys had spent half the night sending messages if this was how they were going to travel to Scotland.

Madelina invited the ladies upstairs.

Stopping Poppy with a gentle touch on her arm, Rhys asked, "Does this meet with your approval?"

"Hera's crown, it's lovely. You didn't need to go to so much expense. I'm not accustomed to grand luxuries." It was true that while Father was rich, he rarely spent anything more than was strictly necessary.

His smile would have made a saint want, and Poppy was no saint. "You should be spoiled from time to time, Poppy. I want this journey to be enjoyable for you. After all, I am trying to convince you to spend your life with me."

Warmth crept up her neck and cheeks. "I am properly impressed by your friends and this lodging."

He bowed, joy reflected in his smiling eyes. "Then I am well on my way to a proper wooing."

It was impossible not to be charmed. "I will see you at dinner." With a curtsy, she ran to catch up with the others.

Mercy waited at the top of the second set of stairs. "I thought you and I would share. You might have had enough prying from Faith and Aurora at this point."

Poppy wrapped an arm around Mercy's waist and squeezed her. "You are a gem, dear friend."

"Come and see the room. It's quite nice." Mercy hugged her back and laughed.

The last light of the long day shone into the well-furnished room. Green wallpaper and light polished woods gleamed in the streaks of sunlight. Two beds, each curtained in ruby velvet, would keep any light out and make a cozy cave for sleeping. A soft rug of summer green warmed the stone floor, and a fire burned low in the hearth.

"It's lovely. I have never seen an inn like this." Poppy flopped onto the bed.

Mercy landed next to her. "He's really making an effort. That is certain."

"You're not going to try to talk me into marrying Rhys, are you? Because I can get that from Aurora." Poppy was half teasing but at the same time issued a warning.

A low laugh shook the bed. Mercy said, "No. I trust you'll do the thing that will make you happy. I was only noting his effort."

The air went out of Poppy. "That speech at George's." A low sigh that she tried to stifle pushed out too.

Mercy rolled to face her. "I've never heard anything so romantic in my entire life. I couldn't blame Faith for her tears this time. He was spectacular."

"And I was ridiculous." She rolled to face Mercy.

"No. Shocked. Surprised. Speechless. Confused." Mercy opened her mouth to continue her litany of adjectives.

"All right, that's enough." Poppy giggled.

Mercy sobered. "Do you remember when we were at school and the boys from the neighboring school came to our ball?"

"I remember they were rude and loud." Poppy scoffed and propped her head on her hand.

Lips tight in a serious line, Mercy leaned in. "No. They were young and embarrassed just like we were. You vilified them because you didn't want anything to do with them. Several wanted to ask you to dance. That boy with the red hair and freckles came over four times, but you scowled and chased him away."

Poppy sat up. At sixteen those boys had seemed quite menacing, but looking back, Mercy was right. They were high spirited, but harmless. If she saw them today, she would think them children doing what children do.

"Do you think I still do this, Mercy?" Had she pushed men away based on some notion rather than the truth? Had she done the same with Rhys?

Snuggling next to her, Mercy pulled her into her arms and gave her a tight squeeze. "I'm afraid so. Most of the time it hasn't mattered. The men who tried to court you were after money or position or just too imbecilic to be bothered with. Rhys is different. You should pay attention to the events about to unfold and make your decision based on how you feel in your heart. Don't let your parents' horrible example ruin the rest of your life."

"You think I should marry Rhys?" The hair stood up on the back of Poppy's neck. It was a fear response. Was she right to be afraid, or just because it was an easy way out?

Shaking her head, Mercy sighed. "I have no idea what you should do. I only want to impress upon you making your decisions based on erroneous information is bad practice."

"Don't tell me even you were taken in by his speech?" If the least sentimental of their group could be warmed, Rhys had outdone himself.

Mercy cocked her head and twirled a bit of hair around her finger. "He may have been ignoring us, Poppy, but he was impossible to ignore. He loves you—even if he didn't say it in so many words, he said it yesterday at George's. He poured out his heart in public and left no mistaking his intent. It was riveting."

A long sigh overtook Poppy. "It was that." Her heart pounded at the memory as much as the fact he was just down the hall and she would see him again for dinner.

Jane knocked and walked in carrying a steaming bucket of water. Her cheeks were rosy from exertion, but her pleasant smile was in place. "Shall we get you ladies dressed for dinner?"

Poppy pulled herself to her feet. She hoped once they arrived in Scotland she could soak in a long, hot bath. For now, she would settle for warm water and a good scrub to wash away the road dust. "I suppose we must."

* * * *

Dinner was a spectacular event. Oslo and Madelina Ionescu dined with them and were the perfect hosts. Food and wine came to the table in a steady flow. Some of it was familiar and some new.

They used the common room as a dining hall and had pushed together several tables to accommodate them. Yet, it had a continuity to it with ruby-red linen covering the table and three tall candelabras lighting the food. Several others were lit in corners of the room as well. The walls were a rich cream color with wood from mid-wall to the floor.

This was no inn, but a home, and all who entered were treated as family.

Poppy delighted in a warm dish called Moldavian stew, a combination of a corn mash, fermented cheese, eggs, pork, sausage, and something tart. It woke all the senses and settled in her stomach like a blanket.

The wine was rich red, and her glass was never empty. If not for the constant laughter and storytelling, she might have felt dizzy from the effects.

Oslo asked Rhys, "Where did you and Mr. Winslow meet?"

Frowning, Rhys drank a long sip of wine. "At school, Eton."

Garrett roared with laughter. "Tell the story, Rhys, or are you a coward?"

With assurance, Rhys put his goblet down on the table. "You want me to tell that story, old friend?"

Mercy laughed. "Now you must tell it. I'll badger you until I know what has Garrett blushing and you hesitant."

"Yes, yes, we are all friends now. Tell your story," Oslo said, slapping the table hard.

A young man of perhaps fifteen came around and filled the glasses.

Madelina took the bottle from him, kissed his cheek, and murmured something in an unfamiliar language.

He bowed and walked swiftly from the room.

Poppy watched the exchange, curious about the life the Ionescus lived.

Madelina caught her gaze. "He lives down the road, and it is getting late. I do not want his mother to worry. I can serve the cake and pour the wine."

"Tell the story, Rhys." Faith's command was uncharacteristic and may have been a result of too much wine.

While two girls in their midtwenties cleared the table, Madelina brought cake and cut slices for each of them.

Rhys said thoughtfully, "It was our first year. I had been at school for over a week before the session started. Father had been in a temper all summer, and going away early was the only way to escape." He gave

Aurora an apologetic smile. "I'd gone to lunch and stuffed myself full of bread and cheese until I was bursting and needed a good nap before I would be fit for anything.

"I opened the door to my room and there was Garrett, in the middle of the room, standing on his trunk, with his wrists bound and tied to the beam, as naked as the day he was born."

Everyone, including Garrett, burst out laughing.

"What on earth had happened?" Faith dabbed tears from her eyes.

Garrett spoke. "The upperclassmen who were supposed to introduce me to my new roommate had a little fun with me. Bound me like a pig to market and left me there to make my own introductions." Garrett's cheeks were red, but he shrugged and laughed.

"What did you do?" Poppy gave Rhys her full attention.

With a deep breath, Rhys picked up his glass and sipped. His eyes locked on Poppy's "What anyone would. I gaped for a full minute, then closed the door and cut him down."

Garrett belted out another laugh. "Ha. First, he asked me a dozen questions about where I was from, who my father was, and what type of sport I liked. I thought he'd never help me. He tromped around the room gathering my clothes, which the older boys had tossed aside, and placed them at my feet. He spoke as if we were meeting over a fine meal rather than with me practically hanging naked from the ceiling. I thought I had a madman for a roommate."

"But then I did cut him down." He and Poppy shared a private smile while the rest of the group laughed and Oslo told the story of how he and Madelina had escaped an uprising in Romania.

They had been landowners, and a change of government had created chaos. They took what they could and fled the country. From the looks of the home they built, what they kept from their old home must have been valuable.

Madelina sat and settled her gaze across the table. "What about you, Miss Poppy? Do you have a story to tell?"

"I am not interesting, and these people know all my stories." Poppy couldn't conjure a single story that would incite laughter. "I fall a lot. In fact, I have ruined more dresses than most women have owned."

"Funny, you don't seem at all clumsy to me. I would describe you as graceful," Madelina said.

Faith finished her goblet. "Actually, I've noticed in the last few weeks, you have not fallen or even stumbled. Perhaps something has changed for you, Poppy." Her hiccup punctuated the observation.

Thinking of the last time she fell brought her back to the night in Geb's cellar.

The warm expression on Rhys's face as he stared across the table at her made her believe he was thinking of the same night.

Poppy pushed the thoughts away. "It's only a matter of time. Once I fell into a very large cake that had been constructed for a ball. Puddings have always been a hazard."

Suddenly tired, Poppy excused herself from the table and walked to the stairs.

Rhys was at her side before she put her foot on the first step. Offering his arm, he escorted her up. "I hope you enjoyed the meal."

"It was wonderful. I'm just tired from everything that has happened in the last few days."

"I understand." When he'd brought her to her room, he stopped.

Turning to him, her pulse raced and warmth seeped into her skin. "I didn't mean to take you from the party."

His lips touched hers like a promise of things to come. He rubbed his lips back and forth over hers, never asking for more but leaving his essence behind.

Her hands went to his chest, and she leaned in.

Touching her cheek, he nipped her bottom lip and then the top before kissing her nose and stepping back. "I would miss a thousand parties for a moment or two with you, Poppy."

With a reach around her, he opened her door.

She stepped inside, and before she could turn back to him, he closed the door.

She wanted to tell him she missed his calling her by her full name. It was clear he took her command never to call her by her full name again seriously. How she missed the sound of it on his lips.

Despite the excitement, her exhaustion won out. By the time Jane helped her out of her gown, she was swaying on her feet. Tucked into the warm bed, she let sleep take her before she could reflect on the events of the day.

Chapter 16

On the second day of travel, after bidding the Ionescus goodbye, Poppy again declined to travel in the carriage with Rhys. The decision was made out of protective instinct and left her wishing she'd been braver as she watched the countryside roll by.

She missed the way he looked at her and the way he smiled when she said something he agreed with. She even missed the frown when he disagreed. She'd somehow become sensitive to his moods and expressions.

The day was long, and they only stopped twice to change horses and eat a quick meal before pressing on to their second stop. It was a very nice inn, but they were exhausted by the time they arrived after dark. The ladies had taken their supper in their rooms and gone to bed.

Poppy nibbled her food and watched out the window at the moon for hours after Mercy had fallen asleep. All her life she had known exactly what she wanted and what she didn't. When Mother had declared she would marry Rhys, she knew being forced into marriage was not what she desired.

This turn Rhys had taken changed things. He wouldn't force her to marry. So, the question had become, whether she wanted Rhys for her own and was willing to give herself to him. It was a far more complicated question and harder to answer.

Movement in the yard below caught her attention. In the full moon's light stood Rhys, gazing up at her. His smile was sad and full of longing. She had questions that needed answers. Her own cowardice had been her enemy these last few days. If she had spent them in a carriage with him, she could have questioned him to her heart's content.

She waved, unable to keep from smiling.

His eyes brightened and he waved back.

A leap was required, but Poppy backed away from the window and climbed into her bed.

* * * *

The farther north they traveled, the wilder the countryside became and the more Poppy's nerves frayed. She had again declined to ride with Rhys. Staring out as the terrain became rocky didn't help, and she closed her eyes.

Startled awake when the carriage stopped, Poppy's neck ached from the unnatural position. "Where are we?"

Aurora shrugged. "I haven't the faintest idea, but it's quite lovely."

Rolling hills of grass were dotted with enormous rock formations, and a stunning lake in the distance reflected fluffy white clouds.

Garrett opened the door. He grinned and bowed. "Apparently, we are stopping for a picnic."

"How nice," Faith said, stepping out.

Aurora gave Poppy a sympathetic smile and left the carriage.

Mercy and Poppy followed. Mercy took her arm. "What do you think his lordship has in store for you today?"

"I cannot even venture a guess."

The footmen set out a large blanket with food and wine. Every manner of food to be eaten with fingers from meats and cheeses to bread, biscuits, and wine. It was a feast.

When she'd had enough to eat, Poppy stood and surveyed the view. The lake was like glass, and then a rogue breeze slipped through, sending ripples along its surface. The same breeze tugged several strands of her hair loose.

She felt Rhys behind her before he spoke. He was like a caress when near. "Will you walk with me to the lake, Poppy?"

With a nod she stepped beside him, and they strolled toward the water.

"How are you enjoying the journey so far?" he asked when they were out of hearing of the others.

"You have gone to great lengths to make it pleasant." She folded her hands together, not willing to risk touching him accidentally.

"That is not an answer to my question."

"It has been very nice. May I ask you something?" She steadied her breathing.

"Anything." He said it as if it should be obvious.

She stopped and faced him. "Why are you doing all of this?"

His frown made her wish she could take back the question. "Isn't that obvious?"

"Not to me." She resumed the walk. "I am not so special that anyone should want to make such a fuss. I'm the unwanted daughter of an earl who longed for a son. I have a reputation for making a mess of everything and have been a constant source of disappointment for my parents. A fact which they have never kept a secret. What could the Earl of Marsden want with me?"

Running his finger down her bare arm sent a chill through her. It was not entirely unpleasant. "When you share these things about your parents, it fills me with anger that I don't know if I can control."

"I was telling you about myself, not them." They reached the water's edge, and she stopped to face him.

Rhys shook his head. "You are not to blame for your parents' bad behavior."

"And what about my own behavior? I have disgraced them by giving my body to you." That night had been so wonderful, and yet, it was her downfall.

Eyes narrowed, he glared at her with thinned lips and a tight jaw. "Your mother knows nothing of our night together. She saw an opportunity to get you married to an earl and that is all she cares about. What transpired between us was a beautiful thing, and I would hate to believe you regret it, Penelope."

The last was said with such sincerity and worry, that combined with the use of her full name, it broke her heart. "Not regret as much as worry. You have been more than kind, but I don't understand why you have gone to these lengths. You need to marry at some point, I was convenient, and you feel responsible for taking my virginity. So why all of this fuss?"

He closed his eyes, and the muscle in his jaw ticked. "At this moment, I'm going to take you back to the others. If we stay here, I will say or do something I will regret. It is amazing to me your capacity for misunderstanding. I have never met anyone who could stir my emotions, both good and bad, to this frenzied pitch."

Rhys spun on his heels and strode back to the carriages.

Poppy was dazed by his anger but had no choice but to follow.

Guilty and confused, Poppy rode in Rhys's carriage. Aurora rode with them to keep things proper, and it was a good thing too or they would have traveled in silence.

"How much farther is Garrett's house?" Aurora asked after a particularly long stretch of quiet.

Rhys grunted.

"I beg your pardon?" Aurora was undaunted by his mood.

He schooled his features and faced his sister. "It will take another two days at least. I have some very nice places arranged for us to stop."

Poppy wished the trip over. She needed to think, and it was not possible with him so close and so many people around. She'd not wished herself alone in a long time, but she needed space, and a carriage or inn was not going to provide it. The mix of his emotions with hers left her in a whirlwind.

It was late afternoon when they rolled down a long drive to a beautiful manor with yellow-and-white stone. Tall columns stood proudly beside the front door. The drive was lined with trees, creating a canopy that opened up into a large yard with a rounded lane for the horses.

They stopped at the front door where a line of servants waited patiently.

"Where are we?" Poppy asked.

"Warwick Manor. My friend David Richmond owns the house and was happy to give it to us for the night. He is not at home, but as you see the house is open." Rhys smiled.

"No inn tonight, what a delightful surprise." Aurora accepted a hand down from the footman.

With a sigh, Poppy moved toward the door.

Rhys touched her arm. "I'm sorry I lost my temper at the lake."

"I try your patience. I understand. It's a common theme in my life." She continued toward the door.

With more speed than she would have thought possible, Rhys blocked her way and closed them back inside the carriage.

Outside, Garrett spoke to the butler and the ladies oohed and aahed over the pretty stone building.

"Poppy." Rhys swallowed and stared at his hands.

She sat back in the seat across from him and waited.

"I was angry for a great many reasons, most of which had nothing to do with you. I thank God every day you found good friends in Switzerland. I can't imagine how you survived the first fifteen years of your life without them. I do not wish to speak badly about your parents, but they have not done their duty by you. It is my hope this trip will show you there is another way to live that doesn't include scheming and threats to get what one wants."

"I learned that from the Wallflowers years ago, Rhys. It is marriage I mistrust. I don't want to be any man's property to do with as he pleases even if that includes beating me to death or ignoring me to seek pleasure in other women." A weight lifted from her shoulders.

Rhys leaned forward and took her hands in his. After kissing each one, he brought his gaze to hers. "Not even if the man belonged to you in equal measure? If the man swore there was no other woman who could ever capture him the way you had. If he loved you to distraction and wanted only to make you happy for the rest of his life. What if this man didn't know how he would go on with the demands of his own life without you in it and your refusal would leave him an empty shell?"

The touch of his hand, and the way his words sliced through her straight to her core, pushed tears from her eyes. Through a tight throat, she said, "I'm not sure I believe any man could feel emotions that deeply."

Closing his eyes as pain washed across his face, Rhys placed her hand against his cheek.

The scratch of the day's beard awakened every nerve and shot lightning through Poppy. She longed to comfort him but feared her own desires and remained silent and still, not even checking the tears rolling freely down her face.

Rhys let out a long breath. "Will you consider my words might be true and possible? Can you do that for me, Poppy?"

Aching deep in her chest, she leaned forward and pressed a kiss to his lips.

His eyes opened.

"I will give the matter and all you have said in the last few days consideration. It is all I have been able to think about, Rhys. You have been more than kind, and I'm sorry to be so much trouble." The old shame washed over her, forcing her to look from his soulful eyes.

With one finger, he lifted her chin so she would look at him. "I am happy to convince you there is another possible life." His playful grin warmed the chill building inside her. "Besides, we have our closest friends, we are on a small adventure, and it has been an entertaining few days. Wouldn't you agree?"

When she pushed aside the battle raging inside her, she had laughed more in the past three days than she had since returning from Miss Agatha's. "You have arranged a wonderful journey."

His expression softened, and he ran his knuckles along her jaw to her chin. "Then we should join our party and continue the recreation."

"Of course."

She waited for him to exit, but he stayed in the carriage with his gaze down.

"Is there something else?" Poppy asked. She wanted to comfort him despite all her doubts.

His eyes edged with worry. "There is, but this is not the place for such a discussion. I noticed at Mr. Arafa's you enjoyed the art and artifacts in the cellar. David has a fine collection in his gallery. Will you meet me there after you have settled in?"

Once she nodded, they joined the party.

* * * *

It had occurred to Poppy to avoid Rhys and whatever he wanted to say, since it had put such serious concern on his face. The one thing she had determined during the long carriage rides filled with gazing at the countryside was, lying to herself would serve no purpose. She wanted to see him, to know what he thought, and if possible, to ease his worry.

She stepped inside the gallery and came face-to-face with a white marble statue depicting Achilles lying on his back with an arrow protruding from his heel. His mouth open in pain, he grasped the arrow's hilt. Agony was etched on his stone face.

"It's quite lifelike, isn't it?" Rhys stood just a few feet away.

Poppy hadn't heard him at all and started at his sudden appearance.

He closed the distance between them. "I'm sorry. I didn't mean to startle you."

Once her pounding heart settled back into her chest at a normal rhythm, Poppy chuckled. "I don't know why I should be so jumpy. I knew you'd be here after all." Another deep breath. "It is a stunning rendition. I'm very fond of the Greek and Roman mythology."

"Is that why you use those colorful expletives?"

She shrugged and walked around the life-sized statue. "It started because Mother forbade me from using the ones I'd heard in the street or the barn. It also annoyed her to no end. Then it just became a habit."

Offering his arm, he said, "Would you care to see the rest of the gallery?"

"I would, but I think I would like to talk before I'm distracted by the art." She took his arm. His warmth reached her through her glove and his clothes.

His frown made her wish she'd just enjoyed a tour of the amazing gallery. The only windows were set very high on the white walls, letting in streams of light yet keeping direct light from harming the treasures within. An added benefit was more wall space for the works of art. A Vermeer hung to their right, its deep colors catching her eye.

A low bench in the corner was cushioned in royal blue. Rhys led her there and they sat.

He kept her hand in his and tugged gently on her glove until he exposed her fingers. Tracing a line from her wrist to her palm before holding her firmly, he said, "I want to talk about my past."

Instinctively she flinched. "What do you mean?"

"Women. I want to talk about the women in my past. I want there to be no secrets between us. I know it was my behavior as a young man that colored your opinion about me."

"You already told me about Melissa." She shuddered at his exposing things she might not be able to forgive. Men had needs. Her mother had told her so many times that men couldn't control themselves when faced with temptation. Yet Rhys had always been in control. Even when they'd made love, he had been gentle and loving, never the brute her mother had hinted at.

"I know, and I appreciate how kindhearted you are toward her."

"What more could you want to tell me? I have no need to know about every conquest of your life, Rhys." The idea of hearing his tales of other women nauseated her.

It was the first time she had seen him blush. "Conquest is a bit too strong, Poppy. That's exactly what I want to make you understand. I was much like most men in my youth. I enjoyed women, and I'll not apologize for it."

Another thing Poppy's mother often said was that men took what they want and made no apology. Poppy drew a deep breath and held fast to her seat even when she wanted to bolt from the gallery.

Rhys must have noticed her restlessness. "Shall we tour the art?"

She leaped to her feet. Ready to rush away, she was stopped when he threaded his fingers through hers.

One wall was covered in family portraits. Each had a small plaque giving the name of the Richmond depicted and the year of his or her birth. A tall man stood next to a chair with a plump woman seated. She gazed up at him adoringly, and he looked equally enamored. Poppy gazed a long minute at the love reflected in their eyes. Donald and Philippa Richmond, 1650 and 1654…even so many years in the past, their love survived in this portrait.

"David looks a lot like Donald Richmond," Rhys said. "Same red hair and narrow chin. They look quite in love."

"Yes." Her voice was small and squeaked with emotion.

Rhys walked on, and she didn't resist the tug of his hand.

"I have not been a saint, Poppy. I told you that, but I want you to understand it was never about conquest and I have never forced myself on any woman nor tried to persuade someone who was unsure. I have enjoyed women who wished to trade pleasure with me." There was a sense of pleading in his voice as if he wanted her to understand something.

Poppy's nausea returned. "I'm not sure I want to hear anymore."

Stepping in front of her, he took her other hand and kissed both. "I'm sorry. This is very awkward and uncomfortable. I would not tell you this, but I know you think the worst of me in regard to relations with women.

It's important that you not create some fantasy of my bad behavior; better to have the truth."

There was logic in that notion. She did have ideas of men going from woman to woman to win some challenge from their birth to bed as many as possible before death. "And what about me, Rhys?"

He cocked his head. "I'm not sure what you mean."

"I came to you willing and wanting just as you describe these other women." Shame covered her like a tattered blanket. A shiver ran through her, and she closed her eyes against a wave of dizziness.

Rhys lifted her into his arms and strode to the bench. He sat with her nestled in his arms. "Listen to me, Penelope." His voice was a warm whisper where he pressed his face against the side of hers, his lips touching her ear like the wings of a butterfly. "What is between you and me is more special than I'll ever do justice to with words. You gave me a priceless gift that night and I cherish the memory. Do not cheapen what was beautiful by making such a comparison. The moments spent with you both that night walking in the dungeons and this time right now are precious. I would spend a lifetime making more moments like this, going on adventures and making love with you, if you would let me."

Something inside Poppy broke, and tears spilled from her eyes. She wept against his chest, shaking, unable to stop.

"Why are you crying, sweetheart?" He ran his hand up and down her back.

"I want to believe you," she sputtered. "I want the things you say to be true and to think you'll want me and only me for our lifetime."

"But..." he prompted.

Poppy pushed against his chest, putting enough distance between them so she could look him in the eye. "Everything I've ever seen from men is colored by violence, greed, and selfishness. I don't know how to alter my opinion."

Smiling, he kissed her nose, her cheek, and then her lips. The pressure there didn't force or push but rather waited and enjoyed until Poppy gave permission for more.

She opened her mouth, giving him entry, and let the kiss take form. Her tongue met his and swirled around. Inside her body melted with desire and love.

She stilled as the thought took form. She loved Rhys.

"What is it, Poppy?" He cupped her cheek and threaded his fingers through her hair.

Unable to tell him her truth, she asked, "Why aren't you angry with me?"

A warm smile spread across his handsome face, making him stunning to behold. "Why do you think I should be angry? You told me your fears. I must endeavor to soothe them."

"I think most men would be furious to hear I believe them violent and selfish." She slid off his lap, afraid she might ask for more from him if she didn't create some distance.

"I know these things aren't true in reference to me. There is no reason to be mad over something you have been taught just because it is incorrect." He stood and offered his hand. "Come. You should rest before dinner."

Taking his hand, she got up. "Thank you for being so honest about your past. I wish I was different, Rhys. Sometimes I wish I was one of those girls who longed for marriage."

"I would not change a thing about you, Poppy."

She stopped their progress toward the gallery door. "You would have me more graceful, more feminine, more accomplished, with a better sense of fashion…."

He silenced her with a finger across her lips. His eyes were wild with some emotion beyond description. "Not one thing," he said with more force. "I adore everything about you including the occasional tumble, torn gown, and habit of saying shocking things. I want you just as you are and would be very vexed if you changed a thing. My only wish is for you to see me as I am and not as your parents have painted men as a whole."

"I will do my best." The agreement came easily to her. Already many of the notions she believed were being tested by his sweet courtship.

* * * *

It was late the night they arrived at Thwackmore two days later. Poppy was so exhausted, she followed blindly behind the housekeeper, and once Jane helped her out of her dress, she fell into a deep sleep.

In the morning, she was disoriented. It took her a moment to remember where she was. Outside her window, drizzle added to the gloom she felt. She'd thought she wanted to arrive and be still, but now she was afraid Rhys would press her for an answer she wasn't ready to give.

Shaking herself, she said, "He has not forced anything and he's not likely to start now."

After washing, she put on a simple peach day dress. The room was covered in a similar color, though the bed curtains leaned toward salmon. A small writing desk with paper, ink, and quill stood near the window.

Gathering her courage, Poppy studied the white gazebo at the far edge of the garden off to the left. Even in the misty weather, it was lovely with hills rolling away. Poppy imagined mountains beyond the clouds and hoped the weather would break so she might view them.

Her stomach grumbled, forcing her to brave Rhys and her friends down in the breakfast room.

The tall stairs went on forever, making her wonder how she had managed them the night before. They led down to a large foyer complete with giant chandelier and the most enormous door Poppy had ever seen. Impossibly, it was another feature she'd been too tired to notice the night before.

A footman stood to the right and with a short bow opened the door for her. "The breakfast room is through here, my lady."

"Thank you." Steeling herself and lifting her chin, Poppy entered.

Rhys, Aurora, and Garrett sat around a round table set for six. White linen hung from the table and sideboard with silver and gold covering everything from the goblets to the window trim.

Tall windows allowed light to flood in from the east, and gossamer white curtains draped like waterfalls.

"What a beautiful room," Poppy said by way of greeting.

The men stood until Poppy sat down.

"Did you sleep well?" Rhys folded the paper he'd been reading and sipped dark aromatic coffee.

A middle-aged butler stepped beside her. He wore a green-and-blue tartan and bowed. "May I get you a plate, my lady?"

"Just some coffee and toast, please. I'm sorry, I don't know your name." Poppy should have paid better attention when they arrived. She was sure the butler had been introduced.

"It's Woolery, madam. I'll see to your breakfast." His accent was rich with a hint of the Scottish Lowlands thrilling the sound.

Poppy returned her attention to the table and Rhys, who watched her with a pleased expression. "I slept very well, thank you. I was so tired, I have no memory of meeting your butler, Garrett, nor climbing those enormous stairs."

Aurora laughed. "I had a similar experience, Poppy. Don't feel bad."

"It was a very long day yesterday," Garrett agreed.

Her toast and coffee arrived; she thanked Woolery and sipped. The warm, rich drink slid down her throat and invigorated her. She'd taken to drinking it against her mother's wishes about a year earlier. Mother felt tea or chocolate was more ladylike. Poppy needed something a bit stouter to start the day.

Clearing her throat, Aurora sipped the last of her tea and stood. "Poppy, when you have finished will you meet me in the gazebo? I would like a private word."

Poppy agreed. Aurora left and the men sat back down.

"What was that about?" Rhys asked over his paper.

Shrugging, Poppy chomped her toast. "Is there a plan for today, or are we able to amuse ourselves?"

Garrett pushed his plate aside. "You may follow your own wishes. Nothing is planned and the weather is not fine. Perhaps if it is better tomorrow, we might all take a long walk."

"That sounds wonderful. Faith will hate it, but the rest of us will be delighted."

"What will I hate?" Faith called from the door.

Mercy was beside her and went to look at the available food on the sideboard.

"A walk," Poppy said.

Pulling a face, Faith joined Mercy.

With the last of her toast eaten, Poppy rose with her coffee. "I'm going to meet Aurora. I'll see you all later."

The men rose and bowed.

Poppy made a quick curtsy and carried her coffee to the garden. She pulled on an overcoat on account of a mist and the promise of rain as she walked to the gazebo. The first meeting with Rhys and no mention of the reason for the journey had set her at ease, and she was determined to enjoy the manor, its gardens, and her friends' company.

The gazebo, while beautiful, offered no shelter from the mist. Poppy tromped up the three steps. "Why are we meeting out of doors on such a day?"

Aurora startled and jumped from her seat on one of four benches set along the walls. "What I have to tell you is difficult and I didn't want to involve anyone else."

Poppy didn't know if she had ever seen Aurora looking so troubled. "Whatever could have put you in such a state, dearest?" She put down her coffee cup on one of the benches and rushed to her friend.

"Oh God, don't be kind. It makes this even harder." Aurora's voice rang with anguish.

Taking her hands, Poppy held them so Aurora couldn't look away. "What are you talking about?"

A tear ran down Aurora's pale skin. Dark rings smudged under her eyes, and her lips quivered. "It was me."

Confused, Poppy didn't know what question to ask next. Her friend was near hysteria and she wanted to help. She tried to lighten the exchange. "All right. It was you.... What was you?"

More tears spilled from Aurora's eyes, and she shook. "I wrote an anonymous letter to your mother informing her about you and Rhys."

Poppy's insides froze. She released Aurora's hands as if they burned. It was hard to breathe. It took her a several beats to push back the wave of lunacy threatening to overwhelm her. She backed farther away. "Why would you have done such a thing?"

Hands opening and closing on nothing, Aurora bit her lip. "It was so obvious when the two of you came back from Mr. Arafa's home you were in love and perfect for each other. I knew you would never accept that you loved him without a push."

"So, you betrayed me? One of the few people in my life I trust, and you deliberately put me in a position to be owned by a man? Did Rhys ask you to do this?"

Aurora stepped forward, eyes pleading. "Rhys knows nothing about this. And would it be so terrible to be married to him? A man who will love you and care for you. A man who will never hurt you. You would be my sister."

"I already was your sister." Poppy's heart ripped in two. The garden spun, and she gripped the post of the gazebo, a splinter digging into her palm. She gripped harder.

"Don't say it as if it is no longer true," Aurora cried in earnest. "I wanted you to be safe from my fate and to be happy."

Chin quivering, Poppy fought to keep her knees from collapsing. "And have I been happy since Mother got your letter? Have you made me or Rhys happy with your subterfuge?"

Aurora's mouth opened, but she said nothing.

Hobbling down the steps, Poppy ran through the garden to the open hillside. Aurora called after her.

Chapter 17

Rhys walked into luncheon after searching the manor and grounds for Poppy. When he didn't find her there either, concern knotted a ball in his gut. "Has anyone seen Poppy?"

Three pairs of eyes gawked at him in innocence, but his sister was less wide eyed.

"Rora, where is she?"

Garrett leaned forward at the head of the table. "She must be in her room. She might have needed more rest after the journey."

"I have been to her room three times over the course of the morning. She has not been there, and Jane, her maid, knows nothing about her whereabouts. But I can see that my sister knows something." Rhys rounded the table until he was next to Aurora's chair.

Mercy narrowed her eyes. "Aurora, if you know where Poppy is, you had best tell us. She might need help."

Picking up the napkin next to her plate, Aurora dabbed her eyes. "I upset her this morning, and she ran from the garden. I thought surely she would return once she calmed down."

"What did you say that would send her running into strange lands?" Faith's eyes were wide, and she stood, though her voice was soft.

Sobbing was the only response from Aurora.

The uncharacteristic display of emotion from his sister forced Rhys back a step. Since they were children, she'd always kept her emotions inside. Rhys's trepidation increased to the point where he had to clutch his hands at his side to keep from shaking the knowledge from Aurora.

Garrett rounded the table in a flash and pulled Aurora into his arms. "You will have to tell us what happened, Rora. Poppy might be in danger. The rain isn't likely to let up, and it will be dark in a few hours."

After several gasps for air, Aurora pulled away and turned to Rhys. Her eyes swam, and the color had drained from her cheeks. Even her hair fell sorrowfully across her face. "I told her I wrote the letter to her mother that started this entire mess. I was planning to take the information to my grave, but guilt forced it from me. I haven't slept since betraying the two of you. I only did it because I wanted you both to be happy."

Faith threw her hand over her mouth, covering her gasp.

Mercy shook her head. "Oh, Aurora."

Rhys put his hand on his sister's shoulder and kissed her cheek. "I understand, Rora, but you must have known Poppy would find it harder to accept. You should have trusted me to do this my own way."

"I just thought to give you both a little push. I didn't think her parents would behave so badly. I thought it would give you the nudge you needed to propose and maybe she would see what a good fit you are together."

Rhys let his breath out and shook his head. "I had every intention of proposing long before you involved those parents of hers."

"I'm sorry," Aurora cried into her napkin while Garrett patted her back.

"Where did she go?" Garrett frowned but waved for the butler with his free hand. "Woolery, his lordship and I will need boots and coats."

"She ran from the gazebo toward the forest." Aurora still wept, but Faith had come around and taken over for Garrett's comforting.

Rhys was torn between his sister's obvious state of despair and finding Poppy out in the dank weather before she caught a chill.

"We will take care of Aurora," Mercy said. "You go and find Poppy." She rounded the table and the three sat.

Rhys gave Mercy a nod and ran for the door. He grabbed the outerwear being held by Woolery in the doorway and donned the cloak as he rushed through the house. At the back door, he changed footwear.

"We'll head toward the woods, then split up and search in opposite directions. Are you certain she's not in the gardens, Rhys?" Garrett buttoned his cloak, his usually affable expression stoic with concern.

"Yes. I searched the house from top to bottom and then the gardens on all sides. She is not within the grounds." His own panic started to churn. Poppy had been gone for hours. She had to be cold and wet by this time. She might have fallen and been hurt or worse.

"Rhys, I see the terrible possibilities rolling around in that head of yours. We shall find her, and she will be fine." Garrett's voice was a command rather than a reassurance. "We will meet back here at nightfall with or without her. If it takes longer, we'll need to gather more help."

With a nod, Rhys mounted his horse and trotted toward the woods, calling Poppy's name. They split up at the edge of the trees, and Rhys headed north. South would have taken Poppy past the manor, which seemed unlikely.

Garrett rode off to the east.

The rain grew harder, and soon Garrett's calls became faint then disappeared into the other sounds of the forest and storm.

Combing the woods this way and that, Rhys found no sign of her. The trees were dense and gave little light. It had been hours, and the daylight waned as his panic returned. Common sense said Poppy would return before dark if she could, but his Poppy was stubborn and hurt. She would need time to sort out her feelings. And there was her clumsiness to consider.

Forcing his darker thoughts aside, he followed the sound of running water.

A creek pushed past its banks blocked his path. It might not have been so high when Poppy came through. She might have crossed. Rhys might drown himself and the horse trying to cross at its current velocity. He walked southeast along the water's edge, looking for a safer place to cross. The rushing water was so loud his calls for Poppy would never be heard over the roar. Still, he shouted until his throat scratched with the effort.

A twig snapped.

Rhys tugged his horse to a quick stop. The last thing he needed was to frighten a wildcat and get mauled. More likely it was a grouse disturbed by his presence near her nest. Determined, he kept on his path to find a better way over the creek, which was more like a river from the rain. "Poppy!"

"Rhys?"

The response was so low, he thought he'd imagined it. "Poppy!"

Stronger. "I'm here."

He jumped to the ground.

At the base of a large tree, Poppy sat soaked and covered in mud. He let out a breath he'd not realized he'd been holding and rushed to her. "Are you hurt?"

She shrugged. Her voice rasped with tears. "I fell. I'm cold. My knee hurts. Aurora…"

Cupping her face, he peppered her cheeks and forehead with kisses. "I know, she told us."

"I'm sorry I ran. I…" She sobbed into her hands.

Female tears were the order of the day, he supposed. "Let me have a look at your knee."

"The creek was too high to cross and I got a bit turned around. I wanted to come back, but then I tripped over a root." She pointed at a gnarled bit of root humped up out of the ground ten feet away.

He lifted the hem of her skirt above the injured knee.

A gash marred her perfect skin. The blood has slowed to seeping, but her lower leg was covered with the sticky remains of a wound. Between that, the mud, and a dark bruise, he couldn't see the extent of the cut. He pulled his blouse out of his breeches and tore the bottom in a long strip. With the very end he cleaned the mud and bits of pebbles and bark away. Once he wrapped the cloth around her knee several times, he tied a knot.

"Any other injuries?" He searched her for some indication of where else she might hurt.

"None you can fix with your shirt." Her hair had fallen from the chignon she'd worn in the morning. It hung around her face in soaking spirals. There was little left of the tattered bottom of her peach day dress, and the charming lace around the collar he'd noticed earlier was missing entirely. The brown overcoat she donned presumably to meet Aurora in the gazebo was also soaked through and hung from her shoulders. Even looking like an abandoned rag doll, he wanted her.

"We shall work on those once we have you dry and warm."

"I'm not at all sure it can be fixed. How will I ever trust her again?" Her despair was heartbreaking.

"You will forgive Rora when you realize she was only doing what she thought would be best for you. I am confident you shall get through this, and I will help you in any way I can. Now let's get you back, if you're ready."

She nodded.

Lifting her, he hugged her a moment before putting one arm behind her knees. He swung her into his arms and put her in the saddle. Swinging up behind her, he settled her on his lap and carried her west, out of the woods. It was several miles back to the manor.

Poppy kept her face buried in his cloak. "I cannot trust anyone. I wish I had run far away as my first instinct told me to. I could be in another country where my parents would never find me by now."

He stopped, the rain pelting them. "Your friends, including Aurora, will be frantic with worry. Then you can calmly think this all through without the panic that sent you into a strange wood alone. And, Poppy, don't ever do anything like this again."

When she just stared back at him, he continued forward. The manor's lights were a welcome sight when they arrived back at the gardens long after dark.

Poppy hadn't said another word and shivered in his arms, her teeth chattering.

"We shall get you dry and warm, sweetheart. Hold on a bit longer." Rhys's temper had waned when facing her becoming ill from the cold. Perhaps if he believed she would not catch a fever, his words would be fact.

Inside, Garrett was pulling off his sopping cloak and handing it to Woolery. His friend sagged against the wall. "Thank God, you found her."

The butler called for more wood on the fire in the great parlor. He yelled for dry clothes for Poppy and both men before turning back to Rhys. "The other ladies are waiting there, my lord. It is the warmest room in the house, and it might be best to care for Lady Penelope there until she has shed her chills."

Rhys stomped through the house and kicked open the parlor door before the footman could open it.

Aurora, Mercy, and Faith all gasped and jumped up from their places around the hearth.

Once he deposited Poppy by the fire, there was a flurry of activity as the girls and maids cared for her.

A glare from Poppy forced Aurora back.

It was not his place to interfere, and he was confident that Poppy would come around. He slogged up the stairs and changed his own sopping clothes before returning to the parlor.

On the rug next to the fire, Poppy wore a nightgown of billowy white and was wrapped in at least three blankets. She sat with her hands around her knees. Faith ran a brush through her damp hair, but Poppy still chattered and her skin was gray.

Rhys moved a large overstuffed chair toward the fire, lifted Poppy, and sat her in his lap on the chair. He held her tight, willing the cold out of her. "Relax, my love. You are safe now and with friends."

By the time Poppy's hair was dry and she fell into a fitful sleep, Rhys felt the heat of a fever coming off her.

The other three Wallflowers slept nearby huddled together on the couch despite the availability of several other pieces of furniture.

Aurora stirred. Her eyes widened when she saw him in the firelight. "What is it?"

"She has a fever."

Waking the other two, Aurora jumped from the couch. "Let's get her to bed. She is strong and by morning she may have fought it off."

* * * *

Rhys spent the night at her bedside. When dawn broke and she was thrashing with fever, he sent for a doctor and was informed the doctor for the region was in another town. It would take three days to reach the man and bring him to Thwackmore.

They kept cool cloths on her head and changed her bedding as she went from sweating to chills several times during the day.

Aurora came in the room. "Go and sleep awhile, Rhys. If you become ill, who will order the rest of us around?"

"You'll call me if she wakes or gets worse?" He stood.

"Of course," Aurora said, turning her attention to Poppy's sleeping form.

Rhys slept hard and deep for hours. The last two days had caught up with him. Someone had entered and left a bowl of stew on the table in his room. He downed the food, dressed, and went to Poppy's room.

Mercy sat with her and gave him a sad smile when he entered. "She is the same. She called for you once about an hour ago, but then fell back to sleep, so I thought not to wake you."

Mercedes always had a direct way of speaking, which Rhys appreciated. He missed her usual sarcasm and wit and hoped Poppy would soon recover and everyone would return to normal.

"Perhaps I shouldn't have dragged all of you up here." He sat on the edge of the bed and picked up Poppy's limp hand.

Rising, Mercy shook her head. "Aurora's interference had already happened. This is not your fault, nor is it Aurora's. This happened because Poppy is afraid to live a life not her own. Fleeing is what she does to protect herself. But I suspect you knew all of this without my needing to tell you."

He forced a smile. "It's still nice to have someone confirm it all."

"Shall I send Faith in?" Mercy asked.

"No. Let her sleep. I will stay and take care of Poppy."

When Mercy was gone, Rhys leaned over Poppy's hand and kissed her knuckles. "Come back to me, my love. What will become of me if you leave?"

Shivers overtook Poppy. Her teeth clacked together uncontrollably, and she thrashed from side to side.

Rhys kicked off his boots, climbed under the covers, and pulled her into his arms. "I have you, Penelope. Nothing will hurt you as long as we're together."

He kissed her hair and tightened his hold, willing his heat into her.

Her usual flowery scent was obscured by rain and woods she'd brought back, but underneath was pure Poppy. If he could live on that alone, he would be happy for a lifetime. Pulling her around to face him, he rubbed warmth into her back. "Come back to me, and I will show you a world you had never imagined," he repeated.

* * * *

The first light of day shone in Poppy's room. The rain had moved off, and the sun crested the horizon. Rhys pressed his cheek to Poppy's and found her cool. When he pulled back to take a look, she protested and tightened her grip around his back.

Unmeasurable joy bloomed inside Rhys. "I think you must be feeling better, my love."

Releasing him, she pulled back. Her eyes were clear though tired. "Is that what I am, your love?"

Her voice was small and filled with worry. His heart was so full, it might overflow. He kissed her nose and then her cheek. "You are my only love and shall be for as long as I live, Penelope."

She sighed and wrapped her arms around him again. "I had very strange dreams, I can't quite remember. I think I was in another world, but all the while you were calling me back. It's all very fuzzy now."

"I was calling you back to me. You scared me, dearest. You had me frantic that I might lose you." He held the back of her skull, his fingers threading her hair.

Her back expanded with air and then released. "That would solve all the problems, would it not?"

Pushing her back just far enough so he could look her in the eye with only an inch between their noses, he said, "No, Poppy. It would not solve anything. It would leave me devastated. How many ways must I tell you, I love you and want to spend my life making you happy? What must I do to convince you that you are the only woman I shall ever want? When will you believe we were made for each other and you would no more be my property than I would be yours?"

Every emotion passed through Poppy's eyes before she settled on something more tender. "I believe you, Rhys."

He stilled, and his heart stopped beating as he waited for her to take her words back. "You do?"

"Yes. No one would go through all of this trouble for a woman he didn't love. I have been a fool and hope you will forgive me." She pressed a simple kiss to his lips.

It sent a bolt of lightning through him. "Does that mean you might consider the possibility of marrying me?"

Her eyes lowered.

Rushing to fill the empty space, he said, "I don't need an answer now. I will not pressure you. When you are ready you can tell me what you want. Aurora will still shelter you if you choose not to marry me. I will pay for you to live however you wish as long as you are happy."

She pressed one finger to his lips, silencing him.

A warm blush crept up her cheeks. "I have been blinded by a past I didn't understand. When I was in the woods and thought I might never make my way back or be found, I had a lot of time to think of you and the way you have cared for me these many weeks. You never wavered. You asked me to marry you before my mother was involved."

"I asked because it was what I wanted, not because we'd made love or out of a sense of duty." He brushed her hair back behind her ear.

"I can see that now. I was so blinded by my own beliefs about you and men in general, I nearly killed myself over this nonsense. But in the woods, something occurred to me."

His heart had lodged itself in his throat, but he squeaked out, "What was that, love?"

"In my twenty-one years, I have seen my fair share of rakes and rogues who took liberties with young ladies both willing and not. Yet none affected me the way what I saw in the forest all those years ago had. When I sat in the mud soaking and catching a chill, I played each moment back in my mind looking for the difference, and all I found was you."

"Me?" Rhys didn't know what she was talking about, but he was enraptured with every word.

She blushed deep pink before returning her gaze to his. "Yes. I think I may have loved you even then."

The word from her lips stopped the world around them. That single moment of perfection made everything else unimportant. Time stopped and held. "You love me?"

A slow nod and a shy smile lit her face. "I love you now as I did then. I think it a short jump from love to hate, and when I saw you with that woman back when I was little more than a child, my love turned. I should have let it go, but I couldn't. Until now."

"What do you feel now, Penelope?" Rhys didn't want to risk losing the moment.

"I love you, Rhys Draper. I shall love you until my death, which I hope will not be for a hundred years."

He laughed and kissed her nose. "A hundred years will do very nicely." She giggled then sobered. "I'm sorry to have frightened everyone. I really had planned to come back, but I got lost."

"No more running, Poppy. If you are afraid, you have friends who love you and will help."

She sighed. "Aurora."

"Will you forgive her?" It was hard not to make Aurora's case, but he thought better of it.

"I don't know. Can it be enough I've had one revelation today?"

Leaning in, he took a long, lingering kiss. Her mouth opened under his without hesitation. He nibbled her full bottom lip, and she did the same to his top as if they were coming together after a lifetime. Her hands skimmed up and down his back, moving lower with each pass.

He pulled her bottom toward him, letting her feel the agony she created within him as well as the promise of pleasure. Lips, teeth, and tongues merged in passion and relief before Rhys came to his senses. "This is not the time or place for this, my love. Our friends will be barging in at any moment to check on your condition."

Poppy swallowed several times with her forehead pressed to his. "Then do you think I might request a bath?"

Laughing, he got out from under the covers. "I will see what can be arranged."

"Don't go," she called when he reached the door.

"I won't be able to stay here while you bathe, Poppy. However, after we're married, I expect you will have to toss me from the room should you want a private bath." His imagination ran wild with the thought, and walking became uncomfortable.

A low, sexy giggle bubbled from her. "I suppose you may go. It's just that when someone realizes they are in love and want to marry, it's hard to watch the object of their affection walk away."

Rhys returned to the bed. "I shall never leave you, not really. My heart will forever rest right here." He touched the space between her breasts with his palm.

Holding his hand tight to her chest, she met his gaze with wide, wanting eyes. "I will always take very good care of it. I promise never to doubt you again, Rhys."

Rhys's heart leaped in joyous celebration. Nothing could have made him happier. Everything he never knew he wanted was in this room with this woman. "You cannot even imagine how happy you've made me. I shall never be able to express it adequately."

The way she looked at him with complete trust called him back into the bed. He pulled his hand away instead. "I had better go and order your bath and tell the house you are feeling better." He turned to the door then swung his gaze back to her. "Do not get out of that bed. You may be feeling better, but you have been very ill for two days and if you injure yourself, I will be very vexed."

"I will wait for someone to help me stand."

"Thank you." He breathed a sigh of relief.

"It's the least I can do after all I've put you through." She winked.

"I have a feeling our life together will never be boring." There was that joy again bubbling inside him like a volcano ready to erupt.

"I'm counting on it." A beautiful smile spread from one ear to the other, making her stunning even with her pallor.

He opened the door.

"Oh, I could eat something too," she called.

His laugh felt as if it had been bottled up for decades as he trotted down the stairs to order food and a bath for his wife-to-be.

Chapter 18

Poppy had expected panic to set in after going against everything she'd thought she wanted, but agreeing to marry Rhys came with a calm sense of right.

Swinging her feet over the side of the bed sent the room spinning. Poppy decided it best to take Rhys's advice in this case. She tucked herself back under the covers and dozed in and out of sleep.

A soft knock brought her fully awake.

Faith's smiling face poked inside. "Am I bothering you?"

"Of course not. Come in and keep me company. I'm hoping some food is coming up soon." Poppy's stomach rumbled in its agreement of the fine idea.

With a running start Faith threw herself atop the bed and sat facing Poppy. "It's a frenzy of activity below to gather food and heat water. I think the tub should be arriving any moment."

"That's good. I feel positively caked with filth."

Nodding, Faith frowned. "You were a mess when Rhys found you. He was frantic; we all were."

"I'm sorry to have caused so much trouble, Faith. I thought to come back, but then fell and became lost. I never meant to worry anyone." Poppy reached out her hand, and Faith gave it a squeeze.

"I know. Just the same, that quick temper of yours nearly cost your life this time, and Rhys his sanity."

The door opened without a knock, and Mercy's gleaming head poked through. She took one look at the bed and pranced over to join in. "I'm glad you are awake. The men are carrying the tub up now. The water will come after you've eaten."

Once Mercy was settled on the mattress, Poppy sighed. "You should know, I've agreed to marry Rhys."

"Have you?" Mercy's green eyes were wide.

Faith squealed. "Wonderful news. It's no wonder he looked so pleased when he ordered your meal."

Bliss formed a rolling ball deep in Poppy's center. As she thought of Rhys being happy, the ball grew, spinning its elation throughout her body. She stilled her thoughts. "I've been a bit of a ninny about the entire thing."

"No." Faith's voice was sober. "You had your beliefs, as we all do. It takes time to form new ones even when faced with evidence to the contrary. Only running to the woods was a very bad idea."

Mercy nodded. "Will you see Aurora and tell her this?"

"Not yet." Poppy's answer came too fast. She might have come to her senses where Rhys was concerned, but she was still not over Aurora's underhanded actions.

Sighing, Faith said, "At least you didn't say never."

"When I was lost and wet in the woods, I imagined never seeing any of you three again and the notion was terrible. I am angry with Aurora and disappointed she would write that letter. However, she, like the two of you, are part of my heart. To cut one of you out would be to chop off a bit of that organ. I couldn't survive." Emotions clogged Poppy's throat.

"You sorted through a lot of things in those hours alone." Mercy plucked at the tawny coverlet. "How will you deal with your parents when we return to town?"

Here was something she hadn't calculated. "I don't know. Their actions were far worse and not done with any thoughts to my best interest. I will need to stew on it a bit longer."

The tub arrived, and two footmen placed it in the center of the room.

Gillian brought a tray of food. Her fair skin seemed lighter, making her freckles stand out more keenly. Dark rings marred the undersides of her eyes, and her hair was tumbling from its cap. "Some nice soup, bread, and cheese if you can manage it, my lady."

Jane brought towels and soap, which she placed on the chair near the tub. "I'll come back after you've eaten to help you bathe, my lady."

"Thank you both. I'm sorry to have worried you." It was obvious her illness had kept the two lady's maids up at all hours. They both dragged their feet, ready to drop. Guilt ratcheted around Poppy's heart.

"We are happy you are safe and well, Lady Poppy." Gillian curtsied. "I'll come back for the tray. Do you need help to the table or shall I bring the tray to your bed?"

"I'd rather eat at the table."

Mercy stood. "We will help her, Gillian. You should rest for a while."

When the maids were gone, Mercy helped Poppy out of bed and to the table. Her knee ached but wasn't as bad as the waves of dizziness from lack of food and the aftermath of a fever.

She started with the broth, which was light but flavored with chicken. She dunked a bit of bread in and nibbled that as well. When the bowl was empty, she gave a bit of cheese a try but decided it was too heavy for a first meal. Leaning back in the chair, she breathed out a long, exhausted sigh. "Who knew eating could take so much out of a person."

Faith got up. "I'll run and tell them to put a hold on your bath. You need to nap for a while. Then you can bathe."

Though she wanted to argue about needing the bath more than sleep, Poppy couldn't summon the energy. Mercy helped her back into bed, tucked her in, and promised to return.

Poppy woke to the late afternoon sun and the scent of more soup. Rhys sat next to the bed, looking rested and pleased with himself as he watched her. "Hades's breath, is it time to eat again?"

He gave her a nod. "You've been sleeping almost four hours."

"It felt but a moment," she mused. "Will you help me to the table?"

Stronger though still wobbly, she was happy for the help. Falling down again was not something she needed at that moment.

The soup was a bit heartier than the last, with bits of meat and vegetables in it. Poppy lapped it all up without a care that Rhys watched her every spoonful. She was too hungry for those silly ideas about ladies not having large appetites. She ate the cheese this time too and the bread. "I feel better."

He stacked the dishes on the tray and put it on the dresser before returning to sit with her at the round table. "I can see you do. Shall I call for your bath?"

"Sit a moment first." Poppy had dreamed of so many things that now rummaged around in her mind. "I would like to talk to you about my parents and what they want."

"What *you* want would be more interesting to me." His frown deepened, forming a crease between his beautiful eyes.

Loving his words made the rest of what she wanted to say easier. "I'm glad to hear it. My parents want a big public wedding at St. Paul's so they can show all their friends what a fine job they've done and they are well rid of me. Of course, we've already ruined it, as tomorrow would have been our London wedding date. However, when we return, it is exactly what they will demand."

He cocked his head to one side. "I suppose that's true, though put a bit more harshly than I would have ventured."

An old anger bubbled inside Poppy. "I'm finished being polite where my parents are concerned. At least in the company of my closest friends I would like to be honest."

No sign of his frown as his face lit in a bright grin. "I'm happy to be counted among those friends."

Her bliss started spinning inside her again. "I want a small wedding with no fussing and fuming. I want to remember the day we promised ourselves to each other as joyful and happy. If we return to London, I shall be forced to stay away from you with only chaperoned visits for weeks until more terrible arrangements are made. I want our life together to begin now and not with all the rules society would apply to us."

Wide eyed, he gaped at her. "You want to elope?"

"If that's what you would call getting married here in Scotland with our friends present and no wild preparations, then yes. I want to elope."

Shocked certainly, Rhys also couldn't wipe the smile from his lips. "When were you thinking?"

"As soon as I'm well enough to walk down the aisle unhindered." Her heart pounded with excitement and a touch of fear. Not that she feared marriage to Rhys anymore, but she worried about the repercussions when they returned to London.

"It's not a death sentence, Poppy." He laughed. "Your parents will be angry but they will recover. Besides, you'll be a countess and there is little they can say in the negative about it."

The bubble spun faster and grew bigger. Poppy didn't think she'd ever been so happy. "Then you don't mind marrying without proper banns and no fanfare?"

In a flash, he was on his knees before her. His cupped her cheek. "As long as it is you I'm waiting for at the front of the church, I would marry anywhere, Penelope. You are the only part of the wedding customs I'm interested in."

"There will be a lot of trouble to face." She combed her fingers through his wild golden hair and reveled in its softness.

"Then we shall face it together, my love. You should be happy on your wedding day, not miserable because of things other people want." He leaned into the touch of her hand.

"What about your mother? Won't she be unhappy?" One of her dreams depicted a raging Dowager Countess of Marsden chasing after her.

He kissed her palm and took a long breath. There was a flash of regret in his eyes, but it was replaced by his previous excitement. "Mother will understand. I'm sure she would prefer the typical wedding as well, but her happiness at my being wed and the prospect of grandchildren will outweigh anything else."

Leaning down, she pressed her lips to his. "It's settled, then?"

Rhys wrapped his hand around her neck and extended the kiss until they were both breathless. "It's settled."

He was still on his knees when Gillian came in to take the tray. She blushed deeply. "I'll tell them you are ready for your bath, my lady."

Giggling, Poppy covered her face. "We must be all the talk in the manor. You should go. Jane will come to help me in a few minutes."

Rhys stood. "I will see you later. I imagine you'll need to rest after a meal and a bath, but I'll check in on you."

As he left, Jane excused herself and entered.

There was comfort in knowing he would always come back. As impossible as it was to believe, she had found someone who would never leave her or stray from his vows. Heart full, she needed to take care of one more thing. "Jane, do you know where Lady Radcliff is?"

"In her rooms, miss." Jane's mousy brown hair was just visible under her cap, and her tan skin showed she'd been out in the good weather, which had arrived that day. "Can you help me down the hall while they fill the bath, Jane?"

Stuffing Poppy into a robe and slippers, Jane kept an arm around her should she stumble on the stone hallway. Remarkably without incident they arrived at Aurora's chamber door.

Poppy knocked.

"Yes?" Aurora's voice called from within.

Jane opened the door.

As soon as Aurora saw Poppy, she jumped up from the French-style lady's desk where she'd been writing in a small book. Aurora always kept an account of her days. "I will help her, Jane. You may go."

Aurora rushed over, but Poppy felt stable enough to cross to the table and sit. The room was similar to Poppy's down the hall. This one was in delicate blues and yellows, with a charming damask on the walls and a rich blue rug. A small round table and two chairs stood near the window, and curtains in the same colors donned the bed and window.

Jane didn't move to leave until Poppy was safely seated.

"Jane, come back when the bath is ready, please."

"Yes, my lady."

Now that she had come, Poppy wasn't sure how to begin. This was her oldest and closest friend. They had met even before Mercy and Faith had joined their foursome. "I hope you're not writing anything too horrid about me in your book."

Aurora forced a smile. "You know it's just the nonsense of my days. Nothing of import."

"I thought it best if we spoke alone."

Aurora's hair hung loose, and her eyes were ringed red. Her usually pink cheeks were ashen. "I'm very glad you came. You understand I would have come to you, but was unsure if you wished to see me."

"I should not have run away," Poppy admitted. "It is a bad habit and I'm done with it."

A tentative smile lit Aurora's eyes. "I'm just happy Rhys found you and you are well. How is your knee?"

"Only twisted. It already feels better. A bit stiff from so much time in bed these last days."

"You gave us all quite a fright." Aurora spoke like they were mere acquaintances.

Poppy couldn't stand it. Frustration boiled to the surface. "I am still vexed with you. You had no right to interfere."

"I know. I should have trusted you would sort it out. I'm sorry, Poppy. I would never want to do anything to hurt our friendship." A tear slid down Aurora's cheek.

Forcing herself not to be swayed, Poppy pulled her shoulders back and lifted her chin. "You must never do anything like this again. I trust in the future, when you have something to say, you will say it and not go behind doors and act the spy."

"I promise. I have more than learned my lesson." She wiped her face with the back of her hand.

Emotion started to well up inside Poppy. "Good. Then that's settled." Poppy used the table to push herself to standing. "Now, I don't know if Faith told you, but I've agreed to marry your brother."

With a high-pitched screech, Aurora flung herself into Poppy's arms, rocking them both. She righted them before they landed in a heap on the floor. "I'm sorry. I'm just so happy."

It was so good to be hugged by her friend, she didn't even care they almost hit the hard floor. "I'm happy too. You will truly be my sister in just a few days."

Aurora stepped back. "A few days?"

Blood rushed to Poppy's cheeks. "We are going to marry here in Scotland as soon as I'm strong enough. I don't want my mother and father to ruin one moment of my wedding."

Wide eyes and foolish smile, Aurora looked quite mad. "I think that's the best news I've heard…well, ever." She grabbed her in another hug.

They sat and talked as if the last few days had never happened. Jane came and collected Poppy at the same time Gillian appeared to help Aurora dress for dinner.

Aurora kissed her cheek. "I will come and sit with you when your dinner is brought up later. Enjoy your bath."

Once Jane helped Poppy into the deep tub and washed her hair, Poppy asked her to let her soak alone for a while.

Each ache and pain from her run, fall, and illness eased in the warm water, and the steam cleared her head of unwanted worry. Thoughts of Rhys and how kind he had been flitted through her mind. For the first time in her life, Poppy knew everything was going to be all right.

* * * *

Rhys had been right about how tired she would be after the bath. Poppy had climbed into bed and slept despite the tray, which turned cold on the table.

When she awoke, she took a bite of the bread, but the rest she left.

Without bothering to take her robe, Poppy slid into her slippers and out of her room. The house was still, making her think it must be quite late. As if in answer, the clock in the foyer struck one.

She shuffled along the stones and past the grand stairs. It wasn't ladylike, but Poppy again knew which door belonged to Rhys's room. At the time, she told herself, it was good to know where everyone slept, but now she could admit the real reason. She loved him and had to know where to find him when she needed him.

The door was like every other in the hall, but it was not the same. Poppy's hand shook as she pushed the latch. Thankful it wasn't locked, she stepped inside and slowly pulled the bolt.

Dwindling coals gave the only light, but it was enough to see a large draped bed on one side of the room. She stumbled on the edge of a rug, but by some strange magic she didn't fall.

Still shaking, she decided it was excitement rather than fear and slipped through the curtains.

As soon as she put a knee on the mattress, Rhys sat up in the darkness. There was a frozen moment. "Penelope?"

"Yes, it's me." She climbed fully onto the bed and toward his voice.

He must have been able to see better in the dark than she could. He scooped her into his arms and snuggled them to the mattress. "You shouldn't be out of bed."

She giggled. "I'm not out of bed."

He breathed deeply against the spot where her neck and shoulder met. A hum of pleasure rumbled along her skin. "You smell like a garden in spring."

"I've had a bath." It came out prouder than was necessary, but she loved the feel of his flesh against hers and the way he reveled in touching and smelling her.

"That does not explain what you are doing in my bedchamber at this hour." The words were scolding, but his tone rumbled with love and passion.

Poppy kissed his forehead. "I knew you would not come to me."

He touched her cheek with the back of his hand. "You haven't become feverish again?"

Turning her head, she kissed his fingers, sucking the smallest into her mouth and humming as it slid out. Her eyes had adjusted to the darkness, and his were wide. "I am perfectly well, Rhys. However, if you are not interested in lovemaking, I shall return to my own room and leave you to your sleep."

He stopped her exit as soon as she opened the bed curtains. Pulling her back to his front, he whispered against her ear, "Don't be so hasty, my love. I'm not turning you away, for that I shall never do. My only concern is because you have recently been very ill and this visit might be too much for you."

"I have been asleep for days and even today, I dozed most of the day between meals and chats."

Rhys got out of bed.

Poppy's heart sank, though his nudity was enough distraction to keep her from complaining about his absence. His broad back bulged with muscles that corded down either side of his spine and led to the most perfect bottom. She couldn't turn away, making her way down long, muscular legs then making her way back up.

The spark of the fire broke the spell he had her under. In all his naked glory, he added two logs to the fire and stirred it back to life. In the firelight's full blaze, he was even more magnificent. Like one of the gods in Greek mythology she'd read about so often in her youth.

"You're beautiful." The words slipped out unbidden.

He turned, surprised but unashamed of his nudity. "You are the one who is beautiful, Penelope. Come and sit by the fire."

It was one thing to sneak down the hall and into Rhys's bed in the darkness and quite another to stride across the room toward a naked man.

The notion of running was fleeting. She didn't do that anymore. Her path was clear. On sturdy legs she rose, and halfway across the room she stopped. Her gaze never left his as she reached up with her left hand and pulled the bow at her right shoulder.

Eagerness shone in his eyes.

Buoyed by his attention, she lifted her right hand and tugged the other tie. With the barest movement the nightgown pooled at her feet.

Rhys's breath caught. "You are the most stunning creature."

Careful not to trip over her own garment, Poppy stepped out of the center and continued until she stood before Rhys. "I'm glad you didn't send me away."

"I never would." It seemed his voice had grown rough and strained. He ran his hands from her shoulders down her arms and took her hands in his. He threaded their fingers together and stepped until their bodies grazed each other.

Poppy shivered. It was like being kissed everywhere all at once. Her skin pricked with awareness and need.

His lips found hers in the gentlest of kisses. First he loved the bottom lip and then the top.

Not wanting to miss one sensation, Poppy remained still until his mouth opened on hers. She could no longer keep her passion at bay. Fingers still entwined, she leaned forward, tightening their bodies. His shaft pressed hard at her abdomen and forced a satisfied moan from Rhys.

The kiss was part battle, part rapture as tongues, teeth, and lips warred, made peace, and warred again. Gasps and groans issued from her own mouth as the inability to use her hands became unbearable.

She struggled to free her fingers, but Rhys held fast.

Breaking the kiss, he planted a string of kisses down her chin to her neck.

Waves of desire flooded, her sending pleasure to her center as his tongue traced her pulse. Lower still, he kissed her shoulder and chest, stopping at her nipple to suckle until her knees gave way. Freeing her hands, he wrapped his own around her to keep her from collapsing.

Poppy hugged him tight, digging her fingers into his strong, smooth back, effectively pressing his head tighter to her breast. He nipped the sensitive bud.

Another wave of want shot between her legs.

Taking a black fur from the chair but not letting her go, he spread it on the rug between the two carved wood chairs flanking the hearth.

Rhys gave the other breast the same attention; only this time when Poppy's knees weakened, he eased her onto her back.

The soft fur enveloped her, and each tiny hair touching her skin heightened her pleasure. Rhys's journey down her body continued as he kissed each rib then dipped his tongue in her navel. This was yet another new sensation, and Poppy yelped with delight and then giggled.

He smiled up at her but didn't waver from his intent. He licked the crease where her thigh met her pelvis before gentling her knee to bent. When she was open to him, he slid his tongue between her folds.

Mind empty of everything but pleasure, Poppy's hips rolled of their own accord. Gripping his soft hair in her fists, she wasn't certain if she wanted to pull him tighter or push him away. Her pleasure surged in ebbs and flows like the ocean until the waves cascaded over her.

Rhys's mouth silenced the cry. He held her until the last shudder no longer racked her and her muscles relaxed against his chest.

"You are magnificent." He kissed her again on the lips, then the cheek, and then each eyelid.

Too spent to open her eyes, she smiled.

* * * *

When she woke, she was in her own bed and the first signs of morning made the sky gray. Frightened it had all been a dream, she sat up in a panic.

"Hush, love. Everything is all right." Rhys pulled her back to him, but there was no touch of flesh on flesh. He'd managed to put her nightgown back on her, and he was dressed in blouse and breeches.

Poppy let out a long sigh. "I meant to give you pleasure, not to fall asleep."

With a deep rumbling laugh, he kissed the top of her head. "You do give me pleasure and we have a lifetime to make love. You are still not fully recovered from your fever."

She snuggled in deeper, unable to keep the joy from showing. "Still, you foiled my plan."

"Your plan was flawed so I came up with a better one. In the future you can show me your plan and I shall be delighted to oblige." He kissed her again and extracted himself from her arms.

She groaned a loud complaint.

"The house will wake soon. I can't be in your bed any more than you should be in mine."

Sitting up, she retied the bows at her shoulders, which he'd made a mess of. "I suppose you're right and your plan was very good." A warm blush flooded her cheeks.

After stealing one more kiss, Rhys stepped to the door. "Since you seem able to walk, you should come down for breakfast today. Be sure to have Jane help you on the stairs, though. Don't do anything heroic. I want your head squarely on your shoulders when I make you my wife."

It was too delicious a portrait to argue with. "I shall be very careful."

Chapter 19

Standing at the front of the small chapel on the property at Thwackmore, Rhys wished it was grander. The simple wood and glass didn't do justice to his beautiful bride walking toward him in a blue gown. The unadorned nave paled in comparison to Poppy. Her hair was curled and braided, and her color was high. A warm smile spread across her face, and she never took her gaze from his. His heart lodged in his throat; breathing was no longer possible.

She reached the altar, and elation reflected in her eyes. They faced the vicar, and still she stole glances at him.

Smiling, he turned toward her. The vicar harrumphed at the unorthodox turn toward the bride but continued to droll on about the seriousness of entering into a marriage.

Poppy kept her eyes focused on him, yet when the vicar came to the vows and asked if Poppy would obey and serve Rhys, she flinched and lowered her eyes.

Bending his knees to catch her gaze, he gave a tiny shake of his head and held one hand up to stop the babbling preacher. "No more than I will serve you, my love. That is my vow and I shall never break it."

Faith wept openly in the first pew with the other Wallflowers and Garrett.

Poppy nodded, smiling, and the vicar blathered on to the ceremony's end.

"With this ring I thee wed, with my body I thee worship, and with all my worldly goods I thee endow." Rhys finished the prayer and slid the simple gold band on her finger.

She glanced at the ring and then at him.

"I had high hopes," he explained. "It was my grandmother's. She and my grandfather were very happy together."

Her smile was enough to steady him for a lifetime.

When the ceremony was over, the Wallflowers surrounded his wife like a gaggle of geese, and they all made their way back to the manor for an informal wedding breakfast.

"I wish it had been a prettier setting for you, Poppy," Rhys lamented.

Her eyes wide as saucers, she gaped at him. "I am hardly a fancy type of woman, Rhys. I thought it perfect. If you want all of that pomp, we can make my parents happy and be married again at St. Paul's."

"No. We wanted this wedding just for us. I'll not overshadow it with anything else. If it was enough for you, then I am satisfied." His heart leaped in his chest. How had she bewitched him so thoroughly?

In a long silence, Poppy toyed with the cuff of his blouse where it poked out from his coat sleeve. "I suppose we must return to London at some point?"

"I think sooner rather than later."

A long groan and sour face reminded him of how she often looked at him before they became friends and long before they became lovers.

"The longer we wait the harder the return will be."

Mercy said, "I'm afraid Rhys is right, Poppy. You should go back and face your parents. They have no power over you now. You are the Countess of Marsden."

It was true, but Rhys shuddered at the scene Lord and Lady Merkwood would make when they heard their daughter married in Scotland without all the social fuss they'd hoped for. "I will be with you every moment."

His ferocious wife lifted her chin and nodded. "Tomorrow, then? We had better start back, for it is a long journey and at least we'll have the time before the horrors of my birth beset us."

Everyone laughed, but there was real concern in Poppy's eyes, and Rhys longed to ease her mind. Unfortunately, until the event, she would worry about the unknown.

* * * *

The Earl of Merkwood's face was purple with anger despite his relaxed stance against the wall of bookshelves lining his study. "I cannot believe you would do this, Marsden. We waited for your return. The church was scheduled. We had to write to our guests and inform them there would be no wedding because the bride had gone to the country for her nerves." He said the last word with disgust.

Rhys was biting his tongue, but it couldn't last long.

"I would have expected as much from that one, but you should be a better man." He pointed at his daughter as if she were a pesky rodent in need of a good trap.

Temper flaring, Rhys stepped in front of Poppy. "My lord, in the future, I suggest you speak of my wife with a bit more respect and courtesy. If you ever refer to her so rudely or point at her again, I will snap that finger from your hand and you will be needing the appendage when I call you out for your insult."

Merkwood's eyes widened then narrowed. He pushed away from the books. "She is my daughter and I'll speak to her and about her any way I damned well please."

Turning around, Rhys checked on his wife. Always a surprise, Poppy did not look hurt or even angry. She met his gaze with a raised brow and amused smile. Of course, she was used to her father's dismissive and harsh regard for her. She didn't seem the least bit offended as she smoothed the lace on her soft green day dress.

Lady Merkwood sat in an overstuffed chair, looking confused but not as enraged as her husband. Like a statue, her stiff back and folded hands appeared practiced and normal for these instances.

It was not something Rhys was used to, nor did he have any intention of accustoming himself to Merkwood's rants. Without returning his gaze toward Poppy's father, Rhys said, "I think we should go now, my dear. It seems you were right and a courtesy call to your parents was a mistake. I had hoped they would see reason and wish us joy, but it seems it is not to be."

"You'll not see a penny of her dowry." Arthur Arrington's lips twisted in a smirk, and a vein in his forehead stood out.

Lady Merkwood gasped, and her hand went to her throat.

The notion this had always been about money and power rather than the happiness of their only child grated on Rhys. He turned.

A triumphant glare made Lord Merkwood even more distasteful. His gray hair and pale eyes gave him the look of a specter, and with his gaunt face red with rage, he might be death himself.

It took Rhys several deep breaths to control his anger. He would not give Merkwood the satisfaction of pushing him into a fit of temper. "My lord, I have no interest in Penelope's dowry. However, if you withhold it after boasting about it all these years as the way of bettering your status and relinquishing your daughter, you will enhance the notion you disapprove of this marriage."

"I do disapprove." Merkwood crossed his arms over his chest.

Rhys advanced until he was only three feet from Poppy's father. "If you make it known you disapprove of a marriage that you arranged, how will it make you look, my lord? Will the men in the House of Lords be keen to listen to a man so changeable in his opinions and wishes?"

"No one cares what happens to a misbegotten waif like her. She's never been accepted in good society anyway."

Unable to bear looking at the hurt he would see in his wife's eyes, Rhys focused on the miserable form of her father. "I will care, sir, and so will all of my friends and acquaintances. She is a countess now. She will be accepted in all society and revered there. You will place those funds in trust for any children my wife and I might be blessed with, or I will see to it you are made a mockery of at court."

Merkwood's face got impossibly redder, the muscles in his neck strained as his jaw ticked, and he muttered something under his breath before he nodded.

"Good." Rhys turned to Poppy, who still looked more amused than hurt by her father's stupidity. "Shall we go, Lady Marsden?"

With a nod, she turned to Merkwood and curtsied. "Father." Then her mother. "Mother." Then she took his arm and walked out of the study.

They were gathering their things from the butler when Lady Merkwood rushed out of the room and gently closed the door. "Penelope, I would be pleased if you would allow me to throw you a wedding breakfast."

"I don't think Father would be pleased about it." Poppy took her mother's hand and smiled.

"Perhaps not, but I'd like to do it anyway and I do run this house. Will you allow it?" Apprehension lurked in her eyes.

Poppy leaned in and kissed her mother's cheek. "Of course. That is very kind of you, Mother. I'm sure my husband and I will be delighted to accept such a thoughtful invitation."

A bright smile transformed Lady Merkwood into a stunning older version of Poppy. "I shall contact you with specifics."

"Come to tea on Monday, Mother. We can talk then." Poppy tugged on her gloves.

Rhys bowed to his mother-in-law, offered his wife his arm, and led them from her parents' home. Guilty of a grievous error, he didn't know how he would make amends. "I'm sorry. You were right. I should not have put you through that. I should have dealt with your father on my own."

"Nonsense. That was the singular most wonderful moment involving my father of my entire life." Poppy preened as she stepped up into the carriage.

Rhys joined her inside. "How so?"

"You stood up for me. No one has ever done that, at least not with Father. Nor have I ever seen anyone threaten that beast of a man. It was glorious." She clapped her hands in delight.

Leaning back against the cushion, Rhys admired her. With a few words she eased his mind and lifted his heart. "Will you never cease to amaze me, wife?"

"I hope not." She giggled.

"Take us home, Patrick," Rhys called to the driver.

"Wait, Patrick," Poppy yelled after.

Patrick's dark brown eyes shifted from one to the other, unsure what to do. Finally, he said, "My lord?"

It was always going to be an adventure with this woman. Rhys shrugged. "Well, where are we going, then?"

"To visit with the Duke of Breckenridge."

* * * *

The Duke of Breckenridge's London home was elegant, enormous, and a bit daunting. Steeling herself, Poppy strode up the steps with Rhys at her elbow.

Rhys gave her a warm smile and banged the knocker twice.

The door swung open, revealing a butler of middle years. His brown hair grayed on the sides, and his dark eyes simmered with mistrust. "May I help you?"

Handing over his calling card, Rhys said, "The Earl and Countess of Marsden to see His Grace."

The use of titles seemed to perk up the butler as he eyed the card. "Please come in. I will see if His Grace is available. You may wait in the sitting room."

The foyer was magnificent with black-and-white marble tiles, which reminded Poppy of a chessboard. Twenty feet above them a chandelier reflected light from the window above the door. The sun caught each of hundreds of crystals and set them aflame. Stark white walls made her worry she might mar something. It hardly reflected the personality of Nicholas Ellsworth and his easy demeanor.

With a definite limp to his step, the butler led them down a hall and into an ornate sitting room facing the gardens. "I am Dumford, should you need anything."

He closed the door.

The room was broken up into three spaces: A table and four chairs in one corner covered in a lace cloth. A conversation area with couch, settee, and three chairs all in the French style with swirling woods and fine upholstery. A pianoforte in the far corner with a golden candelabra perched on it and several family miniatures placed around the top of the instrument. Poppy noted the image of Nicholas alongside an older man with a similar look.

"This is so formal compared to the man." Rhys ran his hand along the back of the couch.

"Yes. I thought so too."

"It is to my mother's taste." Nicholas stood in the open doorway.

Poppy started, having not heard a sound of footsteps or the door opening. She stumbled into a curtsy. "Your Grace."

Rhys bowed as well. "Good afternoon, Breckenridge."

Entering the room, Nicholas's eyes held wariness. "To what do I owe this unexpected honor?"

Perched against the corner of the fireplace, Rhys raised his eyebrows in Poppy's direction.

Taking careful steps to bring them closer together, Poppy swallowed down any fear. "I feel you deserve an apology and an explanation, Your Grace."

He let his expression soften as if he'd given up a pretense. "Sit please, Poppy, and my name is still Nicholas. Tea will take a few moments."

Relieved the warm man she'd met so many weeks ago at the Sottonfield ball was not altogether gone, Poppy sat. "Thank you, Nicholas. Would you let me explain my actions?"

He sighed. "I can't see how it will make a difference, but if it will make you feel better." He inclined his head.

Drawing in a long breath, Poppy started from the beginning. "My friends and I have formed a pact to never let another man harm one of us. When Faith was sold off to a man none of us had ever met, our worry bloomed into panic. Please understand, we did not know you, and you are a man with many secrets."

"She was not sold to me." He bit out the words angrily.

"No. I know. I have had many issues with the institution of marriage that I am now recovering from since Rhys and I have recently been married."

Nicholas's eyes widened. "Yes. Dumford mentioned your title. I offer my felicitations."

"Thank you. I thought if we could get to know your character, we would know if Faith would be safe with you. It would also help if you and she might have developed some regard for each other." Poppy huffed in frustration.

"I agree, that might have been nice," Nicholas said.

"Can you perhaps see, considering our fear of a disastrous fate, your secrets and odd behavior might have set our teeth on edge?"

He leaned forward. "Perhaps, but going to my friend and spending two nights for information-gathering purposes was beyond my tolerance, Poppy."

"We only meant to ask a few questions and be on our way. The weather forced us to stay longer, and I'll not apologize for the extra time. I wouldn't trade meeting Mr. Arafa for the world. He is a most interesting man and not like anyone I have ever met." She lifted her chin.

Rhys laughed. "That is true. I agree with my wife. Mr. Arafa is a fine friend to have."

"Indeed," Nicholas conceded.

Poppy swallowed the lump in her throat. "I am sorry we invaded your privacy, and I hope you will take more time to get to know Faith and let her get to know you. If you decide otherwise, I understand but believe you will be missing out on a lifetime with an exceptional person."

"Oh, and do I have the approval of this group of ladies or am I still on trial?" Derision oozed from Nicholas's words.

Poppy ignored his sarcasm. "If Geb Arafa approves of you, then I do as well. Faith is still not sure, but I shall let her speak to you of her concerns as it is not my tale to tell."

"So, I am just to forgive you and her for spying on me? I have no say in what I wish to tell my perspective bride and what I want to keep from her?" Nicholas stood and crossed the room, planting his hands on the top of the pianoforte and staring down at its shiny surface.

Rising, Poppy went to Rhys and took his hand. "As I am only recently married and can only speak from my own experience, I am not fully qualified to answer that question, Your Grace. However, until I was honest with my husband and he with me, our chances for a life filled with joy and love were nonexistent. So, I suppose it depends on what you wish to gain from a marriage. If you want a broodmare to give you sons and be ignored for all other purposes, then your silence might work. Then again, if it is a companion who loves you and makes your life worth living you seek, you shall have to tell her everything and let her decide if she can live with it."

Rhys lifted her hand and kissed her knuckles. Pride and love shone in his eyes.

"It is a very big risk you ask of me." Nicholas turned to face them. His eyes were filled with conflict, and his knuckles were white where they gripped the instrument.

"I am not asking anything of you, Your Grace. It is only my opinion there is always risk for the greatest reward. Rarely do we get what we want without giving something of ourselves in the process."

Sensing the interview was at an end, Poppy looked at Rhys. He took her elbow, and they walked to the door. "Thank you for seeing us, Your Grace." Rhys too returned to a formal address, taking his cue from Poppy.

Nicholas watched them leave but said nothing.

Outside Poppy's hopes fell. "We failed."

Rhys handed her up into the carriage. "Did we?"

"Faith is perhaps further away from a good match than when we started on this ill-fated journey." A heavy burden settled in Poppy's chest. She had not helped her friend the way she said she would. She had not fulfilled her oath. "Now that we are fully discovered by Breckenridge, we have no means to gather information."

Rhys gave Patrick instructions to take them home. Once the carriage was rolling and they were settled, he pulled her into his lap. "My love, we set out to discern his character and did as well as anyone could have. I know we didn't find a flawless prince under his disguise, but those are very rare. He is liked and respected by his friends. He has a sense of humor. Even when angered, he has not shown signs of violence. I think we did what were charged with. The rest is up to Faith and Nicholas."

The burden lightened, allowing Poppy to breathe. "You are wrong about one thing, sweet husband."

He snuggled into the spot where her neck and shoulder met and kissed her sensitive flesh. "Which part, my love?"

"Sometimes one does discover a prince in disguise." Poppy cupped his cheek and pressed her lips to her own prince.

<<<<>>>>

Meet the Author

A.S. Fenichel gave up a successful IT career in New York City to follow her husband to Texas and pursue her lifelong dream of being a professional writer. She's never looked back. A.S. adores writing stories filled with love, passion, desire, magic, and maybe a little mayhem tossed in for good measure. Books have always been her perfect escape, and she still relishes diving into one and staying up all night to finish a good story. The author of the Forever Brides series, the Everton Domestic Society series, and more, A.S. adores strong, empowered heroines no matter the era, and that's what you'll find in all her books. A Jersey girl at heart, she now makes her home in southern Missouri with her real-life hero, her wonderful husband. When not reading or writing, she enjoys cooking, travel, history, puttering in her garden, and spoiling her fussy cat. Be sure to visit her website at asfenichel.com, find her on Facebook, and follow her on Twitter.

Keep reading for a special excerpt of Faith and Nicholas's story in **MISLEADING A DUKE.**

Chapter 1

The last person Nicholas Ellsworth expected to find at his good friend, Geb Arafa's dinner party was Lady Faith Landon. Yet there she was, Nicholas's fiancée, maddeningly pretty and equally aggravating. She fit perfectly with the lush décor and priceless artifacts in Geb's parlor.

"Lady Faith, I had not expected to find you here. In fact, you and your friends' presence is an astonishment."

"I hope you are not too put out. It seems Lord and Lady Marsden have become fast friends with Mr. Arafa and that friendship has extended to the rest of the Wallflowers of West Lane." Despite his desire to be rid of her, Faith's soft voice flowed over him like a summer stream and he longed to hear that voice in the dark, in their bed. The way she filled out the rose gown set his body aflame and there seemed nothing he could do about it.

He shook away his attraction reminding himself that this was a sneaky, manipulative woman who it had been a mistake to attach himself to. The fact that he longed to find out if her honey-brown curls were as wild as they promised despite her attempts to tame them into submission, shouldn't matter. Nor should his desire to get lost in her wheat colored eyes and voluptuous curves. This was a woman made for loving.

Lord, he hated himself. "I wonder that you're being here with those friends is not some dire plot in the making."

He had reason to be suspicious. When he'd first arrived home from France, in the spring, she and her friends had engaged in spying on him and trying to ferret out his past. It was intolerable. He should have called off the engagement, but the thought of ruining her for good society didn't sit well with Nicholas. Instead he'd offered her the opportunity to set him aside, but she had refused to do so as of yet.

She frowned and was no less stunning. Her full lips longed to be kissed back into an upturned state. "We are here because Mr. Arafa invited us. He's your friend. I'm surprised he didn't mention it."

Nick was equally bewildered by Geb's silence on the matter of Faith and the other members of the Wallflowers of West Land. He had met them on several occasions during his feeble efforts to get to know Faith. Her instant suspicions that he was hiding something may have led to her friends' actions, but he still couldn't let the slight die. Though he did admire the strength of the friendship between Faith and the three women she'd gone to finishing school with. They were as close as any soldiers who fought and died together. Even if they had called themselves "wallflowers" there was nothing diminished about any of the four.

"He is not required to give me his invitation list." It pushed out more bitterly than intended.

Those cunning eyes narrowed. "I think you would like it exceedingly well if he did."

That she wasn't wrong raised the hair on the back of Nick's neck. He had not been able to keep many friends over the years. His work for the crown had made that impossible. Now his friendship with Geb Arafa was in jeopardy as well.

He bowed to her. "I do not always get what I want, Lady Faith."

Head cocked, she raised one brown. "Don't you, Your Grace?"

Geb chose that moment to stroll over. His dark skin, set off his bright tawny eyes and though he dressed in the black suit and white cravat typical of an Englishman, there was no mistaking his eastern background. "Nicholas, I'm so glad you are here. I thought you might be held up with politics."

Nicholas accepted his offered hand. "I finished my meetings and came directly."

Smiling in her charming way, Faith's golden eyes flashed. "I shall leave you gentlemen to catch up."

Both Nicholas and Geb bowed and watched her join her friends near the pianoforte.

"She is a delightful woman, Nick. You should reconcile and marry her." Geb ran his hand through his black hair smoothing it back from his forehead.

Not willing to let his attraction to Faith rule his decisions, Nicholas forced down the desire seeing his betrothed always ignited in him. "She is sneaky and devious. I shall wait for her to give up and call off."

"I would have thought such character traits would appeal to you." Geb lowered his voice. "After all you are a spy with much the same qualities.

You might consider speaking to the lady and finding out the details behind her actions."

"Why don't you just tell me what you know, Geb?" It was obvious his friend new more than he'd disclosed thus far. Nicholas asking for more was futile. If Geb was going to tell him more than he already had, he would have done so months ago when he'd first informed him that Poppy and Rhys, now the Earl and Countess of Marsden were investigating his character.

"I am not at liberty to divulge that information." Geb's white teeth gleamed.

"I didn't realize Egyptians were so keen on keeping a lady's secrets." Nicholas teased.

Grabbing his chest, Geb feigned a knife to the heart. "I would never tell tales of a good woman. There have been a few who were not reputable and those that are part of our line of work whose secrets I had little scruples about divulging."

"Indeed." As much as he wanted to be angry with Geb for befriending Faith and her friends, he couldn't manage it. The truth was, Geb was quite discerning about who he called a friend.

During the time Nicholas spent with them, he couldn't help but like them as well. They were the most spirited and brightest women he'd ever known. He recalled a beautiful blonde in Spain who had tried to put a knife between his ribs and shuddered. At lease he didn't think these Wallflowers were out for his blood, just his secrets. What he didn't know, was why they were so keen on divining his past. He might be a fool to think them innocent. His trust of a sweet face in the past had nearly gotten him killed.

Geb nudged him out of his thoughts. "Talk to the girl."

Glancing at where Faith stood drinking a glass of wine and talking to Poppy Draper, Nicholas mused over if they were plotting their next attempt to invade his privacy. "Perhaps later. First, I would like a glass of your excellent cognac."

"Avoiding her will not make your situation better," Geb warned, his rich Egyptian accent rounding the words and lending a sense of foreboding.

"The lady will decide I am not worth the trouble and find herself a less complicated gentleman to attach herself to."

Nodding, Geb said, "I'm certain that is true. She is too lovely for half the men in London to not be in love with."

Nicholas wished that thought didn't form a knot in his gut. He also longed for a day when Faith wouldn't enter his mind a dozen times. She had gotten under his skin before he'd even met her, and he couldn't rid himself of her spell. Even knowing it had been her mother and not the lady herself who had written to him when he was if France hadn't dulled what he knew and liked about Faith Landon.

"One day you shall have to tell me how you came to this, my friend." Geb signaled for Kosey, his servant.

The extremely tall Egyptian wore a white turban and loose black pants and a similar blouse. He carried a tray with two glasses of dark amber cognac. "Dinner will be ready in ten minutes, sir. Will that please you?" Kosey spoke English in an eastern way.

It gained looks from some of the other guests, but Nicholas liked the formal old-fashioned speech.

Lord and Lady Flitmore gaped at Kosey. Perhaps it was his height as he towered over everyone in the room. It might have been his odd clothes. Whatever it was their shocked regard, needled at Nicholas.

Faith stepped between him and the couple. "Lady Flitmore, it's nice to see you again. I heard your daughter Mary would be here tonight, but I've not seen her. I hope nothing is wrong. I know how she can get into mischief."

Lord Flitmore coughed uncomfortably. "Mary had some trouble with her gown and is coming in another carriage. She will be here any moment."

As if on cue, a footman announced the arrival of Lady Mary Yates.

A slim woman with red hair and flawless skin sauntered into the room. Pretty in the classical way, her long thin nose appeared in a perpetual state of being turned up at everyone and everything. Hands folded lightly in front of her she walked directly to where Faith stood with her parents. In a voice without modulation, Mary said, "Mother, Father, I'm sorry to be late. I hope no one was waiting on me."

The lack of any emotion in Mary's voice made it difficult to tell if she was sincere or just saying what was expected of her. "Thank you for sending the carriage back for me."

Lord Flitmore pulled his shoulder back and beamed at his daughter. "Dinner has only just been announced, my dear girl. Please say hello to, His Grace, the Duke of Breckenridge."

Mary made a pretty curtsy and plastered a wan smile on her rosy lips. "How do you do, Your Grace?"

Bowing, Nick couldn't help but notice the look of disdain that flitted across Faith's face. "A pleasure, Lady Mary. I'm pleased you could come tonight. Do you know, Lady Faith Landon?"

Another curtsy and a smile that likened to a wolf, and Mary said, "Lady Faith and I went to the Wormbattle school together. We have been acquainted for many years. How are you Faith?"

Faith raised a brow. "Very well, Mary. You are looking fine. Your parents tell me you've had some issue with your gown this evening.

Mary's gown was dark blue and threaded with gold. It pushed all her assets up to the breaking point of the material at her breast and flowed down showing off her perfect figure. She blushed. "Just a small issue that my maid and a needle and thread resolved easily enough."

The ladies leered at each other.

Clearing his throat, Lord Flitmore said, "Mary, let me introduce you to our host."

"Of course," Mary agreed and with a nod to Nick, all three Yates's left the circle.

Faith watched after Mary but had schooled her features to a pleasant expression that no one could have noted anything amiss from. Nick had many questions, but none of them were any of his business.

"Shall we go in to dinner?" As they were officially engaged, Nick offered Faith his arm and they preceded the others into the dining room.

The long table had rounded corners and was draped in white linen. Fine china leafed with gold and highly polished crystal and silver made the setting gleam in three fully lit chandeliers hanging overhead and four standing candelabras placed in all corners of the room. The high backed, dark wood chairs were cushioned with a pale blue demask. It was decidedly English, and extremely elegant to appeal to Geb's guests.

At the head of the table, Geb told a story of being on a sinking ship and the diners were riveted despite the fact that most of them would not invite an Egyptian to their own homes. Faith smiled warmly at Geb and Nick wondered if she were different. Would his friends, regardless of their origins, be welcomed to her table?

He shook off the notion. He would not be going through with marrying Faith Landon no matter how much he desired her or how kind she pretended to be. She had betrayed him with her spying and he wouldn't have it.

Another exception to the apparent prejudice against Geb were Rhys and Poppy Draper. The earl and his bride genuinely liked Geb and had become fast friends with him after being stranded at his house in a storm.

"Did you swim to shore from that distance, Mr. Arafa?" Poppy's blue eyes were wide and her dark hair and lashes made the color all the more demonstrable.

Geb's cheeks pinked and he laughed. "I'm afraid nothing so heroic, my lady. I was hauled out of the ocean by a small fishing vessel. My lungs were full of water and I caught a terrible ague and spent three weeks in a Portuguese hospital."

They all laughed with Geb.

Rhys Draper took a long pull on his wine. "I would be willing to bet you were the most interesting thing those fishermen plucked from the Atlantic that day. And you were damned lucky. Not only could you have drowned, but if this had happened a year later you might have been caught up in Napoleon's invasion."

"Indeed, luck was with me that day and many others." More sober, Geb gave Nick a knowing look.

Nick noted his friends careful use of luck rather than invoke the name of the Prophet in a room full of Christians. Knowing how religious Geb was, Nick knew what he was thinking. They had experienced many adventures together and luck, Allah or God had seen them through some things that seemed impossible at the time.

The footmen served the soup.

Nick noted that many of the guests poked at the fine broth, vegetables and bits of tender beef, but didn't eat. The Yates family among those who would not eat from the table of an Egyptian, but would be happy to attend since Geb was a good resource for many business dealings. Not to mention the depth of Geb's pocketbook.

Faith, Poppy and Rhys ate with gusto. Perhaps more than was natural and Nick decided they had also noticed the rudeness of the other guests.

Besides the Yates, Sir Duncan Humphrey, his wife and two sons, Montgomery and Malcom were in attendance as well as William Wharton and his wife. All were well respected among the ton and had obviously not come for the food or company. They didn't speak other than the occasional thank you.

On Nick's right, Faith sipped the last of her soup and turned to Mary. "You didn't like the soup?"

"I'm not hungry. I'm certain it is quite good." Mary narrowed her eyes at Faith.

"It's really too bad, it was the best I've tasted." Faith smiled warmly and turned her attention back to Geb. "Poppy told me how wonderful your cook is and now I can taste the truth of it."

"You always did have a great love of food, Faith." Mary's voice rang with disdain and she peered down that thin nose at Faith's curvaceous figure.

Poppy looked ready to leap across the table and do Mary physical harm.

A low laugh from Faith calmed the situation. "I suppose where I am fond of a good meal you are fond a good bit of gossip. We each have our hidden desires. Don't we, Mary."

It was a warning, but Nick didn't have enough information to know what was at stake.

Mary bit her bottom lip and narrowed her eyes before masking all emotion and nodding. "I suppose that's true of everyone."

A flush of pride swept over Nick. He had no right to feel any sense of esteem for Faith's ability to out think another woman and put her in her place. Yet, he couldn't help liking that she had not been bested by a bigoted daughter of parents who would attend the dinner party of a man they clearly didn't like, but wanted something from.

Turning his attention back to Geb, Nick noted his friend's amusement at the social volley going on at the table. Geb smiled warmly at Poppy as she changed the subject to the delectable pheasant and fine wine.

By the main course, Nick had given up on the other end of the table and was ensconced in a lively conversation among the four people around him. Rhys was well versed in politics and they discussed the state of coal mines. Faith and Poppy both added their opinions, which were well thought out and more astute than he would have thought for ladies of their rank. Perhaps he should rethink his views of what ladies ponder in the course of a day. Clearly it was more than stitching and tea patterns.

Geb too ignored the reticent group at the far end of the table and joined the banter. When Kosey announced that cake and sherry were being served in the grand parlor, Nick was disappointed to leave the conversation.

As soon as they entered the parlor, Flitmore cornered Geb about the sale of several horses and Sir Duncan wanted to know when the next shipment of spices from India would be arriving.

Stomach turning at their duplicity, Nick escaped to the garden.

Geb had torches lighting the paths. The gardens here were one of Nick's favorite places in England. They were orderly and wild at once. White stones lined the lanes meant to guide one through the low plantings. It was a maze but without the threat of being lost. The fountain at the far end broke the silence of the pleasant autumn night. Soon winter would turn it to a wasteland and a good snow would give it the feel of an abandoned house.

Nick sighed and walked on.

"Are you determined to be alone, or might I join you, Your Grace." Faith called from only a few feet behind him.

He must be losing his training for her to have sneaked up behind him without notice. "Is there something you wanted, Lady Faith?"

She stepped closer. Several curls had freed themselves of her elaborate coif and called out to Nick to touch them. "It is a lovely garden." She glanced around and smiled.

"Yes. Geb has taken bits from all his travels and placed them in his home and this garden. I think it brings him comfort."

Faith's golden eyes filled with sorrow. "Do you think Mr. Arafa is lonely in England?"

"It is never easy to live amongst a people not your own." Nick considered all the time he'd spent in France, Spain and Portugal and how much he'd missed the rainy days in England and people who understood his humor.

"The Wallflowers are very fond of Mr. Arafa. We have not entertained much, but I will see that he is added to our invitation list. Perhaps a circle of good friends will make him feel more at home." She'd placed her index finger on her chin while she considered how best to help Geb.

Adorable.

He needed to be free of this woman. "You didn't say what it was you wanted, Lady Faith."

Frowning, she walked forward and down the path. "Must I have a reason to walk in the garden with my fiancé?"

Leaving her to her own devices and returning to the house flitted through his mind, but it would cause gossip and he was curious about the reason for seeking him out. "We are hardly the perfect picture of an engaged couple."

"No. That is true. I wanted to apologize for any undue strain I may have caused you by trying to find out what kind of character you have."

"Is that your apology, or shall I wait for more," he said when she didn't elaborate.

She stopped and puffed up her chest. Her cheeks were red and fire flashed in her eyes. "Why must you be so difficult? Even when I'm trying to be nice, you find fault. The entire situation was mostly your doing. If you had been open and honest, that would have been an end to our query and none of the rest would have been necessary."

Even more beautiful when she was in a temper, he longed to pull her into his arms and taste those alluring lips. He was certain just one tug would topple all those curls from the pins that held her hair in place and he could find out if they were as soft as they appeared. It was maddening. "I hardly see how it was my fault. You and your friends spied on me and involved Geb, which is unforgivable."

As soft and lovely as she was, a hard edge caught in her voice. "I supposed then you will not accept my apology. I see. Well, in that case, I'll leave you to your solitude." She turned to walk away and stopped eyes narrowed into the darkness beyond the gardens, which were surrounded by tall evergreens.

Following her gaze, Nick saw nothing though the hair on the back of his neck rose. "What is it?"

"I felt eyes on me as if someone was watching." She shivered and continued straining to see in the shadows.

"I'm sure you are imagining things." He dismissed her worry.

That hateful glance fell on him before she plastered false serenity on her face. "Perhaps."

He preferred the disdain to the untruthful agreement. Why he should care when he wanted nothing to do with her, he didn't know. "Shall I escort you back inside, Lady Faith?"

"You are too kind, Your Grace, but I can manage the journey on my own." With a curt nod, she stormed away from him toward the house.

Unable to look away, he admired the gentle sway of her hips until she climbed the veranda steps and went inside. Lord, how he longed to hold those hips and slide his hands up to that slim waist and so much more. He shook off the wayward thoughts before he embarrassed himself with his desires.

One thing was certain, Faith Landon would be his undoing.

CPSIA information can be obtained
at www.ICGtesting.com
Printed in the USA
BVHW081118260921
617564BV00007B/231